EYESHADOW

Mark Macrossan was born in Brisbane in 1961. His previous occupations include barrister (Sydney) and film extra (London). He currently lives in Sydney.

He can be found online at www.markmacrossan.com.

EYESHADOW

MARK MACROSSAN

ANTIMERIDIAN

First published by Antimeridian Press in 2025

This edition published in 2025 by Antimeridian Press

Copyright © Mark Macrossan 2025
www.markmacrossan.com

This is a work of fiction and any resemblance to actual persons, living or dead, is entirely coincidental.

Eyeshadow

ISBN: 9781764413008 (e-book)
ISBN: 9781764413015 (paperback)

This version: 2025-12-31

Cover design by Jonathon Eadie
www.eadie.biz

e

Eyeshadow

Attention à l'ombre
à midi, forte et sombre.
Elle vient pour nous.
Elle vient pour vous.

*Beware the sharp, dark
shadow at noon.
It comes for us.
It comes for you.*

1.

The headlights dazzled her eyes.

It was the oncoming traffic, it confused her. Disorientated her. Sydney streets, never the enemy before. It was hard to keep going, but she certainly couldn't go back, couldn't stop even. Because he was there, behind her, following her, and he wouldn't give up until...

Until what?

Up ahead, in the pauses between the blinding flashes, she caught glimpses of towers in the gloom. Or chimneys, the chimney stacks...

Why was he chasing her? She was just a woman, just a girl, she was nobody, nobody at all. Why her, and why couldn't he just go away?

She looked down and noticed that her legs weren't moving. She'd stopped.

She wanted to live.

To live she had to move, and it had to be forward, and it had to be *now*.

She lifted her leaden legs and ran.

2.

Detective Senior Constable Agatha Ducatti, freshly arrived for the day, sat down at her desk at a sunny extremity of the Newtown police station. Not feeling her usual motivated self, but feeling a little out of sorts. She wasn't sure why, it had been a beautiful spring day on the way in. No clouds, but all blue, gearing up for warmth. Best time of year, in Sydney at least. So there was no obvious reason for this heavy feeling.

She scanned the contents of her desktop – the physical one, not the one on her computer which she'd only just switched on – and it was satisfyingly uncluttered, not yet sullied with the new tragedies the day would no doubt bring. New *tragedies*? A bit melodramatic.

Her desk calendar stared back at her, reminding her of her first duty of the day and she flipped its page, so it now read:

Wednesday

16 October

2013

She counted the months out with the fingers of her right hand: April, May, June, July, August, September, October. Seven months, so she was over thirty-four and a half. Closer to thirty-five. And once she'd passed thirty-five, she'd be closer to forty than thirty. Was that her problem?

No. She enjoyed being in her thirties, and the idea of one day turning forty didn't faze her in the slightest. She enjoyed being well clear of that mad frenzy that was her twenties. And all those *men*. Boys more like it, but whatever. The thirties were calmer. Slightly more boring, possibly, but she enjoyed her independence. She was more herself. And the man of her dreams, he was still out there somewhere...

That was it. The *dream*. That was what had been nagging at her. Not only had it been weird and unpleasant – terrifying, even – it had been as vivid as any dream she'd ever had.

She was in Paris in the late eighteenth century, at the time of the French Revolution and the Reign of Terror. She'd just been snatched off a grey street by a roaming pack of Jacobins and then shoved into a busy courtroom, and as soon as she was there her name was called, 'Agatha Ducatti Durán-Delapeña!', and she tried to speak but no words came. The judge's gavel came down with a sharp crack, followed by the words 'The usual sentence' and then he looked her straight in the eye and he added 'for royalist sluts like you'. She was dragged outside where a giant of a man in a hood was beckoning to her. 'You're the first, so it's clean!' he exclaimed, and then she saw he was standing next to a guillotine. She tried to protest, but again nothing came. Which was when it dawned on her that she was dreaming, but she was unable to tear herself loose and wake up. She was roughly pushed down onto the lunette at the base of the frame. They had her facing up and she could see the blade above her when a cavalry officer rode up on a large white horse and proclaimed 'This one's reserved for the Dive!' and the crowd roared its approval. And then she was perched high up on a church spire, with the mob below shouting out 'Dive! Dive!' At this point, the surrounding buildings had morphed from their Parisian grey to a warmer colour, more of a sandy dark yellow, as if they were made of Sydney sandstone, but this was no sign of a reprieve: around her the gargoyles sprang to life, snarling, and when one of them doubled in size and leapt at her, she dived. She tucked her chin and stretched her arms out, a perfect dive into the cobblestones... and when she hit, she sliced through the stones as if she was diving into the warm, azure waters of some tropical sea, and she was — she could see coral and columns of colourful fish — and when she surfaced, there were islanders — Polynesians or Melanesians — shouting gleefully at her in French from the edge of a cliff. And near them she spotted a plump, sinister-looking white man clapping and laughing, managing to look at once both ridiculous and threatening. And vaguely familiar. 'Well done Agatha!' he shouted in English, but with a slight accent of some kind. He was pale and overweight with light-coloured hair and with features — nose, eyes and mouth — all too small for his large round face. Incongruously, given the location, he was wearing a navy suit and dark-coloured trainers. Under the suit, which was unbuttoned, he wore an open-necked blue shirt which had become half untucked with one side flapping free over his fat stomach, and the cuffs of which, at his wrist, he tugged on from time to time. He was squinting severely, clearly uncomfortable in the tropical glare. 'Tchaikovsky's your man!' he went on. 'But don't you worry your pretty little head about it!' Agatha tried to speak, but he shouted over her, 'Welcome to the South Pacific, my dear! Just don't forget the name, it's Smeeton, with a double e! Too *eeasy*! Do you get it Agatha?! Do you get it?! Oh you'll get it all right! You'll get it!' And with that he got up and laughed, and kept repeating this awful refrain *Oh you'll get it all right!* over and over until Agatha eventually managed to pull herself out of her nightmare.

But before she was fully awake, when the dream was still as real as the bedroom she was waking up in, she realized that this man was the man who...

The man who...?

The man who what? She couldn't remember, it was gone. Evanesced into the morning air. All she knew at that moment was he was back again. He was back, and this time she knew, he wasn't going to let her go.

Agatha's computer had just finished rebooting, and when the welcome screen popped up, she entered her password.

As she stared at her computer screen, she thought of how handy it would be to be able to reboot not just her computer but her mind as well. Including now, for example. And rid herself of the sinking feeling this latest dream was giving her. She needed to shake it off, get on with her day.

She was a highly intuitive person and was used to vivid dreams, she'd always had them, but this one had been different. For one thing, she'd never been trapped like that before, unable to wake up. Was that significant?

Furthermore, this man, this Smeeton or whatever he'd called himself, she'd already dreamt of him – more than once – although this was the first time he'd revealed his name. But the dreams always left her shaken up, as though the darkness they carried came with a heightened level of reality.

How long had she been having them for? She had no idea. A year? Or more? And who was he? Where was he from? He had to be from somewhere, surely not simply out of her head.

Surely not.

3.

'He swears it was where he took the photos. Near the chimneys.'

It was later that morning in another room of the Newtown police station, one with no windows. Brearly (Detective Sergeant) was being handed a photograph by Lutger (Detective Constable), whose office they were in, although Brearly would have preferred it if Agatha had been the one doing the handing. Agatha Ducatti Du-whatever-it-was. It annoyed him that he still couldn't remember her full surname after... how long had it been? Since she'd arrived in Newtown? Over two years? Never mind, he thought, concentrate on the photographs.

'The chimneys in the park?' he asked, scrutinizing what was marked as photo number three.

'Sydney Park, yeah,' Lutger said. 'He reckons she was... that wall you can see, the brick wall, it's part of one of the buildings there, the old brickworks. One of the brick kilns.'

'Mm.'

'Where she was, he reckons was kind of hidden. Couldn't be seen very easily from the road or any of the paths.'

Photo number three was similar to the first two. The body of a girl, possibly in her twenties, not unattractive by the look of things, slumped on her side in the dark shadows beneath an old brick wall. The bricks were flatter than modern bricks, the way they used to be made, and they were speckled with moss. The body was lit up, and not by street lighting – the kid, who'd taken the photos with his phone, had clearly used his flash.

The girl herself was dressed only in underwear. Her smooth white skin, lent a kind of spectral purity by the light of the flash, was sullied in places by smears of dirt, possibly from soil or grass. Her underwear was black and lacy and sheer: bra and pantyhose, no panties. In other words, *dead sexy* – excuse the pun, Brearly thought, but he had to admit it, to himself, it was giving him the beginnings of a hard-on. Not appropriate, he knew that – *totally* inappropriate – but what could he do? Think of something to kill it? Like...? No. It was bad enough switching on the news every night. He had enough noise in his head already and he had to *concentrate*, apply himself to the matter at hand. Because something was most definitely not quite right here...

'And this boy...' Brearly said, picking up the next photo himself. It was from a different angle this one, you could see her face and her eyes were open, her pale lips slightly parted. 'The boy who claims he found her. At... seven p.m. last night or whatever it was... was he—'

'Seven fifteen, night before last,' Lutger corrected. '*Monday* night.'

Lutger could be irritating at times. He had a steel trap of a mind, never forgot a thing. Brearly prided himself on only remembering the important stuff (although, admittedly, this included every street name within a ten-kilometre radius of the GPO, his one 'party trick'). Lutger, though, remembered *everything*, even conversations. Word for word. A week later. *Months* later. Which was one of the reasons Brearly rarely went drinking with him. A photographic memory (or whatever you called it) was great for police work, but a recipe for disaster when it came to socializing.

Then again, who had time to socialize these days? These *dark* days. Armies of evil thoughts were pounding on the city gates. He shut his eyes for a moment, as if that would be enough to repel them.

'So why didn't he report it straight away?' Brearly asked, frowning hard.

'Got scared he reckons. He's only thirteen.'

'Old enough.'

The fifth and final photograph showed the girl's backside, and with no panties her buttocks were clearly visible through her gossamer-thin pantyhose... and even her anus? It was all a bit too salacious really, even for someone with Brearly's, how should he put it, *robust* tastes.

'Old enough to be having some fun with us,' he added.

Lutger's face contorted. 'Fun?'

Brearly could almost hear the whirring of the hard drive in Lutger's head.

'The body's gone, right?' he said. 'It's no longer there. And corpses don't just walk off, do they.'

'Not on their own.'

'Not on their own,' Brearly agreed. '*Unless...*'

His colleague finished his sentence for him. 'Unless they have help. Unless someone moved her. But who? The perp? The murderer? He'd be taking one hell of a risk. Returning.'

But Brearly wasn't listening. He was staring at photo number four – the one showing the girl's face – and looking deeply into her sapphire-blue eyes.

'Corpses don't just walk off on their own, *unless*... they're not dead.'

4.

Agatha was having a quiet moment.

Her office, if you could call it that, was small. By any standards. She'd already tried swinging an imaginary cat and it hadn't gone well for the cat. The fact that she now had to share the space with Brearly only made things worse, although thankfully he was out more than he was in. Her modest desk was pushed up against a wall, and as she often did when she needed to think, she swivelled in her chair to face the window, which at least provided a view, through adjustable horizontal blinds, of the adjacent buildings and the sky.

The shadows were shortening outside as the sun rose higher, and then a plane, breaking the relative peace, roared in over the building – the first of many – following the latest change in wind direction.

The quiet moments were when she felt her self-inflicted isolation more keenly.

Most people knew her as Agatha Ducatti, but her full name was Agatha Ducatti Durán-Delapeña. The *catti* was pronounced like 'catty', *Durán* like 'do run' (with a rolled *r*) and the *n* in *peña* like the slippery second one in El Niño, that trouble-making weather phenomenon that crops up in the warm Pacific waters off South America every few years. She was born in Caracas, Venezuela, and following the naming customs practised in Spanish-speaking countries, she was burdened with both her father's first surname and her mother's. Her father was Italian by birth, hence 'Ducatti' (her great-grandfather had added a *t* to his surname after a nasty, ongoing argument with his motorcycle-manufacturing cousins). Her mother was Spanish and *her* father had hyphenated the surnames of his parents so that any surname he passed on would contain both, hence 'Durán-Delapeña'.

Agatha's mother, an actress and her father, an oil engineer, met and married in Madrid where they both lived and worked, and moved to Venezuela when the company Señor Ducatti worked for posted him there. When her mother gave birth to their first child, they named her Agatha because of Señor Ducatti's fondness for Agatha Christie's detective stories. As it turned out, a detective was all Agatha ever wanted to be.

(In fact she'd been told that the name Agatha had also been inspired by the Catholic saint, Agatha of Sicily, which was probably unsurprising given her father's Italian background. It wasn't until she was old enough to understand these things, though, that she discovered the gruesome tale attaching to St Agatha: she'd been tortured by the Romans – which supposedly included having her breasts cut off – and was martyred in the year 251, going on to become the patron saint of, among other things, rape victims. Fun facts that her parents had left out.)

In 1991, after an unplanned pregnancy, Agatha's mother gave birth to another girl: Agatha now had a sister,

Laura, twelve years younger than her. The following year, at a time of political instability and troubles in the oil industry in Venezuela, Agatha and her family moved to Australia, settling in Sydney. Agatha was thirteen. When her parents and Laura moved to Brisbane in 2006, Agatha was already a police officer in Sydney and chose not to join them.

So she'd been living apart from her family for seven years now, and some aspects of that never got any easier. Her sister Laura was studying to be an architect and was too immersed in her life up in Brisbane to pay Agatha much attention. And Agatha was too busy to travel up there except at Christmas, and even then she often had to cancel at the last minute.

And she was single (again) which didn't improve matters.

As she leaned back in her chair, staring at the sky, she could feel her top and her pants stretching and straining. The thought occurred to her that she'd probably been eating too much lately — not that she was a calorie-counter (and more note-taking was the last thing she needed) — and maybe she'd have to consider cutting out the chocolates, or at least cut down. She was fit enough and reasonably toned — she jogged, swam, worked out — so no problem there, but would have preferred to see a smaller number stare back at her when she weighed herself each morning. Sure, she was womanly, and men seemed to like her (no problem there either), but she was still self-conscious about her weight. Maybe it was because she was a little tomboyish, but sometimes she felt as though she was a thin girl trapped in a fat girl's body.

And she was proud of her Venezuelan upbringing and sense of femininity, dare she say it, and her, how shall we say, on-the-table sexuality (or was that on-the-sleeve?), and she couldn't have been anyone else if she tried.

But she was tired. Tired of the struggle of it all. It wasn't easy being a 'foreign' girl, being from another culture, even though she'd been living in Sydney now for twenty-one years. You still had to prove your worth, every day. And homicide was exhausting, people were exhausting, *men* were exhausting. Men, why did they always have to try to control you? Surely they were smart enough to know that they wouldn't like it if they got what they thought they wanted?

But of course, they *weren't* smart enough, were they.

She sighed deeply and leaned further back in her swivel chair, throwing her head and arms back and stretching right out. When Brearly walked in, she could see him upside down.

5.

Oh Lord save us, Brearly thought.

He'd just walked into the office he shared with Agatha. This situation had been in place for just over a week now, and the distraction level was still high. Higher, if anything.

Today she was wearing those tight white pants she often wore, along with a black short-sleeved top, and was stretched out over the back of her chair, flashing her cleavage for all the world, and in particular Brearly, to see. In the circumstances, he couldn't have, if he tried, avoided seeing her bra. It was black lace, or possibly navy. Black or navy, one thing was crystal clear: this was getting ridiculous, she *had* to have known what she was doing, surely. Had she seen him coming? He needed a coffee. Or something.

It reminded him of when Agatha first turned up at Newtown.

A few weeks prior to Agatha's arrival in May 2011, when they'd been keenly awaiting their first look at the new detective, Brearly had remarked to his immediate superior officer at the time, Dan Jeffries, 'Well let's hope it's a willowy blonde, then.' He'd been only half joking. *A female in her early thirties*, was all they'd been told.

As it turned out, Agatha was the polar opposite, the photographic negative, of a willowy blonde. Her hair was dark brown, almost black – like dark chocolate – and fell in bouncing ringlets. Her eyes were the colour of amber, rich and warm, and possessed both a sensual glint and a sparkling ferocity, like a wild animal's. Her olive skin had a depth of colour and smoothness that was almost breathtaking. And no, she wasn't willowy either, but more... curvaceous. She wasn't tall, but she wasn't plump – she was athletic, and at the same time, as far as Brearly was concerned, one hundred percent woman.

That day when Agatha first walked into the 'Big Room', as they called the main meeting room at the Newtown police station – headquarters of the Newtown LAC (Local Area Command) – she was wearing a pair of trousers a size too small, looking like they'd give way any second, so tight they were in danger of becoming transparent. Brearly had been explaining something to Dan and had lost his train of thought. In the awkward moments before their boss arrived, Agatha sniffed the air disapprovingly, or so it looked to Brearly.

'I'm sorry.' It was Superintendent Perrick, following her in, looking vaguely flustered. 'Introductions are in order. Agatha, this is Detective Sergeant Dan Jeffries, and Detective Constable Peter Brearly. Gentlemen this is...' He paused, took a breath. 'Detective Constable Agatha Ducatti Durán-Delapeña.' He'd been practising. 'Where's Spanner, er... Simon?' Brearly and Dan both shrugged. 'Anyway, bit of historical background, I'm sure she won't mind, Agatha is, as you may already know, originally from—'

'Buenos Aires,' Brearly said, nodding.

'No, no, she's—'

'Argentina?' Agatha looked aghast. Brearly immediately had a vision of her shooting him right there, in the middle of the police station – these Latinos and their hot blood, you never knew. He did like the way she said 'Argentina' though, pronouncing it the Spanish way and stretching the middle *i* to breaking point. Like her trousers.

'Agatha's from Caracas, Brearly. *Venezuela.*'

'Jesus, Brearly, get your facts straight,' Dan said.

'Right.' That was about all Brearly could say. He'd never been to Venezuela, or anywhere in Latin America for that matter. His only experience with native Spanish speakers was a quick trip through Spain on a Contiki tour in the nineties. They spoke *fast*, was about all he remembered.

Also, while not approving of the habit in others when he encountered it, and he was almost ashamed to admit it, but he was finding it hard to resist having his attention constantly snatched by Agatha's admirable physique – and her backside in particular – especially every time she twisted this way or that. Or moved at all. It was probably a good time to step out for coffee... if only he had the strength to.

'Although I *have* been here for nineteen years,' Agatha clarified.

'You're a regular Aussie now,' Perrick said. 'Like the rest of us.'

There was a pause, a conversational gap which begged to be filled.

'Right, then,' Perrick continued, 'I'd better let you lads and ladies get on with it.'

'Ladies?' said Brearly. 'The Superintendent must mean Agatha and *you*, Dan.'

But Brearly wasn't looking at Dan Jeffries. He was smiling at Agatha and those coruscating amber eyes of hers – eyes which were telling him everything was going to be, if not all right, then at the very least just that little bit better.

Agatha sprang back upright, flinging her hair forwards, and then back again out of her face. After a couple of beats, she swivelled her chair around, presumably to see if he was still there. One guess.

'Peter,' she said.

She never used his first name. Neither did anyone else. For good reason.

'Brearly,' he replied.

'That's you.'

'Listen. Agatha.' He paused, knowing how comical this was going to sound. 'You may have noticed there are quite a few Peters around here.'

'You. And...'

'Lutger...'

'Peter Lutger. True.'

'Lutger, and then there's...' He waited for her to twig. 'Perrick.'

'Oh yeah. Peter, Peter and Peter. The Three Petes. That's so funny.'

'No it's not. It's a freakin' pain in the neck. I've tried to work out what the chances are of three of us in the one... Does my head in.'

'Be easy enough to work out. You just take the—'

'Anyway. The upshot? The Peters all use surnames.'

'Huh. I always thought the surnames thing was some kind of macho act.'

Brearly snorted. 'Perrick started it. When I arrived. Said it'd be too weird if he called me Peter. Be like talking to himself. That's Perrick for you.' He smiled and shook his head. 'Macho act. You must think we're a bunch of idiots.'

There was a short silence.

'That's fine by me, Brearly,' Agatha said and got up and walked over to a filing cabinet. As always, Brearly did his best not to remove her pants with his eyes (an impossible task anyway, they were too *tight*).

'So anything more on the body?' she asked.

'You mean the Pantyhose Woman?' He shook his head. 'Nah, I reckon our body walked off on its own.'

'You don't think she was dead?'

Brearly shrugged. 'That's where my money'd be. And I wouldn't be surprised if that *kid* had something to do with it, too.'

'So it could be just... a prank?'

'Could be.'

'Hmm.' Agatha frowned and sat down again. 'And so the boy? Is he——?'

'He's coming here later, after school. His mother's bringing him in.'

'He's coming here?'

Brearly nodded. 'I think you should speak to him. Alone. Might be a bit less threatening.'

'OK. Sure. No problem.' Agatha paused for a moment. 'Why, because I'm a woman?'

'Partly that. And, you know, you're Argentinian, so...'

'Venezuelan!'

'Same difference.'

'It is *not* the same difference. Be like me calling you a *Pom.*'

Brearly smiled at her playful enunciation of 'Pom', and the gymnastics of her lips. And she was so beautifully easy to bait, this heaven-sent jewel of a woman. There was no doubt about it: his life was a brighter proposition altogether since Agatha's appearance.

'So how does being Venezuelan or Argentinian or whatever you think I am make me less threatening?'

'The Latina types are more empathetic. Everyone knows that.'

Agatha shook her head. 'Just give me the file.'

Brearly pointed to a pile of manila folders on the floor. 'It's the top one.'

And as Agatha got out of her chair and bent down to pick up the file, Brearly couldn't help but catch the angling

of her bottom in his direction, pants stretched drum-tight,
and then the consequential straightening of her form as she
rose again and left the room.

Lord save us all.

6.

'George?'

They were seated in the police station's interview room and the boy was looking down at his feet. He'd hardly looked at Agatha since she walked into the room. Just once or twice, little furtive glances. With an adorable little twinkle in his eye. Or a cheeky one, she wasn't sure which.

'George?' Agatha repeated. 'You haven't done anything wrong, OK?'

He nodded.

'It's really important that you tell us about all the little things. The details. They can make a big difference. To our... investigation. Do you understand?'

Another nod. He was shy, Agatha thought, especially for a thirteen-year-old. Not so shy, though, to have run away without taking photos on his phone. Not so shy to have kept it to himself. Not so shy to have been unable to smile at her when she first walked into the room. It was a brief smile, but he liked her, it was obvious. He was plainly attracted to her. So no, not so shy – or at least, not *that* sort of shy. So what was he doing at the kilns?

She looked down at her notes again. There wasn't much there yet, not of substance, but whatever it was she wrote it down. Because she was terrified of forgetting. Not just what George said, or the work-related stuff, but anything. And so Agatha wrote everything down. The thing was – and she knew this was illogical, was against the evidence, she was only thirty-four and, she knew it herself, sharp as a tack – she had somehow convinced herself she was getting Alzheimer's, or was destined to. There was no compelling reason for believing this, but she just accepted it, or at least feared it. Any time she forgot something, she blamed it on Alzheimer's. And so because of this fear she wrote everything down so that she'd never forget it and always be able to access it. Her flat was filled, absolutely bursting at the seams, with her notebooks. Not police ones, they were kept at work, but her personal ones.

But every cloud had a silver lining, and Agatha had a particular talent that more than made up for this perceived flaw, whether real or not. She had a remarkable ability when it came to processing information. It was all intuitive, but she could pull an answer out of a hat – a correct answer – just like that, and have no idea how she did it. She could look at a puddle of water on the footpath and tell you straight away, not only how long it had been since the rain had fallen, but how long it had rained for and how much rain there'd been, to the millimetre.

(Of course just as every cloud had a silver lining, every silver lining had a cloud, too. Her potent intuition may have landed her with a detective's superpower, but it also, she guessed, was to blame for her dreams, which were almost more vivid than reality itself, and usually more terrifying – at least it wasn't the other way around! But the dreams tended to linger and impose themselves on her reality. Case in point: she was still having trouble getting the previous night's dream out of her head.)

Sometimes she wondered about the apparent contradiction between this preternatural intuitional power of hers and her obsessive note-taking. It occurred to her one answer might be that the cause of the note-taking, her fear of getting Alzheimer's, may simply have arisen from a fear of losing her superpower. After all, didn't we all fear losing what was precious to us?

There was, of course, a darker alternative: that her intuition was in fact *predicting* she would get Alzheimer's, like some kind of prophecy. A most unpalatable thought indeed.

'So why did you go to the chimneys in the first place? Why were you in the park?'

George shrugged.

'Were you exploring?'

A pause, and then a nod.

'Do you often go exploring on your own?'

'Sometimes.'

'Had you explored around these buildings before? The kilns?'

He shook his head.

'But you knew of their existence? You knew they were there?'

'Just the chimneys.'

'So you knew about the chimneys, you went to check them out... you came across the buildings there... and then you saw the body. Or the girl in the underwear.'

George was nodding.

'On the concrete,' Agatha continued. 'Next to a brick wall. As we see in the photo. OK. So when you first saw... her... what was your first thought? Were you scared?'

A shrug. A pause.

'A bit.'

'Right, so, you were a bit scared... Why didn't you just leave? I mean... why did you take the photos?'

Another shrug.

'We just... I just thought I should.'

George's face had gone the colour of a Rose of Venezuela.

'You said *we*.'

'No I said *I*.'

Agatha looked at him for a moment.

'You were with someone,' she said.

'No.' His eyes darted to one side.

'George.' She waited for him to look at her. 'You were with a friend, weren't you.'

He scratched his face. 'Mm.'

'What was his name?'

'Her name, she's a she.'

'OK. Name?'

A frown this time, but he was obviously only pretending to think.

'Nessie,' he said eventually. 'Ness.'

'Where's Ness now?'

'I don't know.'

'George...'

'I really don't. She hasn't called me back.'

George looked up and stared at her with his big brown eyes. He looked heartbreakingly sad and Agatha wondered what was affecting him the most. The girl in the pantyhose, or Ness.

7.

'He's telling the truth.'

Agatha was back in her office. Or rather the one she shared with—

'Sure,' Brearly said.

Brearly. With his dark hair and piercing green eyes. With his solid build and solid personality. And his sense of humour. She could have done worse.

'*Now* he's telling the truth,' he went on. 'He wasn't before.'

Not what you'd call a pretty face, but no doubt many women would find him cute in his own way. Or at least attractive in his... masculine-ness. Or was that masculinity?

'Only about his friend,' Agatha replied. 'He was just embarrassed that he was with a girl who's since snubbed him. He'd only just met her, that evening I think, and she hasn't returned his texts.'

'Hasn't...' Brearly shook his head. And under his breath: 'Poor bastard has a lot to learn about women.'

'I heard that.'

'I know, Agatha. You hear and see everything.'

And there it was again. Brearly's eyes flicked down, quick as a blink, onto her breasts and back again. A subliminal act of capture, the image stored in his head like a photograph, no doubt. And probably involuntary, but even so. Agatha sighed inside.

At which point she happened to notice, over Brearly's shoulder, a poster she'd glanced at countless times to the point of overfamiliarity. Against a dark blue background, and stamped in large yellow letters over a red circle with a cross through it, were the words 'SEXUAL HARASSMENT', and under that, in slightly smaller lettering: 'In case you're wondering who has to put up with Sexual Harassment… the answer is NO ONE!'.

'I have no doubt,' Agatha said, 'that even if we could find this Ness, there's little she'd be able to add. They were just two kids who came across an odd sight, there's no indication they had anything to do with this. It looks like they ran off, went to their homes, George told his parents, and by the time the father had arrived at the scene the body had gone.'

Agatha was leaning against her desk, and Brearly was standing in the middle of the room, hands on hips. Out their shared window, the rays of the setting sun were hitting the dark red bricks at the top of the old building across the street, making it look like it was coated in blood.

'The thing is,' Brearly said, 'if we're to believe him, she wasn't breathing. Meaning she was dead.' He made a face. 'And I dunno, but… there's something about those photos. Do they look like photos of a dead woman to you?

Agatha picked up one of the photographs lying beside her on her desk, and scrutinized it.

'She might have been breathing without them realizing it,' she said. 'They didn't check her pulse, didn't even touch her.'

'I mean,' Brearly added, 'she's clearly not doing *well*. Seen better days, no doubt. But dead? I'm not buying it.'

'She's been running.'

'Sorry?'

'She's been running.'

'Running?'

'In her pantyhose. Look at her feet.'

Brearly examined the photograph that had just been handed to him. After a few moments' careful consideration of what he was looking at and its implications, he breathed out heavily in a hiss and shook his head.

'I get the feeling...' Agatha began. She was looking at a photo and kept staring at it, and when she eventually put it down, she looked up at Brearly.

'I think she's another one of our girls. Another...'

She suddenly couldn't think of the word they'd been using, the word for the women on her and Brearly's ad hoc, unofficial missing persons list. Their word for the disappearing girls and women of eastern and inner western Sydney.

The list was unofficial, because the official line was still that the disappearances weren't linked and that there was nothing to suggest otherwise. But Agatha and Brearly, who had been involved in a series of investigations for over two years now, weren't so sure. And in the case of the Pantyhose Woman as Brearly called her, despite the fact they couldn't be sure if she'd been alive or dead when the photographs were taken, she'd certainly at the very least disappeared, and even though she couldn't have given you her reasons, Agatha was one hundred percent sure that they had another one to add to their list.

But what list? What was that word? The answer was too obvious to ask Brearly – he'd been the one to come up with it initially, but it was a common word and they used it all the time – she'd feel like a fool, he'd think her mind had gone. They'd been talking about it only a few days ago. It was ridiculous, she was having a complete mental blank.

Los Desaparecidos, The Disappeared list... The Vanished list.... The Missing... The Gone... Absent... Hidden...

Her Alzheimer's or pre-Alzheimer's or pretend-Alzheimer's was driving her crazy.

'*Poof*,' Brearly said. He was nodding slowly, and looking out the window again.

'What?'

'Into thin air. Yet again.'

Agatha's thoughts were at a dead end, and her face must have appeared correspondingly vacuous because Brearly was looking at her strangely, presumably wondering what was going on in there. And who was this woman he'd been landed with.

'I'm agreeing with you,' he continued. 'Could be another one for our list. Another Nowhere woman.'

The *Nowhere* list!

Agatha made a mental note to do something as soon as Brearly wasn't looking: pull out her notebook – her personal one, not her police one – and quickly jot down the phrase *Nowhere list* so she would never forget it again.

8.

Pippa was having a drink with a friend, Jay-Lee, in a pub – the Rose Hotel in the hip and grungy inner city suburb of Chippendale.

'Just talk to him, Pippa. At least thank him.'

'Uh-huh.'

'You have to. He won't... you know, *bite* or anything.'

'Yeah.'

'I'm sure he's a nice guy. Go on.'

Great help Jay-Lee was. Pippa snuck another look across at the pale man in the dark grey suit who seemed to be constantly tugging on his blue shirt cuffs. It definitely looked like there was a potential for biting there. He was a biter for sure, he actually looked a bit like a shark in that angry grey suit. A pretty plump one, too. And one that left half its shirt hanging out. Who wore a suit in the middle of the day – a *Saturday* – into a pub like this anyway? A real estate agent? Funeral director? Maybe a racegoer, but they usually roamed the city in drunken packs. And this one was wearing runners. With his *suit*. Weirdo.

Still, she had no choice. Not really. Not after he'd bought her three drinks. Not that she'd known it was him, she'd actually assumed it was the Robert Pattinson clone over in the corner (served her right). If she'd known it was him in the first place...

Pippa slid off her bar stool and straightened her dress, and pulled it down. It suddenly felt way too short, she should have worn her jeans (she almost did, too). Jay-Lee must be laughing her head off inside, she thought, but it's not funny. Not even after three mojitos or whatever they were. *Especially* after three mojitos.

She walked across the room, weaving around some tables of happy people, absorbed in their lives. She hoped they stayed absorbed. She certainly hoped she didn't know any of them, this was seriously embarrassing. It was only about ten metres but it felt more like ten kilometres, or like she was wading through molasses, and she couldn't have sped things up if she tried.

Eventually, as she was duty-bound to do – seemingly by some obscure law of physics as much as the sense of obligation which by now seemed farcical (must've been the alcohol talking) – she arrived at her destination.

He was plumper up close. Fat, more like it, but powerfully built too. His pale skin shone like a lighthouse and he had beady eyes that were grey and washed out and strange. This was getting worse by the second.

'Hi,' she began. 'Look, I just wanted—'

'You're Pippa,' the man interjected, allowing no room for denial or qualification.

How did he know her name? He must've overheard them talking, the busybody. Now he was looking back across the room at Jay-Lee who… Pippa couldn't believe it, she was leaving! The total *bitch*, she'd kill her for this. Not funny. Not. At. All.

'Is your friend leaving?' the man asked, stating the fucking obvious. Was there an accent there?

'She'll be back in a minute,' she lied.

The cow was doing a runner, leaving Pippa to try to squirm her way out on her own. Jay-Lee had spotted some friends in the beer garden when they'd arrived and that was where she was heading right now, as sure as one and one made two... or *three* probably if this creep was to have his way... *Euuwh!!*... now there was an unpleasant thought, why did she have to go and think of that? Imagine that. Gross. *So* gross.

'I fear you may have lost your wingman,' the suit said.

OK, she thought, that does it. Eject!

'Listen, I just wanted—'

'Go home,' he said.

'What?'

'Go home, to your flat. There's a letter, sitting on your bed. Once you've—'

'On my *bed*? What are you talking about?'

'More like a set of instructions perhaps. Trust me. Everything will be clear once you've read it.'

'Is this a joke? Because...' But he didn't look like he was joking.

'Trust me,' the man repeated, finishing his drink and standing up. 'And you're very welcome to the drinks, by the way.'

He pulled at his shirt cuffs so they fully extended from under his suit sleeves and covered his wrists, and picked up his fat wallet. Which was when she noticed the beginnings of a very mean, very sarcastic smirk forming on his lips.

She was speechless.

'Be seeing you Pippa,' and with that, the fat man and his fat wallet left the pub, and Pippa joined Jay-Lee and her friends in the beer garden.

By the time she and Jay-Lee eventually left an hour or so later, she'd forgotten all about the man's insane claim about there being a letter on her bed. And if she'd thought about it, and if she'd been asked about it, she would have simply said it was the worst try-on she'd ever come across, and she'd come across a few.

Laughable, she would have said.

9.

Her timing could not have been worse. Ten minutes either side and…

It began like any other Monday morning for Chalaise. Dreamt of her boss – again – and woke up wondering what his latest floozie looked like, and whether he'd taken her away yet, on his yacht. (Crappy yacht, by the way, barely floated.) Dragged herself reluctantly out of bed and into the shower, found another grey hair (which was crazy-insane, she was only twenty-nine), fed the dogs, applied her make-up, got in her car.

She usually left at seven-thirty but this particular morning Gangster was in a bad mood. Her Jack Russell. (With the other one, the Pomeranian-cross, you could never tell, she *always* appeared to be in a bad mood, but it was all an act, the good-for-nothin' little rat-faced tart.) So Chalaise took the trouble of feeding him, Gangster, an extra treat. Which meant getting the packet out again, re-sealing it, etcetera. And of course Duchess wanted one too, didn't she. All in all, sixty seconds lost. And then someone had left the bottom gate open, so she had to go and close it. Another two minutes gone. Both things probably contributed to her only just missing the set of traffic lights at the top of the hill, and by then the rot had set in. She was now five minutes late. Throw in the thickening traffic at that time, and one particularly slow driver in front of her, and there's your ten.

Ten minutes either side, that was all it would have taken.

So at 8.35am, ten minutes late, she arrived at the car park in the basement of her building. By the time she'd 'exited her vehicle', to use police parlance, there was no one around. No one, that is, except for the man sitting in his car – a beaten-up black BMW with no number plates, which was a bit weird in itself. As she walked past him, she could see that he was just sitting there, not doing anything. Except watching. She couldn't see his face, he was little more than a silhouette. About all she could make out was that he was white with a hefty build, or at least a large head.

Which was when the lights went out. Everywhere or just in the car park she had no way of knowing, but it was dark as midnight with only the emergency lights providing dim illumination. She wasn't the type to scare easily, but with that man there like that, Chalaise had already been a little uneasy *before* the lights went out. So when it all went dark, she was actually pretty nervous.

She continued walking past the BMW towards the lit-up green EXIT sign next to the lift, with nothing else to hear but the sound of her high heels on concrete, echoing around the car park.

But then there was the sound of a car door opening and closing – very rapidly, with a *click* and a *thwunk* – and although she couldn't hear his footsteps, she knew he was there, following her.

She tried not to show fear, or walk faster, but easier said than done. She reached the lift with her heart in her mouth, and then to her utter dismay the lift button light didn't come on when she pressed it and it seemed as if the lift was out too. Which only left the stairs.

At least there was the emergency light over the stairwell. She got to it at the same time the man did, she could hear him now, the padding of his feet or whatever he was wearing on them. She turned to face her worst fears, determined to win whatever battle it was she would have to fight. Because if you're anything you're a fighter, she told herself.

She couldn't see his face, it was in shadow, but he was wearing a suit, which made her feel slightly better, and trainers, which didn't. And he was handing her something.

'I think this must be yours,' he said in an odd, strained voice. He was holding a black cardboard folder.

'Mine?' Chalaise asked hesitantly. She took the folder, opened it, but there was nothing inside.

And when she looked up again he wasn't there, but that was when she felt the arm across her neck, cutting off the circulation, breathing, everything, because he was strong, so strong, and as she began to faint she was aware of something being put over her face, and then everything went black. Properly black, this time.

And in the slender seconds, and fractions of seconds, between the arm across her throat, and unconsciousness, her brain rapidly processed what was now, in all probability, as things were panning out, useless information. The gist of it though was that, as so often happens in Life, it all comes down to timing. Ten minutes, in this case. If she'd arrived twenty minutes late instead of only ten, it could have been Harriet instead, who always arrived at the office precisely nine minutes late every day and, in fact, was due right about now. (*Hurry up and get your lazy ass down here Harriet!*) If on the other hand she'd been on time and arrived ten minutes earlier, she definitely would have beaten the power cut and probably the man in the BMW, too. All she would have needed was enough time to get to the lift and away, to freedom.

And ten minutes would have been more than enough. No worries.

10.

In about an hour, the sun would be setting and darkness would once again reign. About time, Agatha thought, this daylight saving business was overrated – she'd never been a fan. It messed with reality, somehow.

'They all disappeared without a trace,' Brearly was saying, 'and they're women. OK, young women, attractive, but that's it, there's no other link, that's all they've got in common.'

'Something will emerge,' said Agatha. 'As we've said all along.'

'Yeah but when, though. I'm starting to think maybe we're kidding ourselves with this Nowhere list of ours. For one thing, no one else seems to agree with us.'

She caught him looking at her chest again. She wasn't even wearing a low-cut top for godssake. And it wasn't as if her boobs were gigantic or anything. Maybe these snatched glimpses didn't matter in the greater scheme of things, but they were becoming more frequent and longer-lasting, gradually inching their way across that dividing line (impossible to pinpoint but we all knew where it was) between socially acceptable peeks (compliments, really) and insultingly provocative stares. Not that Brearly was doing the latter. Yet. But maybe she should nip things in the bud and say something. Or maybe just let it go through to the keeper, as they say. For now. In the meantime, she decided she'd just have to man up.

'This latest flurry of disappearances——' she began.

'Not exactly a flurry.'

'Well it's more than a normal... *fluctuación*... fluctuation, it's a bit of a big spike actually, and how to explain that? Coincidence? I don't know about you, but I don't believe in coincidences.'

'Oh *I* do,' said Brearly. 'Because they're all part of the chaos and randomness and pure shittiness of life.'

'Jeez Brearly,' Agatha said. 'You're in a dark mood.'

Brearly threw her a look which she couldn't decipher. One of resignation, possibly.

'Anyway,' he said. 'It's only a coincidence if they coincide. But I agree with you on one thing. It *is* a bit of a big spike, statistically speaking. And with big spikes, you know what they say...'

Agatha waited for the second half of a tasteless double entendre – she had a feeling Brearly was about to push things too far here, about to... what was the expression?... over-egg the pudding – but she needn't have worried. This time.

'They require big explanations,' he said. 'And I don't see any. Take the last couple of cases for example.'

When Brearly bent down to pick up a couple of manila folders from one of the piles on the floor, Agatha couldn't help but notice the line of his underwear showing through the seat of his trousers. She stopped the train of thought – it didn't bear thinking about really – but he did have a pleasingly robust physique. (Enough!) And then she noticed his stomach, just slightly pushing over his belt line, and the line of thought continued, but then it suddenly flipped and she realized that this new uncomfortable feeling stemmed from the way it recalled the previous night's dream and that horrible character she kept dreaming about. What had he called himself again? She'd already forgotten. She should have written it down, along with *Nowhere list,* so she wouldn't forget it. Too late.

'Three weeks ago,' Brearly said, after opening one of the files. 'Philippa Richards, student, known as Pippa to her friends. Last seen leaving the Rose Hotel in Chippendale. According to a friend she was having a drink with,' and he paused as he looked for the name, 'one... Jay-Lee Morton... there was a guy there who was buying her drinks and who she spoke to briefly, but he left well before she did.'

'And we still don't have a description. Of the guy.'

'Nope. What the friend told us is still all we've got. Older. Wearing a suit.'

'That's right,' Agatha said, remembering. And getting an odd feeling.

'So not much to go on there. And neither hide nor hair of her has been seen since.'

The words *hide* and *hair* stuck in her mind for some reason.

Brearly slapped the file down on Agatha's desk and opened the second file.

'Even less with the next one,' he said. '*Two* weeks ago. Chalaise Corlay, travel agent. Twenty-nine years old, works in an agency in East Sydney. Never made it in to work although her parked car was found in the basement car park there.'

'I was just about to have a closer look at that one.'

'Well it won't take you long. Thinnest file in police history. The only eyewitness, if you could call her that, noticed an unusual vehicle parked in the car park, a knocked-around black BMW with no number plates. Or none that she could see, the lights were out, and she didn't stop because she was running late. So there you have it. Possible suspect driving an old black Beemer, that's it. Vehicle was probably stolen anyway, no visual of suspect, no prints, no DNA, nothing.'

'*Poof*,' he added, this time making a theatrical gesture with his hand, before slapping that file down on top of the first one.

'Still no CCTV?'

'This ain't London. As I'm sure you're realizing. Dunno what it's like in Argentina...'

Agatha just sighed loudly and shook her head. Picked up the Chalaise Corlay file.

'And now we have the Pantyhose Woman,' Brearly said, pointing to the photographs still laid out on Agatha's desk. 'Or we did have, and now she's gone. Like some kind of double act, two for the price of one. Any new missing person reports by the way?

But Agatha was thinking of something else. She was looking at a file photograph of Chalaise Corlay. Blonde hair, blue eyes – undoubtedly attractive – but she imagined she could see something in the way this girl was looking at the camera. (Girl? Or woman? If a woman looked young, could you call her a girl?)

'Who took this?' she asked.

'No idea.'

She opened the Philippa Richards file and pulled out a photograph.

'These?'

Brearly shook his head.

Looking at the photo of Philippa – or Pippa – Agatha got the same feeling as the one she got when she was looking at the picture of Chalaise. Wasn't sure why, they were quite different looking, Pippa had dark hair and brown eyes. It was something in the eyes, perhaps...

'There's a link,' she said.

'Tell me.'

She shook her head. 'Something...' she muttered. A multitude of simultaneous thoughts and ideas were rushing through her brain like a tidal bore up the Amazon – a *pororoca*. Or like a passing train skipping the station, not stopping for passengers...

'We see what we want to see,' she said.

Brearly had a look on his face that said *And what am I expected to do with that?*

'Pardonnez-moi!' someone said in a bad French accent.

It was Detective Senior Constable Terri Spedding – she'd just stuck her head in. Terri, who held the same rank as Agatha (although more recently promoted), was blonde, relatively tall, probably over 170cm, but certainly not what you'd describe as willowy, for example. She had, how should one put it, a sturdy build, although not fat or stocky exactly, but almost. Maybe 'athletic build' would be fairer (but who needed to be fair?). And she had the severe eyes of a Victorian-era headmistress. To sum up, fairly average looks in Agatha's view. And she made a habit of speaking in badly pronounced French. She was studying it, apparently, although you'd never have guessed.

'Terri,' said Brearly.

'You're still here,' Terri said, stating the obvious, and then added 'This is late for you, isn't it Agatha?'

Agatha simply forced a smile. She knew what Terri was up to: always trying to cut her down to size. The competitiveness was, frankly, embarrassing.

And to Brearly: 'So how are you finding your new digs?'

'Bit small, company's good. Speaking of which, how *did* you score your own office, Terri?'

'You just have to remember to bat your eyelashes.'

'I must work on that. And by the way, happy birthday for... was it last Sunday? The big four oh?'

Terri appeared lost for words.

'You look *great* for forty,' said Agatha, not meaning it.

'Thanks,' Terri replied with a false smile.

'*Really* not looking forward to that one,' Brearly said.

'How old are you?' Agatha asked him.

'Thirty-eight.'

'Forty's not so bad.' Terri said, looking at Agatha. 'It'll be like ripping off a band-aid. When is it?'

'I'm thirty-four.'

'Oh right,' said Terri, feigning surprise.

There was a pause which Terri must have relished, cut short by Perrick who suddenly appeared behind Terri – like a ghost, he was moving so silently. He should have been a spy, Agatha thought, but then again, wasn't that what most cops were, in their own way?

'Here's trouble,' he said, startling Terri who uttered a muted *Oh!* 'So Brearly, you still coming to the Rose?'

'Yep'

'Agatha?'

'I'll have to pass on that one, thanks.'

'Next time. Terri? You coming?'

'I...' Terri seemed lost for words for a moment. 'I might *not* tonight...' She was raising her eyebrows at Perrick who seemed to be trying to decipher the Morse code. 'I... might... head off, I think.'

There was an awkward moment.

'No problem,' Perrick eventually said. There was something Agatha couldn't quite decipher in his dark brown eyes. And those eyes... He reminded her of her father – same eyes, same even temperament, equanimous. Kept his own counsel. She liked that. 'No problem at all. Right then. Brearly, see you there in twenty.' A last look at Terri, a muttered 'OK', and he was gone.

'See you tomorrow,' Terri said to Brearly and Agatha, and then she was gone too.

Agatha strolled over to the doorway and checked they were out of earshot. 'What was that about?'

'What?'

'Between those two.'

'Yeah,' Brearly snorted. 'You didn't know? Must be the worst-kept secret in Newtown.'

'Terri and *Perrick*?'

'Mm hm.'

'Jesus Christ in a barn. I thought I must have been imagining it.'

'To be honest, it's not really the worst-kept secret. I was actually privy to some... inside information.'

'Perrick told you?' Agatha shook her head. 'So *that's* why she got her own office.'

'And the penny drops.'

'Isn't Perrick married?'

'He is that.'

Agatha puffed out her cheeks and exhaled heavily.

'Nature,' Brearly said. 'Red in tooth and claw.'

'Where's that from?'

'Some poem. Is that Terri, or what?'

Agatha was impressed that Brearly even read, let alone read poetry.

'Or Perrick,' she said. 'The sneaky bugger.'

'Sneaky. That may be giving him too much credit.'

'So... you read poetry, then?'

'Poetry? Hell no.'

'But you do read.'

'Very funny.'

'I'm serious. Do you *read* read?'

'Yeah. If you mean... Yeah. I *read* read.'

'What kind of stuff? Who by?'

'Just... thrillers, mainly. By... I don't know... guy who wrote *The Da Vinci Code*...'

'Dan Brown.'

'Yeah. And that Scandi guy... Norwegian... writes crime thrillers...' Snaps his fingers, trying to remember. 'What's his name?'

'Jo Nesbo?'

'Exactly. Not usually a fan of police procedurals, though. Too inaccurate. And boring. Oh and there's an American I *love*... wrote in the seventies, called... John D someone or other.'

'Jeez Brearly, your memory's terrible.'

Brearly threw her a look.

'Anyway,' he said. 'Perrick and Terri. So when Terri got transferred here in February last year, and Perrick had something to do with that, she was still a Constable, and you'd just been promoted to Senior Constable. One month later and she's promoted to Senior Constable as well. My theory is... OK, it's not a theory, I got it from the horse's mouth... she was promoted so you didn't outrank her.'

'Me? What?'

'And you can guess who was behind the promotion.'

'Far out.'

'Still, for all his shortcomings, Perrick's pretty fair.'

'Fair?'

'Well you and I got our promotions. Lutger's still waiting for his, admittedly, even though he arrived at the same time as Terri. He's still a bit miffed about that, actually.'

'Lutger? I've never heard him complain.'

'Never would, never will. Not the type. Anyway. I'm off. Sure you don't want to come?'

'No thanks.'

And with little more than a flash of his green eyes, Brearly was gone.

In the fading light, the dark red bricks at the top of the building opposite were beginning to take on a darker hue. Soon the city would undergo its daily transformation, and the daytime crowds would give over to that other breed, the nighttimers.

Nighttimers and nightmares.

A mental shiver rippled through Agatha as she recalled yet again the previous night's experience. Which was ridiculous, it was almost a day later, why was this one affecting her so much?

She pushed any further dark thoughts from her mind.

But all that did was leave thoughts of the Nowhere women.

11.

Brearly was standing in the middle of a crowded pub. With the hubbub. The pub in question was the Rose Hotel, Perrick's chosen venue. Funnily enough it had also been the chosen venue of Pippa and her friend Jay-Lee.

Brearly scanned the faces, checked the 'older guys' in suits (it did occur to him that from Jay-Lee's point of view, a student's in other words, 'older guy' pretty much covered the field). A good cop never clocked out, he reminded himself for at least the thousandth time. The thought tired him out then and there, which was timely because he'd just spotted his superintendent.

'What's the acronym for Sydney after dark?' Perrick said as soon as he sat down. 'S.A.D., sad.'

Looking around the room, it didn't look sad. Obviously said more about Perrick.

It had been Brearly's shout, and over a Carlsberg light ale they settled back to discuss matters demanding their attention.

'You a bit on edge, this week?' Perrick asked.

'Me? No, why?'

Perrick nodded smugly.

'I've said it before and I'll say it again, Brearly. Leave your woman trouble at home. It's no business of mine if you're pussy-whipped or not, but it's plain as day and it's a waste of good energy. It's a *waste*... of a good *cop*.'

Brearly looked at him for a moment, and then nodded slowly. *I was thinking of saying exactly the same thing about you.*

'Wow. Your intuitional powers... *sir*... are nothing short of staggering. If I may say so.'

'No. You may not. Not if you're going to take the piss, *Detective-Sergeant*.'

'Trouble is... I don't know what the hell you're actually talking about.'

Perrick just nodded and smiled at that, in the supremely annoying way of his. For Brearly, when it came to 'woman trouble', he'd have begged to differ about the 'waste of good energy'. The way he saw it, nothing to do with women was ever a waste of good energy. No doubt the recent Agatha distraction featured prominently in his reasoning, but of course, in all the circumstances, he'd keep those thoughts to himself. And as for 'pussy-whipped', yes, true, probably guilty as charged on that one, he *had* been, but not anymore, that was all behind him now...

'So how *are* things with Drianna?'

Drianna was Brearly's wife. Well, ex-wife really: they were separated, the division of property had been agreed, and the divorce was only a rubber stamp away. No kids, so it made things considerably easier. Having been married for thirteen years didn't. Drianna was Croatian too, and as far as Brearly was concerned, that said it all. Thirteen years with a Croatian was like twenty-six years with anyone else. In both the good sense and the not so good.

'Almost there. The divorce, I mean. And the fact that she hasn't stabbed me through the eye or had a contract taken out on me is a major bonus. Icing on the cake, if you will.'

'The divorce cake. And how's the new place? The flat in Darlinghurst.'

'Yeah, good. Darlinghurst is... well you know. Bit urban, bit... inner-city chic and all that, but it's fine. Full of gays, but they're good people.'

'And Drianna's still...?'

'In the old place. The house. Yeah.'

'Funny old world,' Perrick said and didn't elaborate.

'It definitely is that,' replied Brearly, mainly to fill the gap in the conversation.

'What do you think of the Portuguese?' Perrick asked. It was one of his typically tangential thoughts. No way of knowing where it came from and better not to ask. The *Portuguese?*

'Can't say I've ever given them much thought, to be honest. Ask me about the Argentinians.'

'You really have to lay off that one. You're gonna drive her up the wall.'

The two of them took swigs of their beers at the same time, and looked around the loud, crowded space, filled with student-types. No old dudes in suits. Just two old coppers.

Well... *Perrick* was old. Turned fifty last year, but Brearly, still under forty, could comfortably slot himself into the younger half of humanity. Just.

'Things OK with Agatha?' Perrick asked. 'Sharing an office?'

'Yeah, it's good.' Brearly said, a little too quickly. 'We get on well.'

'Not *too* well I hope.'

Brearly made an 'as if' face.

'I think I explained at the time,' Perrick continued, 'that normally, as you outrank Terri, you'd have been the one to get the office to yourself, but I figured it was smart to keep the women apart.'

'I understand.'

More swigs of beer.

'Agatha's bright,' Perrick said.

'I know.'

'Her instincts are... spot on.'

'I've noticed. She's good. Sharp.'

'And this theory about the disappearances. Being linked, I mean. You and Agatha still favouring that?'

'Well Agatha certainly is. I have a few reservations—'

'I have to say it's not exactly... a *popular* view at the moment. It's certainly not something we'd be announcing to the press in any big hurry.'

'I know. And I have my doubts about it. There's still very little in common between the cases.'

'*Except...*' Perrick said. 'They're all women. All young women.'

'Even so. There's no evidence of any kind of modus operandi in common or anything like that. And you'd think by this time—'

'There still could be something in it. It's a real cluster, looking at the last couple of years. Quite abnormal. There are these two recent ones, Philippa Richards, and, er...'

'Chalaise Corlay.'

'Chalaise Corlay. And what's this business about a body of a woman spotted near the chimneys and then disappearing again?'

'The Pantyhose Woman. Truly bizarre that one. Agatha has a feeling about it. Being linked. I'm not so sure.'

'Well I approve of you and Agatha thinking outside the box. We need to cover all bases. In case they *are* all linked. You know I've put it out there, tried to get the other Area Commands interested, but no takers yet.'

'I'm not surprised.'

'In the meantime, keep me informed about your theories. We could have a serial killer on our turf and we'll look pretty bad if we miss the signs.'

'That's true.'

'Once upon a time,' Perrick said after a pause, with a distant look in his eyes, 'the predator was a noble creature. *Lion*-like. Heroic and ferocious.'

'You mean animals, or...?'

'Nowadays, in these faithless times, the predator is ugly, selfish and cowardly. Where did we as a culture, as a race, as a species... where did we go wrong?'

Brearly assumed the question was rhetorical, but then Perrick turned and looked at him, waiting for a response.

'Can I phone a friend?' Brearly asked.

55

12.

Nightfall. No current predictions of rain. No cloud to speak of either and the newly risen moon would soon be visible. And when it was, everything would take on that eerie, dead, half-light, as if the night was trying to put a new perspective on things. And right now, for those who could see it, the moon would be hanging just above the horizon, and would be large, round, and orange, and slightly obscene.

With the exception of just one of their number, all the detectives operating out of the Newtown police station had left for the day, most of them still travelling home, still en route, either directly or via their chosen source of alcohol or other release. The exception was still in her office.

Agatha was musing about how the stupidest things had a habit of invading and occupying her mind, and the current one was the question of whether she was out of clean work clothes, and whether there'd be time to put the washing on when she got home or if she'd need to handwash a top and let it dry overnight, and iron it first thing in the morning...

While she was thinking these thoughts – as clear a sign as any that her work was done for the day and it was time to head home – she was sitting with her chair swivelled and facing the window. The wall of the building opposite, not yet touched by moonlight, was still in darkness, and Agatha could clearly see her reflection in the glass.

She could just make out the building and the details of its brickwork through the reflected image of the room around her. She kept staring at these two images, at the building outside, and herself in her room, and observed the way they merged into each other.

And for a brief moment, the image of the building, superimposed on that of her and her office, morphed into the man from her recurrent nightmare. For an instant it was him right next to her, staring back at her.

She closed her eyes. Opened them again and he was gone. And so had the building opposite, and all she could see was herself.

And then, for some reason, she thought of Jay-Lee's 'older guy in a suit' who had been chatting up Pippa, and experienced a sudden and sharp sensation that this admirer of Pippa's and the man that she herself had conjured up – summoned into existence in her nightmares – were one and the same.

This notion, however, was baseless and clearly absurd and, thus, merely fleeting.

13.

Carol had just stepped out of the shower when the doorbell chimed.

Ding dong!

It gave her a bit of a fright. It was 9pm on a Wednesday night and she hadn't been expecting anyone. Where she lived in Woollahra – one of Sydney's most affluent suburbs with its big trees, big houses, big cars and big, big bank accounts – her neighbours weren't the type to knock on your door for a cup of sugar. It couldn't have been her boyfriend Anthony who was away on business in Tokyo – she'd only spoken to him a couple of hours earlier. No, she couldn't think of anyone it could have been, and decided not to answer it. Pretend she was out.

She quickly dried herself, slipped a bathrobe on, and began drying her dripping wet hair with a towel. Told herself to ignore it, but her heart obviously had other ideas, and continued to race—

Ding dong!

Great. Whoever it was had pressed the doorbell a second time, and for good measure they knocked as well, three times, with their knuckles (bypassing the brass door-knocker). They were three hard, insistent knocks too.

She was annoyed now. It had been bad enough getting those irritating calls earlier, but she had an early start in the morning and was looking forward to a pleasant, undisturbed night in, accompanied by a glass of wine, a plate of roasted vegetables and the latest episode of *Borgen*, followed by an early night in bed with her newly washed and ironed, satin sheets...

And then it hit her: the pharmacist. That's who it was going to be. She'd totally forgotten. She'd dropped in yesterday with a prescription. He said it could take a couple of days (for some reason) and would that be OK. Of course, she said, it wasn't urgent, and then forgot about it. He'd done this before – dropped pills in at her home, and his Bondi Junction pharmacy wasn't so far away. (He'd told her previously that her place was on his way home; she wasn't sure if she believed him, but it didn't worry her – she just took it as a compliment.)

She tiptoed down the stairs – luckily she'd left the lights off down there, so whoever it was wouldn't be able to see her.

He was a strange man, her pharmacist. He was certainly good at his job. Good, not just because he knew his compounds and brands and illnesses – he always knew what would help you – but also because he had the most amazing memory, or appeared to. He seemed to know what everyone wanted as soon as they walked into his store and not because he could somehow mysteriously divine their illnesses, but because (she assumed) he could instantly recall what prescription they'd brought in on their previous visit. He virtually had the box slapped down on the counter before you had a chance to get your prescription out of your handbag. Just about.

Carol looked through the peephole – being careful not to make a sound, not even to breathe – and sure enough there he was, standing in the sickly yellow gloom of the front entrance lighting. As always, he was wearing a suit and running shoes, just as he did in the pharmacy. In fact it was all she'd ever seen him in. And there he was tugging at his cuffs, it must have been a nervous habit of his. She had no idea about his age: if she had to guess she would have said he was in his fifties, but he could have been forty and he could have been sixty. He had short, light-coloured hair (maybe sandy?), thick ears, smallish eyes and a large, roundish head. Other than the roundness, and the smallish eyes, his face was difficult to describe. If she were ever asked to help with one of those Identikit images of him, she'd have no chance, she'd be hopeless. He looked like many men of his age – large, a bit rotund (although in his case fit-looking too), and, yes, she had to say it, plain in almost every sense.

Yesterday, when she'd walked into his pharmacy, she'd been heading out for drinks and was wearing her favourite dress. Sheer, white, and a bit daring – you could see her underwear through it. More importantly though, it em-phasized her eyes in a most exceptional manner – even if she did say so herself! (:o LOL). Her eyes were her best feature. And her dress set off not just her eyes, but specifically her eyeshadow as well, which she knew because the pharmacist of all people made a comment about it.

About her eyeshadow. She couldn't remember what it was, but it was something complimentary. Which was a bit strange and made her feel a little uncomfortable – it was certainly a bit of an odd thing for a pharmacist to be going on about, if you asked her. Although maybe it was just as well he'd commented on her eyeshadow and not her eyes, because that really *would* have been weird.

This late in the evening though was a first. Last time he'd dropped off a box of pills it had been around 6pm, not 9. He'd obviously been working late, but why couldn't it have waited for the next day? Maybe he thought she was desperate, but he'd already warned her it could take a couple of days. He was a strange man.

She was halfway into the process of turning the front door handle – past the point of no return, as it were – when an unpalatable thought occurred to her. The pills. They were contraceptive pills this time, that was the prescription. She was thinking how inappropriate it all was, and had a frown on her face when she pulled the door open, but just in time she managed to turn it into a sparkling smile when she greeted him.

'Oh hello!'

14.

Five days later, Agatha was having a sudden coughing fit.

She wasn't sick, it was an externally based intruder, and it had made its way down her throat and had lodged there and was creating havoc. Agatha had no doubt who the perpetrator was: a London plane tree, her mortal enemy. Or rather one of those fine, hairlike bits of seed called 'trichomes' – little fibres of pure evil – that fell off the trees, especially on windy days. And Woollahra was full of plane trees.

On their way in, driving along Ocean Street, she and Brearly were welcomed by them on either side, as if the trees were presenting arms, like some sort of sinister honour guard. She was clearly 'behind enemy lines' and she wasn't even meant to be there. Woollahra was outside their usual jurisdiction, but it was looking like they had another disappearance on their hands – yet another one for their Nowhere list. Perrick was still trying to get the other Area Commands to take an interest in the possibility of a serial offender, and this was his way of hurrying things along. So he had sent Agatha and Brearly over to have a look. Or rather to 'have a gander' as he put it, but as she said back to him, she didn't know what geese had to do with it. By the look on his face, he thought she was being serious.

That was the trouble with retaining an accent: people always assumed you were still catching up.

They arrived at their destination, and wouldn't you know it, there was a massive plane tree sprouting up out of the footpath outside. Adding insult to injury, when she stepped out of the car the smell of burnt wood hit her immediately: the air was contaminated with not just trichomes but bushfire smoke as well, from the recent fires in the Blue Mountains. This wasn't a great start to her week.

Brearly had gone ahead and was already chatting to one of the local officers outside the front door. Apparently the woman's boyfriend had called the police three days ago, on Friday, concerned that he hadn't been able to contact her. He was overseas – in Japan for work – and they spoke most evenings unless one of them was otherwise busy, but he hadn't spoken to her since last Wednesday evening.

The woman herself – Carol Shelly – was forty-one and possessed, according to her boyfriend, 'the most beautiful blue eyes you're ever likely to see'. She was a quiet woman, he'd told them, on the point of being a loner and 'counterintuitively, she was largely shunned by people because of her beauty'. 'You see that a lot,' Brearly had said at the time while looking at her photograph and had then gone silent. Agatha hadn't been sure if he'd been silenced by Carol's blonde-haired, blue-eyed beauty or by a genuine empathy for a fellow human being (not something she'd seen often, in Brearly). As for Carol's looks, Agatha could see that she was, indeed, extremely attractive.

The police officers from the nearby Paddington police station (Rose Bay LAC) had attended the house on Friday and again today, Monday. When they'd first turned up, the front door had been locked. They'd rung the doorbell without obtaining an answer, and then broken in. The burglar alarm hadn't been set and there had been no sign of a struggle, they said.

Brearly waved Agatha over and the pair headed inside in silence. The two Paddington officers remained outside.

The house, despite being two storeys, was small, particularly for the area. You'd almost say tiny. It was a brick stand-alone, not a terrace house, and a bit too cutesy, reminding Agatha of an English cottage. It could have been lifted straight out of the nineteen fifties – it was so old-fashioned, she could scarcely believe a woman like Carol lived there. And owned it too, along with all the old-world furniture. Carol was a solicitor, a junior partner of a large Sydney law firm, and you'd have expected her to be a little more up with the times, but this woman certainly wasn't. And not a thing out of place either, as far as Agatha could see, after a quick scan of the place downstairs and up. Not a crumb on the floor, not a dirty dish in the sink, and her bed was made without the faintest wrinkle. Bathroom tidy. Mirrors clean. Five-star-perfect.

There were undoubtedly no signs of a struggle. And the neighbours hadn't seen anything, either. Brearly was soon bored.

'Seems patently obvious what's gone on here,' he said, after they returned back downstairs. He was staring at a large, framed photograph of a tropical fish hiding in coral.

'And what's that?'

'Look around you.'

Agatha did, and shrugged.

'Nothing,' Brearly said.

'Gee, Brearly, I really love these riddles first thing on a Monday morning.'

'Nothing's gone on here,' he said, 'because she hasn't been here.'

'So where is she?'

'At her lover's place. Cheating on her boyfriend.'

'You think? Why is it, then, that she didn't turn up for work this morning? Or Thursday or Friday?'

'Two reasons, Agatha.' He held up an outstretched thumb. 'Great...' Followed by his forefinger. '... sex.'

'Ha.'

'I'm serious. That's all it takes. You see it all the time.'

'OK. So why was the burglar alarm off then?'

'Plenty of people forget to put their alarm on.'

'I'm not sure, there's something not right.'

'Oh here we go. But I'm gonna jump in first. This house for one thing, this place is definitely not right. Gives me the creeps. The whole area does, let's get the hell back to Newtown... What's with the cough?'

Agatha had begun another coughing fit.

'I'm fine,' she croaked, once she'd finished. 'Something in my throat.'

'That's what *she* said.'

'What I mean is,' said Agatha, ignoring another typical Brearlyism, 'this place, it's too tidy.'

'Too tidy.'

'It's not normal.'

'You're right about that.'

'No what I'm saying is, she might have been tidy, but this is *too* tidy. Something happened here. I can feel it.'

'Feel it.' Brearly raised a sceptical eyebrow and looked around, hands on hips, his signature pose. 'So what you're trying to say is... there *was* a struggle and the wrongdoer has cleaned the place up. *Over*-cleaned.'

'I don't know. I can just feel it, that's all.'

Brearly stared at her for a moment and nearly said something. Apparently thought better of it, and just nodded.

'Well,' he said. 'If this *is* another disappearance, another one for our list... it'd be nice if just *one* of them turned up so we could at least get our hands on a fucking *body*.'

'Then they wouldn't be vanished, they wouldn't be a Nowhere.'

'Call me a dinosaur,' Brearly went on, 'but I prefer the olden days when you had a *murder* and a *body*. This vanishing shit's just plain weird.'

'We had a body, remember? And we lost it.'

Brearly grunted. 'Bodies aren't meant to walk off on you. I still think it was a prank. Anyway. Even if something untoward really has happened to this woman, I don't reckon she's in the same category.'

'Why is that?'

'It's obvious isn't it?'

'Maybe you could make it obvious to *me*, as I'm a little slow as you know.'

'Carol's forty-one. The others? All young women.' He shrugged rhetorically.

'I have to disagree with you here. She might be technically older, but she looks much younger than she is. And she's quite beautiful. You have to admit.'

'Maybe,' Brearly conceded.

'Maybe? Come on. If this guy was after young attractive women—'

'Why do you assume it's a guy?'

'If it's pretty young females they're after, then Carol is definitely going to qualify.'

Brearly grunted again.

'So what about me?' Agatha asked.

'What.'

'Would *I* qualify? Would I make the cut?'

'You? Ha! Well there's a loaded question if ever I heard one.'

She was teasing him of course, and enjoyed watching him squirm. Brearly attempted to leave it at that, but noticed Agatha was still staring at him, waiting for an answer.

'Sure you would, Agatha. I don't know about Terri, but you? For sure. But hey, I'm not sure that's a list you really want to be on.'

And for once, Brearly had a point.

They continued looking around, almost idly, not sure what they were looking for. Agatha found herself heading for the front entrance. As if there was something there for her.

'We leaving?' Brearly asked. 'Best idea you've had all morning.'

Agatha looked at the large white door. Not a scratch, as you'd expect – it was pristine, like everything else. Even the doormat for wiping your shoes was spotless. Had Carol's abductor stood on it? It was definitely too clean for a front doormat. And then she found that her attention was being drawn to the doorbell button. She got really close, as if she could see a fingerprint there, or could smell it.

'Have you spotted something?'

'We should get Forensics in.'

'Forensics? We don't even know there's been a *crime* yet,' Brearly said. 'She could be about to stroll down that front path as we speak.'

Agatha ignored him and Brearly sighed.

She shot him a glance and she noted his inner turmoil: torn between wanting to hold his ground and wanting to give her some latitude. In other words, between not allowing a precedent to be set on the one hand, and getting into her pants on the other. She was getting used to this dynamic and made a mental note to harness it.

'Sure,' he said. 'But the request comes from you.'

Rob, one of the Paddo cops, was heading down the front path towards them.

'Just been speaking to a local, an elderly gentleman. He was returning from walking his dog last Wednesday night—'

'Poodle no doubt.' Brearly threw in. 'Or a Jack Roodle.'

'He reckons he saw a man hanging around outside. Outside this place.'

'Description?'

Rob shook his head. 'Too dark, so not much to go on. But he thinks the man was white, or had quite pale skin, and he was possibly hefty, and he was wearing a suit. But other than that...'

Agatha felt something ripple through her – it was physical, like an electric current. It was unpleasant. And it immediately brought to mind not so much Jay-Lee's 'older guy in a suit' – although there it was again, the suit – but her nightmare last week, with the guillotine and the dive into the cobblestones, and of course the man clapping her, pale and overweight, and who called himself the name that still escaped her.

And yet beyond Jay-Lee and Pippa, and beyond the dream, there was something else. Something in the far recesses. Was it a previous dream? It felt more like a previous lifetime, but whatever it was, she had no idea.

Only that it felt like it was being *hidden* from her, with intent.

15.

By the next day, Tuesday, Brearly eventually caved. Because Carol Shelly *didn't* walk down that path. She didn't come home. She didn't turn up at all.

Another Nowhere woman.

Meanwhile, Lutger had managed to track down Chalaise Corlay's ex, one Shane Jeldry, and Agatha and Brearly's next task was to have a word with him. This involved a short drive to Maroubra, an unhappy little suburb by the sea: physically attractive with a wild and generous headland jutting out with confidence into the blue expanse of Pacific Ocean, but also home to more than its fair share of gang warfare, although most of it these days was confined to the water and minor arguments between empty-headed surfers.

Their 'person of interest' lived in a share household there, and when they pulled up outside, Agatha was surprised to see how rundown the place was. She didn't know what sort of house Chalaise lived in, but the comparison with Carol's house in Woollahra couldn't have been more stark. Shane's place was made of brick – which is where the similarities with Carol's ended – and had an enormous diagonal crack down the brickwork of its street-facing wall, at least one broken window, and weeds in the front yard so high it appeared they'd been granted protected species status.

Brearly pressed the buzzer, which didn't work, and then knocked loudly, and the front door eventually opened to reveal a skinny, heavily tanned creature in boardshorts and thongs that to Agatha looked more like a shaved meerkat than a human being. With more than its far share of emerging lines and wrinkles, his sun-damaged face had plenty to show for its 31 years, and his dark hair was cut mullet-style – short on top, long at the back – and had some half-hearted blond streaks put through it.

'Gedday mate how are ya?' Brearly's standard front door greeting.

'Pretty good. What can I do you for?'

They interviewed him in the murky haze of his living room, reeking of bong smoke and instant coffee and unshiftable BO. Agatha was intrigued as to what Chalaise had been doing with him, their worlds could hardly have been more incongruous. And then, she figured, that had probably been the point. There was often zero logic in some people's choice of partner. No formula could ever account for it.

Shane Jeldry didn't do it.

He knew who did, though. And he was willing to explain in agonizing detail how it was done, and could even give a physical description of 'the accused' as he called him, so accurate that it would take their police artist, so he assured them, 'multiple hours' to complete the picture.

But Shane didn't do it.

Despite the patent idiocy of all this and how absurd it sounded, Agatha and Brearly were duty-bound to go through the motions and check out everything he said, ostensibly because they were short on leads, but mainly because you'd be reamed out if you were found to have ignored a genuine one.

Shane was also willing to take them to the precise spot the body was buried. Or where he reckoned it was. Never mind the dogs, he said, he'd beat the best of them any day when it came to sniffing out a stiff – he'd leave Rex looking out of his depth, leave him with a big doggie question mark hanging over his floppy-eared head – because after all, he had the inside running on this one. He'd find their body all right.

But Shane most certainly did not do it.

He was adamant about this. Aside from the fact that he claimed to have no recollection of what he'd been doing on the day Chalaise disappeared, or where he'd been – not a rock-solid alibi in sight – he was at great pains to insist that he hadn't raped the girl, hadn't strangled her, hadn't cut off any of her limbs and buried her/them, and he absolutely categorically had to insist that he hadn't been a part of any plan to do so. He nevertheless knew who had.

Who? Well there's this bloke who was always sniffing around her, dunno his name, dunno where he lives, but he's got a shaved head, muscular build and woodchopper's arms, and he's covered in tats. With a bit of time, the name might come to him...

And why hadn't he reported any of this earlier? Was he not concerned about what might have happened to Chalaise? Of *course* he was concerned, and he *knew* what had happened, and to prove it, with his help, instead of sitting here on their arses, they could be exhuming the poor girl, *right now*, from her grave of clay and schist.

Agatha made the point to Brearly but out loud, so their person of interest could hear – that Shane seemed strangely unmoved by what would normally be regarded as a significant event in a person's life, namely the brutal murder of their companion, partner and lover, albeit an ex. 'Nearest and dearest', as Agatha put it. And Brearly said yes, he too noticed this and yes, it was difficult to fathom. Unless he was *acting* (catching Shane's eye when he said this). Unless Chalaise had never been his dearest after all. Just his nearest.

And all the while, he gave not an inch. Because Shane did not do it.

'So Shane,' Brearly said. 'How did you two get along when you were going out? When you were together?'

'Who?'

Brearly left a pause.

'You and Chalaise.'

'Good.'

'No fights?'

'Nuh.'

'Never?'

'Nuh.'

'The odd, cross word maybe?'

'She did, I didn't.'

'Got cross?'

'Nah. Did crosswords.'

Brearly closed his eyes for a moment, which Agatha assumed was an attempt to calm himself. She felt the same way. Patience was a non-negotiable requirement in any murder investigation – if that's what this was going to turn out to be – particularly one with persons of interest as bewildering as Shane Jeldry.

'OK,' continued Brearly. 'So you two had been... seeing each other for... what was it...?'

'Two years.'

'Two years? That's a while.'

'Flew by. And time flies when you're havin' fun, right?'

'Right. And no arguments, nothing like that? We're not going to find anyone who witnessed you two fighting?'

'*You're* not gonna find anyone? No idea. But nup. Nothing like that. Although...' He left a long pause as he looked to the ceiling as if they had a second floor and there was someone up there. 'There was one time. Just over this... thing on my laptop.'

'Porn?' Brearly asked wearily.

'Nah! It was just this news item about, I dunno, migrants, that sort of shit. We just, you know, didn't see eye to eye. You get that with mates.'

'Mates. Right. But she was more than mates, wasn't she? Chalaise was your *girlfriend,* correct?'

'Girlfriend? *In*correct.'

'She wasn't your girlfriend?'

'Nuh.'

Brearly threw Agatha a questioning look, but she just shrugged.

'She was my ex,' Shane added.

Agatha noticed the muscle in Brearly's left forearm stand out as he clenched his fist. He looked ready to either throttle the guy or leave, depending on which wolf he decided to feed. She decided now would be a good time to jump in.

'I still don't understand,' she said, 'how you can help us find where she's buried. If you had nothing to do with her disappearance.'

'Instinct,' Shane replied. 'You hear things, you know, grapevine shit, but yeah. Instinct.'

He tapped the side of his nose and stared straight at Agatha, the faintest of smirks daring to show itself.

Agatha and Brearly left soon after, and didn't speak until they were back in the car.

'What a total fucking scumbag,' Brearly said eventually, shaking his head.

'Mm. He's smarter than he looks.'

'Well *that* wouldn't be hard.'

'He went to uni.'

'You're shittin' me.'

'It's in the file. Did computer science but dropped out. Got good grades.'

'Good grades.' Brearly was shaking his head again.

'Distinctions. So I wonder what happened. He just… cracked up?'

'So to speak.'

There was a pause.

'Crack?' Brearly said.

'I got it. But do you think he's lost the plot or just playing with us?'

'He's definitely playing with us. He's got a record, it's all drug-related isn't it?'

Agatha nodded. 'And plenty of court experience.'

'Exactly. And this is his pathetic little payback. Doesn't mean, of course, that he's not actually cut up inside about Chalaise.'

Agatha wasn't too sure about either of those propositions, but she couldn't have said why.

In any event, they decided to leave Chalaise's 'bit of cracked-up rough' as Brearly put it, in the capable hands of Detective Constable Lutger, who would, no doubt, spend the next couple of days looking for a patch of earth on a golf course somewhere, and eventually tick Shane Jeldry off their list.

Because Shane didn't do it. And there was no evidence to suggest the little troublemaker knew who did, either.

'Troublemaker' was Agatha's word. Brearly's was cruder.

16.

As Agatha was heading home for the day, she suddenly realized there was something that had been bothering her. One of Carol's neighbours had reported hearing the phone in Carol's house ringing persistently around the time of her disappearance or possibly the night before, but over a fairly short space of time. It had sounded to the neighbour as though the phone had been answered each time, and whoever had been calling had continued to ring back. Agatha made a mental note to check this report more thoroughly in the morning, in case anything jumped out at her.

In case anything jumped out at her. Another thought she'd have to bury.

For now, though, it had been a long day – particularly with the Shane Jeldry episode in the afternoon – and she was pleased to be shot of the whole show: Shane Jeldry, the Nowhere list, buried bodies, buried thoughts, everything.

The after-work commute had taken her a bit longer than usual this evening: her car was in for repairs and she was using public transport, namely a bus and two trains to Newtown and the reverse on the way back to her place in Sydney's eastern suburbs. She'd stopped off at the local gym as well, in Bondi Junction, but her heart hadn't been in it and she made an early exit and a beeline for home.

Home was the suburb of Tamarama, a vertiginous grouping of apartments and houses nestled among cliffs overlooking the ocean. Home, more specifically, was a rented apartment, a modest flat in a white, nineteen-thirties Spanish Mission style building with arched windows. The few things she had of any value (or value to her, at least) were a collection of paintings, all of them nudes, that she'd bought from a female painter friend a few years back, the large southern windows that opened out to trees and the ever-present ocean, and her red leather couch.

And right now, the red leather couch, along with a glass of wine, was all she needed.

Her thoughts turned to home. Not Tamarama, not Venezuela, but her other home, Brisbane, where her family lived, her parents and Laura. Who she rarely visited. She should call them... but then look at the time. They'd be in the middle of dinner.

And then yes, she had to admit it, she began feeling sorry for herself. No boyfriend, no family around her, not much of a social life to speak of outside work... there were plenty of grounds.

And it wasn't all her fault. It was Sydney's fault, too. Because Sydney was a hard city. Friendly on the outside – as friendly a world city as any you're likely to find – but tough at its core. Cutthroat tough. The truth was that Sydney had a smiling face and a cold soul.

Which is what she was thinking about when her house phone rang, her landline, which rarely rang and which she rarely used and it gave her a jolt as it snatched her attention.

And as she got up off the couch and walked over to pick up the phone, an image flashed into her head: it was of that woman in her underwear, bra and pantyhose, lying there, to all intents and purposes, naked and lifeless.

And what *were* the intents and purposes?

'Hello?'

There was a long pause and Agatha was about to put the phone down when a distant voice – they sounded foreign, maybe Indian – chimed in.

'Is this Miss Ducatti?' It was a man.

'Who is this?'

''How are you today madam?'

'Who is this?'

'Well I'm ringing about your computer. We believe that you may be...'

'No, sorry, I'm not—'

But the man continued without stopping. '... having problems with your Windows. Now if you will bear with me, I will demonstrate how the problem—'

'Excuse me, now *you stop right there*,' she said, raising her voice. And the man stopped, finally. Was this a bad line or plain pushiness? 'Now I know what this is about, and not only am I not interested, but I'm a police officer, so as I'm sure you will now *appreciate*, you have obviously dialled the wrong number—'

'Yes, we know that.'

'I'm sorry?'

'You are Agatha Ducatti Durán-Delapeña am I right?'

He paused, waiting for a response, and continued.

'Detective Senior Constable Agatha Ducatti Durán-Delapeña of the Newtown Local Area Command?'

'Who is... who am I talking to?'

'We can help you fix the problems that you are encountering with your—'

Agatha slammed the phone down. Impossible. It was impossible they could know all that. She'd take this up with the Superintendent the next day.

She was just in the process of getting up to go to the kitchen and refill her glass when the phone rang again. She looked at it for a moment before picking it up.

'Hello?'

Once more, the long pause. They had to be kidding! She was about to slam the phone down again but her back was up now, she was angry, and she was going to have a piece of this guy.

'You shouldn't have done that.' It was him. The same voice.

'Excuse me?'

'You shouldn't have hung up on me like that.'

'Oh yes? And why is that?'

Another pause, a very long one this time.

'Because I know where you live.'

She hung up. Her pulse rate was up, and she was starting to sweat. Was it anger? Or fear? And then she remembered the phone calls to Carol...

She wished she had her gun with her, and cursed the stringency of the rules about detectives bringing their weapons home. And then she thought how ridiculous she was being. Nevertheless...

She went to close the one open window all the same.

Which was when the phone rang again.

She stared at the ringing telephone, but made no move to pick it up. She wasn't so much afraid to answer it for who might be on the other end, as for what it might precipitate.

Once the ringing had stopped, she went to the window – very cautiously – and pulled it shut. Hooked the latch. And then just before she turned around, in the window's reflection, she thought she saw something move.

She spun around.

There was nothing to see but an empty room, the telephone sitting silently but full of threat on the side table.

It rang again.

She charged across the room, furious now.

'*What?*!!' She almost screamed it.

'Freakin' Jesus!' It was Brearly. 'You could improve your phone greeting, Agatha. Is that an Argentinian thing?'

Brearly had rung to discuss with her the way forward on a couple of their investigations. Agatha didn't mind – on the contrary, she was relieved to hear a friendly voice – but it didn't escape her attention that these things could easily have waited for the morning. Was he lonely?

He also added that he gave her full credit for 'getting it right on the night with Carol'. He'd never question her instincts again.

She doubted that, but appreciated the gesture. He possibly even half-meant it.

Agatha didn't mention the phone calls, she'd probably been overreacting and she hadn't wanted to seem like just another scared female.

That night, however, she dreamt of *him* again.

In her dream she was closing the open window in her living room, just as she'd done earlier. This time though, when she turned around and looked back, towards the doorway, towards the hallway to the rest of the apartment... he was standing there. In his navy suit and trainers and untucked shirt, tugging on his cuffs. There he was with his plump body and his fat stomach, with his large, pale face, and this time she could see his eyes, and they were dull and grey. Striking, in their dullness, and greyness. And there he was with his smile. If you could call it that, it was more of a grimace. For some reason she had no doubt, in her dream at least, that this was the caller from earlier. This was despite the fact that there was nothing Indian about his looks, and that from his telephone voice she'd pictured the caller as being slim, almost emaciated – *escuálido* – and there was nothing thin whatsoever about the man standing in front of her. 'Agatha,' he said. She instinctively reached for her gun, but of course she already knew it wasn't there. 'I know I shouldn't be here,' he added. Which was when she realized she was dreaming. Once again though, she wasn't able to wake herself up – as with the last time he stepped into her dreams, this man clearly wasn't going to let her go until he was good and ready. He smiled again. And his navy suit and his hideous grin merged, and then the suit looked like it was being sucked into his mouth, as if pulled through an old washing wringer. He was a fat snake swallowing its tail, his genitals under his belly suddenly splayed in front of her, in front of her face: his thick cock, and his large, hairless balls, and his gaping anus...

The next morning, and all day at work, that image stayed with her, wouldn't fully leave her. The fat man's splayed genitals. And that smile. That frozen sneer.

17.

The man was smiling at the woman in front of him. At the back of her head, her narrow shoulders. He sensed, once again, the limitless power of *him* – of his presence, of his strength, of his sexuality. And her fear – or the fear she ought to have been feeling if she were fully appraised of the situation – only added to it, fuelled it. He was grinning from ear to ear. He felt almost human again.

Agatha, he thought to himself as she paid for her ticket and walked away from the queue, heading off towards the escalators and the trains.

He approached the ticket window, the beginnings of an erection growing hard against his trousers and now, pushing against the wall beneath the glass – the glass that locked away this other woman, this new woman before his eyes, so safely, and just as well, because she too had pretty eyes, although hers weren't nearly as pretty as Agatha's.

'Single to... I don't know, where should I go to?'

'I'm sorry sir?'

She was very white for a, how should he put it, gentlewoman from the subcontinent. It was of no importance to him though: black, brown, yellow or white, they were all just women to him. But not, of course, *just* women. They were never *just* women. As far as he was concerned, all women deserved a pedestal. For their beauty, and for what they had to contend with.

'Where do *you* go when you leave here?'

She looked perplexed, poor thing.

'Never mind,' he said, to put her out of her misery. 'Next time perhaps.'

He flashed his weekly rail pass at her and turned and started walking towards the trains.

Agatha – surely the girl of the dreams of many – was, for now, nowhere to be seen. But he'd find her again easily enough.

Particularly as he knew *exactly* where to look for her.

18.

Brearly slapped the newspaper down on Agatha's desk.

Prior to that, her morning had been a relatively pleasant one.

She'd woken in her Tamarama flat with its stress-releasing ocean view out her living room windows. And what a view it was this particular morning. The sun was out and the sea was like a huge jewel, a giant shining slab of lapis lazuli. Her car was still being repaired, so she'd caught the bus into Bondi Junction and from there travelled by train. And she'd bought a luscious Kensington Pride mango from a fruit shop on the way – they were in season and were simply out of this world – and she'd just begun to taste its delights at her desk when the newspaper came slapping down and broke the spell of her mini-orgasm of taste.

'It's official.'

'What, that you're an idiot? You scared me.'

'The gods are against us.'

'What's happened?'

'Why are *you* so jumpy this morning?'

'I'm not. So?'

'Yeah well, see for yourself.' Brearly stabbed a rod-like finger down. 'Even *Dan's* got one.'

It was an article in the morning's paper. Police had reported that a body had been found yesterday in a park in La Perouse, the southernmost suburb in Sydney's east, which sits at the entrance to Botany Bay. In fact the body was found in some bushes on a golf course. Not buried. And not a female, the victim was male, suspected cause of death a drug overdose. According to Detective Sergeant Daniel Jeffries…

Dan Jeffries. Agatha suddenly got a strange sensation, not about the body oddly enough, but about the mention of Dan Jeffries' name. The sensation was like falling.

Brearly was staring at Agatha and frowning. 'You do remember Dan, don't you?'

'Of course I do. He only left last year, my memory's not *that* bad.'

Dan Jeffries had been Newtown's Detective Sergeant up until he abruptly left in February the previous year – when Brearly was promoted into his position. He was transferred to Maroubra. Agatha never found out why he left so suddenly.

'So what's the big deal?' Agatha said. 'You're not suggesting this might be related? To our—?'

'No no, my point is it's a body. Dan's got a fucking *body*. Which is more than we've got.'

Agatha tried to reconnect with the strange feeling she experienced, but it had gone.

Poof.

Just before lunch, Brearly arrived with some news, relevant this time, and it was big: they'd found one of them. One of the Nowhere women. Alive.

It was the Pantyhose Woman. The one who'd been photographed by George at the chimneys, the so-called corpse that had walked off on them.

'Finally,' Brearly said. 'Something concrete. If not a dead body, the next best thing.'

19.

Half an hour later, Agatha and Brearly were in a women's refuge in Woolloomooloo.

Fiona, the woman who appeared to be in charge, was wearing jeans and looked like the host of a children's television show, and she ushered them into a kind of sitting room. It looked as though the room's occupants had only recently been cleared out.

A pale, tired-looking blonde woman was sitting in one of the equally fatigued, faded-green armchairs. She got up slowly to greet them. A smile was clearly beyond her, not that she owed anybody one, Agatha thought.

She had the same sapphire-blue eyes as the woman in the photographs.

'Samantha, this is...' Fiona began. I'm sorry, I've forgotten your...'

'Detective Senior Constable Agatha Ducatti,' Agatha said, holding out her hand. 'And this is Detective Sergeant Peter Brearly.'

The woman looked like she'd been crying recently.

'Most people call me Sam,' she said. And then, with a sad little laugh: 'I think. I mean... so I'm told.'

'Sam's been having trouble with her, um, recollection, haven't you Sam.'

'Well...'

'Thanks Fiona,' Agatha said. 'It might be better if we spoke to Sam alone.'

'No problem. Absolutely no problem at all. I'll just be, um... If you want me.'

The refuge – meaning Fiona – had called the police earlier that day when it had appeared there was more going on with Sam than they'd previously assumed. Someone from the refuge had come across her on Monday night of the previous week, the night George found her, wandering around virtually naked. That's to say, in the same attire she'd been photographed in (which was using the term 'attire' fairly loosely, Brearly had suggested). She was found in St Peters, not far from the Sydney Park chimneys.

Sam had no recollection of any of it, or anything much at all – she didn't even know her own name – and was in a real state. As if she was drugged or drunk or both. Completely out of it, in other words. She was known to the refuge, she'd ended up there after a relationship break-up once and it had just been assumed she was going through something similar again. Asked why they hadn't called the police as soon as they'd found her, Fiona confessed it was because they knew Sam had had 'the odd run-in with the cops... sorry, the police... in the past' and they hadn't wanted to get her into any more trouble. It was only when her memory began to return and she muttered a few things about some man who'd been following her that they thought they'd better tell the authorities.

The authorities. Sometimes Agatha had to remind herself that was her.

Sam still couldn't recall her own surname though, or where she lived. Fiona had already told them that as far as they knew, her full name was Samantha Jane Poole, and that she lived – or at least used to live, this was a couple of years ago, she could have moved – not far from Newtown, in the adjoining suburb of Marrickville, in a flat on her own.

'So Sam,' Agatha began. 'Do you remember your surname?'

Sam shook her head.

'Or where you live?'

'No.'

'Do you still live in Marrickville?'

Sam shrugged her shoulders in the slow, exaggerated way a child might. And then she looked, all of a sudden, even more distressed. Pain began to surface. Agatha didn't want to do this.

'With people...?'

Tears were coming.

'OK.'

Brearly during all this was remaining unusually and gratifyingly quiet.

'They found you,' Agatha continued, 'on Monday night last week, so nine days ago, near Sydney Park. Do you know where Sydney Park is?'

Sam shook her head, pathetically.

'The chimneys.'

Sam frowned at this but said nothing.

'OK. Do you remember what happened that night? The night they found you? Anything at all?'

'No. No I can't... I don't. I don't even know where I am.'

'You're in a women's refuge in Woolloomooloo.' Agatha let that sink in, and forged on. 'And you told them, told Fiona out there, that a man had been following you.'

Sam's face began to slowly contort – her eyebrows crept upwards, her eyes and mouth widened and she looked as though she was either going to scream or burst into a torrent of tears. She did neither but began to tremble. Started slowly shaking her head.

'I...'

But that was it, she had nothing else.

'You better show her the photographs,' Brearly said, breaking the long silence.

'I'm not sure she needs to see them right now.'

'What photographs?' Sam asked.

'We have to, Agatha. We need something here. For the sake of the others.'

'What others?'

He was right. 'OK,' Agatha said and produced the photographs that George had taken. It was easy to see that it was Sam in them, dressed in those transparent pantyhose.

'Oh God,' Sam said, once she'd had a chance to look at them properly. 'This is me?'

'Yes,' Agatha said.

'And when they found me...?'

Agatha just nodded.

'I was walking around like this? In Newtown?'

'St Peters,' Brearly said, as if this was somehow a comfort.

'It was near the park,' Agatha said. 'It was dark—'

'*What happened to me?!!*' Sam wailed, and then began to quietly sob.

No medical examination had been conducted at the time. Sam hadn't said anything to indicate one might be necessary, although she may have done if the police had been given a chance to question her at the outset. That failure to inform the police was now looking like a serious mistake. It still wasn't too late to conduct an examination though. Agatha explained to Sam it'd still be a good idea to carry one out. But Sam would have none of it. She insisted there was nothing wrong with her. She'd gone from fearing the worst to convincing herself that nothing had happened.

And so that was all they could get out of her, all they could glean. For the moment at least. Maybe with time, her memory would return. Her memory of that night.

And then Fiona came in and took them aside for a moment, said she remembered that Sam had mentioned someone's name when she was talking about the man who'd been following her. The name she'd mentioned was something like 'Smeedon' or 'Smeeton'. That was all, and she had no idea whether it was a first name or a surname.

Smeeton.

That was the name. The man in her nightmares.

Agatha could barely speak. Her stomach was turning and she was short of breath. Brearly asked if she was OK and she said she was fine, and got him to take over.

They tried to speak to Sam again, but all she wanted to do was go back to sleep. The only thing she was able to add before they left was that she remembered being in traffic with cars all around her and headlights in her eyes. And being very, very afraid, but of what she couldn't say. She was convinced though that whatever it was, she'd narrowly escaped it.

Agatha wasn't so sure.

20.

William Tremsur spotted the man as soon as he, William, set foot in the Club's sitting room. Unfortunately he'd been intending to sit in the precise area of armchairs that the man was now sitting in – *what was his name again?* – and would have swiftly changed direction, and even rooms, but it was too late, he'd been spotted, signalled by a limp wave, and it would have looked too obvious. He'd just have to 'suck it up', as his children would have said.

What *was* his name?

The room was commonly called the Smoking Room, although those days were long gone. It still contained ghosts from those times, William thought to himself as he weaved his way between the mainly empty armchairs and coffee tables. The paintings may have changed (although the old favourites remained, mainly Australian landscapes) and the colour scheme may have been tweaked from time to time, but the ghosts remained. What a crowd they would have made if they were all alive and in the room today, and he wished they *were* all here. It was a bit hard to avoid talking to someone you knew when there was next to no one else around. And unfortunately the after-lunch crowd had yet to spill through from the dining room.

The man whose name William couldn't remember – which was ridiculous, by the way, he knew him well – was unnaturally pale, and large too: the armchair in which he was seated only barely contained him. He was wearing a black suit and blue shirt with its top button undone, and an old tie that looked like it had been borrowed from the Club. He was sitting over by the large windows, and the blue-grey city light that percolated through them from Macquarie Street seeped into the room and lent an even greater strangeness to the sight of this man's bulky form. William imagined for a moment he could see an 'aura' around him (not that he was susceptible in the slightest, as a rule, to that sort of mumbo jumbo). At the same time, somewhat disconcertingly, William could see that the man's beady eyes were still locked onto him and had been from the moment he entered the room. William had never liked being stared at.

He doubted the man liked being stared at either. He was the type who'd always made sure he was the one who did the staring. He didn't like being asked questions either, William had observed. Probably for very good reason.

As William approached the man (who hadn't bothered to get up), he was still trying to remember his name. He noticed the man's black shoes were in fact black *running shoes*. There was no accounting for taste, as they say.

'Well they just can't keep you away, can they,' he said, to neatly cover for the lack of a name to call him.

William extended a hand. There was an awkward moment where it looked as though the man wasn't going to offer his own. He did though, and William shook his plump, sweaty paw. A flicker of a smile passed the man's lips, but the tiny, blank-grey eyes were unwavering.

The man's handshake was clammy and soft, and unexpectedly cold, and as soon as there was physical contact, William had a sudden and disturbing flash of... something metallic... and a woman afraid... He was relieved when he got to withdraw his hand.

'William,' the man said. 'How good it is to see you again.' He spoke in a forced tone – almost too 'small' for his size – and pulled at his shirt cuffs, a nervous habit of his that William now recalled. 'You look well.'

'You too, you too. How have you been?'

'Oh you know, bit of this, bit of that, do you find it hot in here?'

'Well... not really—'

'I've asked them to turn the temperature down and they said they would, but... I think they might have been humouring me.'

I don't blame them, thought William. He noticed that the man's shirtfront was half-untucked and remembered that about him as well – it was as if his stomach were constantly trying to break free.

The man still hadn't bothered to get up, which suited William down to the ground: it gave him the excuse to escape early, once this quick round of pleasantries was over. (Pleasantries, he thought, was there anything less pleasant?)

'So how's business?' he forced himself to ask. 'Selling lots of drugs?'

Even though William still couldn't remember the man's name, he knew he was a pharmacist, and even though he was well aware this little jest of his was a cliché, anything to clear away the cold fog that seemed to be perpetually settled over this person.

The man curled his lips in a way that suggested he was bored with the cliché.

'Selling mountains of drugs, William, that's right,' he said in a loud voice. 'And raping lots of women too.'

Aided by his peripheral vision, William was aware of at least one other person in the room looking over in their direction. Which was hardly surprising. The man looked serious too, even as he smiled. Serious, as though he meant it.

And there it was again. The image of something metallic, something sharp, and a woman crying... or choking...

'William? Are you with us?'

The image was harder to shake this time. Where was it coming from? And why for heaven's sake couldn't he remember the man's *name*?

'William? I'm not *really* dating lots of women, don't look so *shocked*. As if. The closest I get to a woman these days is feeling her contraption.'

'Her...?'

Filling her prescription is what he said. Of course William knew that perfectly well. His hearing was fine, his memory good, but his brain, it seemed, was trying to tell him something.

Oh get a grip, he told himself before proffering up a couple more pleasantries and finally, at long last, making his escape.

21.

Later that afternoon, they finally got their body.

It was a real one too, this time. It was dead and it didn't move. Didn't run away. It may not have belonged to any of the women on their Nowhere list, but it was 'a good old-fashioned dead body and beggars couldn't be choosers' according to Brearly.

Agatha wasn't so impressed with this development, but if it made Brearly happy, then that was something in its favour.

It was midafternoon, still Wednesday, and it was turning out to be quite a day.

Agatha was out of the office again — she was spending more time out than in these days, which she suspected had something to do with Brearly — but she wasn't far away. She and Brearly were standing in a small backyard of a house around the corner from the police station. In Eliza Street, the very backstreet that the windows of their shared office overlooked.

Weatherwise, at least, the day was fulfilling its morning promise — sunshine, a gentle warm breeze, an air temperature of at least five degrees above the Sydney monthly average maximum for October of 22.8°C. Maybe hotter than ideal, though, for what they were doing.

Because they were looking at the body of a young man, maybe in his late twenties or early thirties. Caucasian, short dark hair, and although she couldn't see his eyes – his cap had been pulled down, or come down, over them – Agatha suspected that he was quite handsome. Apparently fit, too. What was the expression? Well-proportioned – despite, that is, a degree of abdominal bloating, to be expected in the early stages of decomposition.

Death diminishes you, she thought. But first it bloats you.

He was wearing a black T-shirt with large white lettering on it, the three words one on top of the other with the letters individually boxed within a square:

V E N I

V I D I

V I C I

'I came, I saw, I conquered,' Brearly said.

The two of them contemplated that for a moment.

'I didn't know you spoke Latin,' Agatha said, in a rare showing of giving Brearly a taste of his own sarcasm.

'What's that in Argentinian? Oh sorry... Spanish.'

It was clearly, for him at least, the joke that kept giving.

The body had been found under a blue tarpaulin which was now lying close by. Apart from a small building skip filled with broken bricks, there wasn't much room in the backyard for anything else. There was a head-high brick wall lined with a row of half-dead plants in ceramic pots separating the street from the yard, and the double storey house to which the yard belonged was an old and rundown duplex. Beige and dilapidated. The tenants, apparently a pair of dressmakers, had both been away, and returned to find the tarpaulin, which had been covering the building skip, apparently blown off. It went without saying that the woman who went down to replace the tarpaulin received quite a shock.

Apart from the black T-shirt, the man was wearing a dark blue Deus Ex Machina baseball cap, olive green cotton shorts, and saffron-yellow work boots (although he didn't look like he worked in the construction industry – you could tell by his hands).

Agatha tried hard to avoid looking at what appeared to be a startlingly large erection bulging up under his shorts. Maybe that's not what it was – was that even possible? – but either way that was certainly what it looked like, and she hoped Brearly had at least an ounce of tact, that perhaps he might, on this occasion, be able to resist the urge to——

'Impressive boner,' he said.

There were no obvious signs of injury. Brearly whipped out a glove and without putting it on, used it to gingerly lift the baseball cap. The man's eyes were closed and he could have been asleep. Even though the paramedics had attended the scene before them and had only just left, and though they hadn't been troubled for long as the body had clearly been dead for quite some time, Brearly still checked to confirm there was no breathing and no pulse.

'Drug overdose?' Agatha said, but Brearly didn't reply straight away. He was looking at something.

'Bruising.' Brearly was pointing to the man's neck, and sure enough there were the faintest signs of trauma to the neck region, suggestive of a less than peaceful end.

'So strangulation, then.'

'Maybe.'

'How long do you think he's been here?'

'I dunno, shall we ask him?'

'Brearly...'

'Hey. My last body walked off on me, then turned up alive, so cut me some slack here, OK?'

Touchy. She hadn't needed his assessment anyway, she'd just been curious to compare it to her own which, even if she did say so herself, was always going to be the safer bet.

Nine days was the answer (or thereabouts), although, as usual, she couldn't have explained how she knew it.

'A few days at least,' Brearly said. 'Forensics'll tell us. They're on their way.'

Something caught Agatha's eye.

'What's that?'

'What's what?'

'That.'

The man's right calf was resting on his left ankle, and pinned in between was a piece of plastic, or cardboard. Brearly put on the glove he was holding and went to extract the object.

'Shouldn't we wait for Forensics?'

'Fuck Forensics.'

He slowly and carefully freed the object from its trapped position and gently lifted it up with his white-gloved right hand. Agatha wasn't used to seeing such delicate hand movements from him.

It was a cardboard beer coaster. With a picture of a palm tree on it, overlying an Islamic-style lattice pattern, and accompanying the word 'Zanzibar'.

'It's from the Zannie,' Brearly said.

The Zannie, or the Zanzibar, was a bar located little more than a hundred metres away, at the end of the street. And just around the corner from the police station too, so their local in other words.

'Looks fresh,' Agatha said. 'As in, not rubbish. And strange that it was *on top* of his ankle rather than under it.'

'Yeah.'

'So it probably isn't just rubbish that was lying around the yard.'

'No.' Brearly's responses were slow ones.

'So it must have either ended up there in the course of the struggle, or it was intentionally placed there.'

Brearly looked at Agatha. 'Why would anyone want to intentionally place it there?'

Agatha shrugged.

Brearly looked around the tiny backyard. 'It doesn't look like any struggle took place here. In which case whoever killed him probably dumped the body here. It was probably at night, pitch black, couldn't see, so maybe the coaster just fell out of one of their pockets at the time.'

'Could be. So one or both of them were in the Zanzibar?'

'Hang on,' Brearly said. 'There's something written on the other side. Look.'

He held up the coaster for Agatha to see. In blue pen and clearly discernible against the white background, there was written the simple notation: '5am'. And beneath it, a phone number.

'Five a.m.,' Agatha said. 'And a phone number. So... what, whoever this belonged to was arranging to do something at five a.m.? Not at the Zanzibar obviously, it closes at midnight...'

'Hm.'

'But they were probably at the hotel when they wrote it down. So... a meeting of some kind? But who meets at five a.m.?'

Brearly was staring at the coaster. Staring hard.

'You know what?' he said eventually. 'It's not a 5. It's an S.'

Agatha took another look at it. And Brearly was right. There was little doubt, once you examined it closely. It didn't say '5am' at all.

It said 'Sam'.

22

Brearly was doodling on a Zanzibar coaster – obviously a fresh one, not the one they'd found in the yard up the street – when Agatha rejoined him with the next round of drinks. He had to be honest with himself: he always enjoyed it when it was her shout. Not because of the illusion that the beer was free, but because he liked watching her walk to the bar in those tight cotton pants she often wore. He'd always liked watching her and felt he always would. Which was probably a large part of the reason he suddenly realized he wanted to marry her. That and her incisive mind, of course. Come to think of it though, the fact that she was just as smart as him – OK, let's face it, fair enough, even smarter than him – was probably the reason he *wouldn't* end up marrying her, because she was smart enough to realize what a bad prospect he was.

That and the fact he was already married.

Only technically, of course, he'd be 'free' again soon enough, but to all intents and purposes, he'd still be married. Because to her, wouldn't he be damaged goods? Emotional baggage and all that?

He still loved his wife Drianna, and she probably didn't deserve to be married to a selfish prick like him – she had a heart of gold (viewed in a certain light, at a certain angle) and deserved much, much better. But she had a heart of hydrochloric acid as well, and their arguments towards the end there had been scaring the neighbours. (She was Croatian, it's a package deal.) He knew he should have taken her away on more holidays, she was always complaining about it, but then again, thinking about it now, it did occur to his darker side that it would have been the perfect place for her to have rid herself of him – somewhere foreign where lives were cheap and death was more your best friend or brother than a distant acquaintance or someone you'd only see on TV. Not that she ever *really* would have done something like that. He didn't think.

But god how he was besotted with Agatha. He'd die for her, no question. Maybe in a parallel universe out there, somewhere, he and Agatha were fucking: maybe they were on a king-size bed with white, hotel-smooth sheets and a view of the Colosseum or the Eiffel Tower (or Coogee Beach, he didn't care), and feather-light, wispy-white curtains fluttering in the breeze behind them, and Agatha, with her honey-brown skin, sprawled out like a map, *unfurled* for his pleasure (and hers), limbs stretched out to the four corners of the bed, and the globe too, the world being their oysters. And her oyster being his. Maybe he was diving into her at that very moment. Maybe—

'Coopers OK?'

She was back with the beers, proving they were in the Zanzibar in King Street, Newtown, and a king-size bed was not currently featuring in that particular universe.

'Cheers.'

'Cheers.'

They clinked their beer bottles. The bar was reasonably busy for a Wednesday night. Students, most of them, or so Brearly imagined. Didn't they ever study? Isn't that what students were supposed to do, study? He should have stayed at Uni longer.

'There are the guys,' Brearly said, indicating the clientele, 'who put the *newt* into Newtown.'

Agatha smiled and nodded. She probably hadn't got it. Being Venezuelan.

'As in... *pissed as a newt?*' he added.

'I know.'

She always seemed to be a step ahead of him. He should've known better by now. Being so obtuse, acting like a numbat, this was no way to get into her pants.

Get into her...?

He had to snap out of it, not even *think* this stuff, this woman read minds. From now on, he had to not just act professional, he had to think professional too.

'They've ID'd the dead guy,' he said.

'That was quick. They're good, Forensics.'

'What would we do without them. His wallet was in his back pocket.'

'Oh. So who was he?'

'Benjamin Deane, thirty-one. He'd been working for Microsoft and was recently let go. He was living in Glebe in a share house. His flatmates hadn't reported him missing because they assumed he'd either got lucky or gone home to his parents in Victoria without telling them.'

'And we still don't have a cause of death?'

Brearly shook his head. 'I dunno, I've seen a lot of dead bodies, but never one as healthy as that.'

'Apart from it being dead.'

'All I've heard is that strangulation wasn't necessarily the cause.'

'So, what, a heart attack? Or some drug?'

Brearly shrugged.

'And the coaster? Do we think it's the same Sam?'

'Well if it isn't...'

'... it'd have to be a weird coincidence.'

And then you took the words right out of my mouth, as the song went, *it must have been while you were kissing me.*

'Which reminds me,' he said, attempting to purge the thought. 'I have to hand it to you Agatha. You nailed the time of death.'

'Nine days?'

'Yep. Well, eight to ten, they said. Impressive. Something tells me that wasn't just a lucky guess.'

Agatha smiled, and seemed to appreciate the compliment.

'More importantly,' she said, 'nine days ago was Monday the fourteenth. The night of... whatever it was that happened to Sam.'

They both thought about that for a moment. Then Agatha continued:

'Has anyone tried calling the number on the back of the coaster? And tried to establish if it's our Sam?'

'Lutger I think. Tried, but no answer. Still looking into it.'

'And to see if it's her handwriting, too. Because what if... she met this guy at the Zanzibar, they got friendly and she gave him her phone number. And then the guy gets killed because of it.'

'Why? A jealous ex?'

Agatha shook her head. 'What happened to Sam that night, that's not a boyfriend or an ex doing that. Maybe the guy, this Benjamin Deane, maybe he got in someone's way. Someone who had... designs on Sam.'

'Designs.'

'Yeah.'

'Well there's not a whole lot of evidence to back any of that up.'

'Not yet.'

They both fell silent. A short time later:

'Do you think it's possible,' Agatha said quietly, 'to die of amnesia?'

He scrutinized her. 'You been forgetting stuff? Don't worry about it, you're doing fine.'

'No, I mean... Sam. I just had this crazy thought. I know shock has been known to bring it on, bring on memory loss, but what if... it was being used as a weapon?'

'If what was being used as a weapon?'

'I don't know, some drug that does that to you.'

'You mean a date rape drug?'

'I guess. No. I don't know what I mean.'

They fell silent again and Brearly looked around at the students. The newts. Apart from them and a couple of older locals, that was it. The *old* older locals had been pushed out further afield and away from the frenzy of King Street. He surveyed the room with sad eyes: looking for clues, for links, anything that wasn't simply coincidental. Something loaded with meaning. There was nothing more depressing than working on a file where the victims outweighed the leads by more than five to one.

Could have been worse though. He could have still been lumbered with Lutger. Please God, he thought, don't take Agatha away from me. But something told him God wasn't listening. Maybe in the parallel universe where he was a martyr and a saint, but not in this one.

'Have you noticed how loud the cicadas have been lately?' Agatha asked out of the blue.

'Cicadas? Not likely. Not in the urban jungle *I* live in.'

'Doesn't have to be a jungle. So where do you live again?'

The question made him both hope and dread the subject would turn to his and Drianna's marital home.

'Darlinghurst,' he said, and then wondered if she'd think he might be gay.

'Are there no cicadas in Darlinghurst? Well anyway, did you know that in *fact*... they're singing for sex?'

Took him a moment. 'Yeah?'

'They're males, advertising their virility, trying to get some... action, but it's a signal for predators too, so by doing it they're risking their lives. Better chance of getting lucky, but better chance of being eaten.'

'Cicadas, huh?' There was so much he could say, and yet, by the same token, there was so very little.

So he shut up and tried to focus on the sex lives of cicadas. But all he could think about was Agatha, and what he'd give to know what she was thinking right then. Because her face, her beautiful face, offered no clues.

'I've always been meaning to ask you,' she said suddenly, and he eagerly awaited a question about sex. 'When I arrived at Newtown... two years ago... Simon was still around—'

'Spanner?'

'Yeah. And Dan, too. They left really suddenly. Was there some story behind it that no one told me about?'

Inspector Simon Banner, or 'Spanner' as he was known – Perrick used to joke, whenever he wanted to keep him out of the loop, 'let's not throw a Banner in the works' – and Detective Sergeant Daniel Jeffries left Newtown a little over a year and a half ago, in February 2012. Their departure was abrupt, no reasons given. At the time, Brearly sensed some dissatisfaction on the part of Spanner and Dan, but they remained pretty upbeat about it, which was typical in the Force. And anyway, Brearly got his promotion as a result, so he wasn't bothered.

'No idea. That's what happens around here though. You worked that out yet? When things happen, they happen quickly. Why do you ask?'

'It was just that article in the paper this morning. About Dan, in Maroubra.'

Agatha had a thoughtful look and Brearly didn't even bother to guess what was going on in that head of hers. She probably didn't know herself. And that's what women's intuition was, right? Instinct. Raw cunning. Mercilessly clever bastards, women, when they wanted to be. And even when they didn't.

'Any overseas holidays planned?' Brearly asked idly. 'A trip back to… South America?' he added. He knew he was pushing it with the Venezuela/Argentina joke, and he certainly didn't need Perrick to tell him that. But pushing was what he did. And anyway, she barely blinked anymore.

'Not at the moment. Long-haul flights freak me out anyway. Over all those vast continents and dark oceans. It's like a night without end. That's what being dead is!'

'Just watch the movies like everyone else.'

Agatha left him again – for the toilet this time – providing an opportunity for another eyeful (to put it candidly), it was his lucky night. He had no control over this, it was completely involuntary, a reflex like an eye blink – maybe it was the same for those cicadas – but his eyes locked onto her departing backside like two heat-seeking missiles as her buttocks squirmed beneath her tight white pants, receding into the distant interior haze. Were they the same white pants she usually wore? Or were they a different pair? How many pairs did she have? Or maybe these ones were cream. Beige? Ivory? Champagne? How would he know, did he *look* like a fashion designer?

Brearly allowed himself to settle back into a warm, alcohol-assisted reverie, but he hadn't been relaxing for long when a man caught his eye. The man was passing through the bar – on the other side of the room – and heading towards the front entrance. He wasn't looking in Brearly's direction, so Brearly didn't get to see his face. He was, however, 'older' and wearing a black suit and trainers. And he wasn't thin.

Which wasn't particularly odd in itself (except, perhaps, for the suit and trainers combo), but he recalled Jay-Lee's description of an older guy in a suit, and the eyewitness outside Carol's who reported seeing a pale, hefty man, also in a suit. *And you never know, do you.* If his job had taught him anything, it was that. *You never know.*

And then Agatha was back. She was fast. He liked that about her.

'Funny thing,' he told her after she'd sat down, 'but a guy walked out just then wearing a suit. I didn't see his face, but he was a little hefty-looking, so... you never know, do you.'

Agatha looked perplexed, or startled.

'As in the eyewitness outside Carol's?' he said. 'Being hefty, and... What? What is it?'

'What colour was his suit?' There was a sense of urgency in her voice that he hadn't been expecting.

'Black. I think. Or dark, at least.'

'What about his shoes?'

'His shoes? Jeez. I dunno, maybe... black as well? They were trainers.'

Her eyes widened to two moons. 'They were *trainers?*'

'Yeah...'

Agatha sprang off her chair like it was suddenly red hot, and she bolted for the door.

'Hey! Where are you going?!'

But she'd gone.

Trainers?

23.

Agatha ran into the street and looked both ways. People everywhere, but more to the left, to the north, and she ran in that direction, with her pulse racing, her heart in her mouth.

Faces flashed past her, students, new age hippies, drunks and school kids. No one in a suit. Maybe one or two, but bankers or lawyers out of their comfort zone or in the drunk zone, off their turf or off their faces. But mainly hipsters and thongsters, and ferals as Brearly called them, or newts, and the seekers of healing stones and falafels and booze. A few wholesome couples looking for cheap Thai food, and many, many criminals and ex-criminals, some of them well out, some of them just out, some of them on the run.

But no large, pale man in a dark suit and trainers. No 'Smeeton'.

24.

The man was standing just inside the front doors of the bookstore next to the cinema, beside a narrow book carousel, with one eye on the latest fiction offerings and another on the street outside.

And then Agatha walked past, and his heart would have skipped a beat if he'd been of a more nervous disposition. Her head was twisting to the left and the right, alert and searching. Like a predator in her determined strides, like prey in her awkward twitching glances.

The man smiled and waited.

A minute later she walked back again, still seeking and not finding.

Not detecting.

He wanted to ask her, excuse me, but have you lost something? Has your child run off? Is that fear I see in your eyes?

After she'd gone, he waited a few more minutes, then left the penguins and picadors and random houses, and stepped into the street again. But he didn't head in the direction she'd gone, not this time, he hailed a taxi instead. When one pulled over, he got in and issued a one-word command:

'Tamarama.'

25.

It was just after 9pm when Agatha's taxi pulled up in the small dead-end avenue outside her building in Tamarama – it wasn't late but the sun had long since set and the night was dark. Pitch black, you could say: no moon yet, and not even a visible star. But thanks to the miracle of electricity, it wasn't completely pitch black in her street – there was a solitary streetlight. It stood right next to the bottom of the short driveway to the garages at the foot of her building and her taxi pulled up under it.

After she paid, the driver wasted no time, he was out of there, obviously had an attractive fare to chase. And after the red taillights had vanished down the narrow street, she stood for a moment in the warm glow of the overhead light and breathed in the salt-laden sea air. She could hear the waves in the distance gently pounding the shore. The ocean was black. And the air was still: there was no detectable movement whatsoever. It was a warm, almost tropical, night.

But not a beautiful night. Because something felt wrong. Out of place, and she couldn't quite put her finger on why. It was possibly because of what Brearly had told her at the Zanzibar, about seeing a large man in a dark suit and trainers, but it felt like something more than that.

The neighbouring flats and buildings were all dark and lifeless, and the street – the whole area – was so deserted it seemed like everyone in Tamarama had gone away on holiday. Or just vanished.

She turned and walked up the driveway, and by the time she'd reached the front entrance, the feeling she had moments earlier came back in a toxic wave, and only worsened when she pushed open the unlockable front door.

Her building was an older block, at least compared to most of the others in the area – an area that was being rapidly modernized as the wealthy elite became younger and increasingly shifted its focus from the harbour to the ocean. Being an older building, the level of security was relatively low. It wasn't something that had ever really bothered her, but it was suddenly bothering her tonight.

She climbed the stairs and reached her apartment. Turned the key, opened the door and flicked the light switch. Her first thought when she stepped inside was it was good, at least, to be home, to be indoors. Her next thought was maybe not.

Everything was as she'd left it that sunny morning, as far as she could tell. As far as she could remember. The light, though, seemed harsher than usual, and the paintings on the walls, her much-prized nudes, seemed to have acquired a nasty edge to them – as if they'd mutated somehow, in some barely detectable way, from beautiful to ugly. The southern windows were closed but the curtains were open – outside there was the solitary streetlight with the pool of light at its base, the houses across the street dimly lit in the ambient light, but beyond that, simply darkness.

She opened a window and cold air poured in – like a postcard from winter, the chilled air was far colder than the air down in the street had been – making her change her mind about opening up the flat. She was about to close it again when she thought she heard something, possibly outside. Maybe a cat or a possum, or a fruit bat.

And then a fleeting moment of déjà vu, but of course opening the window was something she did every evening...

She turned around – deliberately ignoring the reflection in the window because it suddenly felt like reflections held terrible things for her, things too awful to contemplate – and she walked back into the room. Looked around again. Something was definitely wrong, but what?

She cast an eye over her red leather couch and its cushions, and then surveyed the coffee table: there was the usual mess including the travel section of the weekend paper, the remains of her morning's coffee in her coffee mug, an empty wine glass, half-dead flowers in a vase, coasters...

Or rather, a coaster. There was a beer coaster on the coffee table. From the Zanzibar. And there was no way she'd put it there.

She knew with one hundred percent certainty she couldn't have put the coaster there: she'd never taken any notice of their beer coasters until today, after the body in the backyard business and the 'Sam' coaster, and it wasn't as if she could have inadvertently brought one home that evening either – she hadn't even put her things down yet.

And so without making a sound, without even breathing, and straining to hear the slightest noise, anything at all, she slowly put her handbag down on the floor and padded over to the coffee table.

She bent down and carefully picked up the coaster. It was clean with no marks, maybe never used. Smelt it. Just cardboard and ink. She turned it over.

And there, written in blue biro, was a word – one single, dreadful word.

Agatha.

She let go of it, horrified – as if it was infected – and it fell to the floor.

And at that moment, before she'd had a chance to think through the full implications of the discovery, her house phone rang.

The sudden noise was heart-stopping – she could have sworn it nearly killed her, the shock of it. Answering it was out of the question, so she just watched it ring – it seemed loud, so loud that she wanted to smother it with something, but she wasn't going to touch it. Just let it ring out.

And it rang on, as if it was never going to stop. And then when it eventually did, the silence that followed was, in its way, equally loud.

Her first thought was to go and shut the window she'd just opened. This now brought to mind the dream she'd had the previous night, which had followed the phone calls she'd received earlier that evening, and all of this, in turn, only reinforced the sense of déjà vu she'd felt earlier.

When she reached the window, she again tried to avoid looking at the reflection in the glass but it was impossible, and she could see the living room stretching back away behind her but then, superimposed on that image, was the image of a man standing alone outside. He was down in the street below, bathed in a puddle of light. And looking up at her.

The man was wearing a dark suit and trainers.

It was him again. No question. It was Smeeton.

He wasn't smiling or nodding. He wasn't moving, wasn't doing anything. He was just standing there, staring. It was almost as if he wasn't looking at her at all, but looking at something else, such as an architectural feature or a bird. He was staring like a predator stares at its prey. A picture of complete concentration.

Agatha backed away from the window, too scared to close it, and then stopped and stared at the open space, fully expecting the man to appear, climbing in. Her body didn't know which way to move, was caught in a terrible moment of indecision, but she had to get a grip and snap herself out of it, it was ridiculous, she was Venezuelan and her father's daughter, and on top of that she was a police officer, she was *the police*.

She forced herself back to the window.

He was gone. Maybe he was never there? Another hallucination, like a week ago when she was sitting in her office in the evening? Not this time. She closed the window and re-hooked the latch. And then she had a horrible thought: that in her deep-seated fear of there being someone in her flat, she may not have re-locked the front door when she walked in.

She looked into the window's reflection – she couldn't help it – and thought she saw a face. This time though it wasn't outside. It was behind her.

She spun around.

And there he was.

Smeeton. Straight out of her nightmares: in a black suit and black trainers, and a half-untucked blue shirt extending over his fat belly, and his large pale face and small, dull grey eyes. And smiling now, that disgusting smile. The very same man, but this was no dream. If only.

He said nothing. She wanted him to speak, as he did in her dreams. But he remained silent, which was far more terrifying.

He began to walk slowly towards her, and she could see the sweat on his bland, bloated face, his tiny nose and shark eyes. And all her training vanished – she was acutely aware of this as it all unfolded – and again she froze, truly rooted to the spot this time, like a bird watching an approaching snake. Hypnotized and paralyzed. In other words, the perfect prey.

And while that last thought – of being, herself, prey – was enough to spur her into action, she was too slow. She knew it too, even as her muscles clenched and gripped as a precursor to sudden movement, even as she turned and made for the window, and even as she unhooked the latch and gripped the window to open it. Because even though she knew, somehow, what was coming, knew it had to be avoided at all costs, knew that her best avenue of escape was out the window, there was a scintilla of defeatism in each and every one of her actions, a realization that this man who'd been seemingly pursuing her for so long was upon her – a destiny as inescapable and inevitable as that of the clipped and stumbling gazelle ahead of the pursuing lion.

With both hands gripping the bottom of the window she looked up for an instant and that horrible face was there, in the reflection, directly behind her own. Lightning quick, that he was fast for a fat man was all she could think, all she had time to think because an arm was already across her throat. She was fast too, though, the adrenalin was kicking in, and she ducked and twisted and fell, and skittered across the floor like a cockroach before finding her feet and bolting for the door. But he was on her, had a hand on her upper right arm painfully squeezing her biceps, and she twisted again, tried to tear herself free, and for a moment – or rather moments, it felt like minutes – they were dancing, a waltz at first, then everything was a whirling blur, a frenzy, and furniture was crashing and she was on the ground, kicking at everything, a chair, a couch, a man's leg, and then up again, but too slow, she kept thinking, *I was too slow*, and eventually he had her, over near the window again, back where they started, and the arm was there again too, only this time it was clamped around her throat, as taut and hard as a crooked steel bar, with the V of the elbow squeezing tight, and even though she was stamping her heel, she kept missing his feet, and it was too late anyway because she was soon immobilized. Her limbs flailed around for a few more seconds, but her strength drained quickly from her body as if it was being syphoned out of her.

As her consciousness slowly ebbed away and her vision became blurred, she could see Smeeton's smiling reflection in the window – or maybe now it was more grimace than smile – all arm and shoulders and round head, the pallor of his ghostly face reflecting back the light oddly. She was suddenly angry, furious with herself: why hadn't she screamed out when she'd had the chance? She couldn't even breathe now, let alone shout.

And then something was placed over her head, a mask of some kind or a bag. Everything went dark and she had just enough time to feel a heartbreaking sense of regret about not calling home one more time – not calling her parents, or her sister, she'd been so neglectful. And in the slowed-down seconds she had left, she had just enough time, too, to think about all the other girls, or women – the Nowhere women – and wonder whether she was about to join them and what would become of her.

What would become of her body.

And as an extension of that, she thought about the one who'd returned, Sam, and her amnesia, and she thought no, this couldn't be happening to her. Amnesia, worse than death, living without a memory, what did you have if you didn't have memory? What would become of her body?

What if she woke up and she remembered nothing?

What if it was all gone?

Worse than death...

Pray for it...

Death...

...

.

26.

Mornings had never been Brearly's favourite part of the day, less so when they involved long discussions with Perrick. The Superintendent was thorough, but had a way of taking twice as long as anybody else to say something and of throwing in a dash of dull at the same time. It was a heady brew and not at all hangover friendly. To make matters worse it was a particularly warm morning – Sydney was experiencing one of its hottest Octobers on record – and Brearly wasn't great in the heat, even without a hangover.

After Agatha had left the Zanzibar the previous evening, Brearly had stayed on for a 'quick one' before heading home. If there was one thing he'd learnt in life, there was no such thing as a quick one – not when it came to alcohol anyway. Not for him. Maybe for others.

It was around 10am. They were sitting in Perrick's office, initially discussing yesterday's drama – the discovery of the body in the backyard just around the corner. Perrick wanted to know if Brearly thought this latest development was in any way linked to the disappearance of the women on their Nowhere list. Brearly told him about the coaster with the name 'Sam' on it, and said it was a tenuous link and that they still hadn't confirmed who the phone number belonged to. And then their conversation turned to Carol, and how few leads they had there.

'Her boyfriend,' Perrick said, 'who was in Japan, I think he's a venture capitalist or something, isn't he? I'm pretty sure. So anyway, as you'd expect, he's flown back, and he's been calling non-stop.'

'So I hear.'

'He's worried sick. Unsurprisingly. I mean it doesn't really...' Perrick trailed off, which was a habit of his. 'I don't too much like her chances, do you?'

Even in his best moods, Brearly made a point of not answering Perrick's questions unless absolutely necessary. It was a time management issue.

'And we're still...' Perrick went on. 'We've still got nothing concrete? Nothing linking them? Other than... young women, and... disappeared?'

Brearly left a good pause, but Perrick was staring at him, waiting for an answer.

'They're not all *that* young. Carol's forty-one.'

'She looks a lot younger than forty-one, you've seen her photo. So what else have we got? Nothing? We must have *something*.'

Brearly shrugged and wanted to leave it at that, but Perrick's eyes were boring into his.

'Except it's a guy who wears suits,' he said. 'Which, I know, hardly narrows it down—'

'Hardly narrows it down much, no. But it's something.'

Perrick swivelled in his chair and looked out the window for a moment, and a look of great sadness seemed to pass over his face. Brearly followed his gaze, out the windows of his office, over Australia Street to the big blue southern sky that greeted them that morning.

'Something strange happened last night,' Brearly said, mainly to break the uncomfortable silence. Talking actually made him feel less queasy than listening. 'Agatha and I were having a beer in the Zannie, and I told her I spotted a guy in a black suit and trainers leaving the place, and she just... bolted outside. I wondered what the fuck... what the hell was going on, no idea what had got into her and when she returned I asked her about it. He'd gone of course, whoever he was, but she seemed to place some importance on the trainers.'

'Really?'

'Not sure where she got that from, the trainers thing, she wouldn't elaborate, said it was just her gut instinct.'

'Really.'

'I think maybe she's been working too hard.' As soon as he said it, he regretted it, the last thing he wanted to do was dump on Agatha. Of all people. But she had been acting strangely, even for Agatha. And you could only listen to this intuition stuff for so long. Not without evidence backing it up. And anyway, Perrick had a mysterious way of squeezing this stuff out of you, like water from a sponge. Resistance was futile.

'And for sure,' he added, 'these disappearances have us all on edge to some extent. But it did freak me out a little bit.'

'Still. You've got to pay attention to the pulses. Those pulses you get, you know what I mean?'

'Pulses?'

'In this job. They're what count. Like a heartbeat, coming from deep in the earth. Like little warnings. Or invitations.'

'Pulses. No, sure.'

'And so the, er... Pantyhose Woman,' and Perrick checked his notes, 'Samantha Poole, who turned up, which I suppose technically means she's no longer a Nowhere woman—'

'A Somewhere woman.'

'You and Agatha got to talk to her yesterday I take it, but she wasn't able to shed much light on anything?'

'Not too much. It was mainly what she'd already told the supervisor. About a man she reckons was following her. Called Smeedon or Smeeton.'

'Smeeton?'

'Smeedon or Smeeton, yeah. Something like that.'

'First name?'

Brearly shook his head.

Perrick appeared pensive. 'Hm. Bit vague. Without anything else.'

'To say the least. Multiple spellings of the surname. No first name or further description. We'd need more resources to—'

'Try to get more. Leads, I mean. Keep working on it. Especially this... Samantha Poole. Maybe her memory will improve. Given time.'

'We have to hope. She's the best thing we've got at the moment. That's even assuming, though, it's the same perpetrator. Or, in her case, whether there *is* a perpetrator.'

Perrick raised his eyebrows. 'You don't believe her?'

'I've always had a funny feeling about this one – or pulse, if you like. There's a smell about it, I don't know.'

'Well *who* knows. But we keep all avenues of inquiry open. And stay vigilant. Because something'll turn up. As sure as night follows day. Something'll show itself and rear its ugly head.'

Another thoughtful pause. Brearly wished Perrick wouldn't keep the integrated window blinds up. They were there for a reason. The glare was now definitely an unwanted friend this morning.

Then a thought occurred to him. Inspired by something Agatha had said. His instinct was to keep it to himself but again, this was what Perrick did to you. Squeezed it out of you without appearing to try. Good superintendents did that, in his experience. Seen it plenty of times.

'We were... I was wondering. With Sam, if there wasn't some kind of drug involved. I mean I know the memory loss thing... in theory it can be a sudden shock that does it, or even more commonly, some kind of alcohol or drug abuse, or a combination, but what if it's a particular drug *designed* to make someone lose their memory.'

'Oh yeah?'

'Seeing Sam like that. Made me wonder... Well, to be honest, it was Agatha's idea, but you have to consider the possibility that someone might have done this intentionally. Whether the memory loss thing, the amnesia, was the point. Or part of it.'

'Part and parcel.'

'Yeah, part of their, you know, modus operandi.'

'Hmm.'

'And if so, who?'

Perrick was frowning, almost looking as though he was thinking of something else altogether. Another trait Brearly had noticed. Supers had to juggle a lot of shit. A lot of data processing had to get done.

'I'll tell you who,' Perrick said. 'A fucking good chemist!'

They both laughed. For once, Brearly found something Perrick said funny. Not because he'd said anything funny in itself – he hadn't, he'd just stated the obvious – but because Perrick never, as a rule, swore.

'By the way,' Perrick added. 'Where *is* Agatha?'

'Haven't seen her. Don't think she's in yet.'

'It's after ten o'clock!'

'Not in Argentina.'

Perrick sighed and shook his head.

'*Venezuela*,' he said.

'Whatever. They're all on *castanet* time, that lot.'

27.

The woman was lying on the floor of the apartment when she woke up. She didn't recognize the place but had a vague feeling it was hers. The thing that puzzled her most, though, was what she was doing on the floor. And why she was naked.

There were clothes strewn about. A chair lay on its side.

Her head hurt. She was hot. Was she hungover? And her neck hurt too, the muscles on both sides, almost like someone had tried to strangle her. What had she done? Where had she been the previous night?

She propped herself up against the red leather couch that was next to her and tried to piece it all together but came up with nothing. She couldn't, for the moment, even remember her own name, but this scared her too much and she tried to think of something else.

She took another look around her. Other than the clothes and the chair, a broken wine glass and a section of newspaper lay on the floor, and a vase filled with old flowers had fallen over on the coffee table and lay in a shallow puddle of water. It looked like there'd been a wild party, but there were no empty bottles or plates lying around.

She decided the clothes were probably hers and that she ought to get dressed. Regardless of whose flat it was, she figured there could have been strangers in the other rooms, people around. Right now, the world was a stranger.

She stood up – unsteady on her feet, she felt like she was going to be ill and prayed she could hold it together at least until she got some clothes on. Which made her think of the word 'pray' and it seemed significant for a second or two – she couldn't think why – and then the feeling was gone again.

A pair of lacy black panties was lying next to the chair – she shuffled over and retrieved them, and then stepped into them, one leg at a time, and pulled them up using a nearby side table for balance. Her bra – or a bra she assumed was hers – was draped over an arm of the couch and she tried to put it on. She couldn't do it. Had no idea how the clip worked all of a sudden. Couldn't understand how you could forget something like that. (Come to think of it, she couldn't even remember the word that 'bra' was short for, although she knew there was one. A name came into her head, she could picture the spelling – Maroubra – but she knew that was wrong and had no idea what it meant.) She had to pull the back of the bra around to the front and even then it took her quite a few attempts of trying to thread the catch. It was like she was a teenager again, learning for the first time. Not that she could picture it, being a teenager. Right now, she couldn't picture anything.

She had to sit down again for a few moments and decided to leave the white pants and black top, piled on top of each other in a heap across the room, for another time. The underwear would have to do for now. Everything was an effort.

She wondered if the bed was made up or not, wherever it was. It occurred to her it could possibly provide a clue as to whether she'd gone to bed (and who with) and then got up, or not yet gone to bed at all.

Found a doorway and looked into the dark room beyond it. There was a bed and it looked unslept in: it was large (queen-size?) with an off-white bedspread and a cluster of colourful cushions thrown over it. It looked like the *kind* of room she would have as a bedroom, and it sort of looked familiar, but then it sort of didn't, too.

There was a built-in wardrobe, but when she opened it, she didn't recognize any of the clothes. She retraced her steps back into the main living/dining room, looking for anything to bring it all back to her, whatever 'it all' was. The longer she looked, the more frightened she became. A rising panic began to take hold. What if it didn't come back? What if she would never remember?

Again she tried to think of her name, and again she had to stop and think of something else. It felt like if she kept trying to remember her name and she kept failing, the effort and the fear would kill her.

She'd been naked, and on the floor, and apparently hadn't slept in her own bed. Had she had sex with a stranger – or for that matter a friend or a colleague – and they'd left? (Assuming it was her flat in the first place that is, but something told her it was.) It didn't *feel* like she'd had sex, or not sexual intercourse at least, but... She didn't want to think about other possibilities. The easiest thing was to assume she'd been drunk and hadn't made it to bed. As simple as that. Just passed out. Knocked a couple of things over in the process. It was as good an explanation as any.

The woman walked over to the windows at the end of the room. They were closed. This seemed significant but she didn't know why.

She found the latch on one of the windows and unhooked it. Pulled the window open. Fresh air.

It appeared she was on the second floor. It was beautiful outside – a warm morning, an *equatorial* morning – and you could see the ocean, and trees and houses of every description. Flats, old and new. It looked like a nice area, comfortable and well-to-do. It wasn't Caracas. It didn't look like Venezuela.

Caracas. Maybe she was from Caracas? There were cars in the street, but she couldn't read the details on the plates and couldn't tell where they were from.

Some of the books in the flat were in Spanish, the rest English.

Something on the floor caught her eye. The word 'Zanzibar'. It was on a beer coaster. She knew Zanzibar was in Africa. Maybe she'd even been there.

She picked up the coaster which had a representation of a palm tree over the name Zanzibar, and turned it over. A girl's name was written on the other side.

Agatha.

She frowned. It seemed familiar, that name... and not familiar. She tried again to remember who she was. Where she was. But nothing came, only tears. And an overwhelming sense of dread.

28.

The woman looked up as a plane flew over. Wondered where it was going to. She watched as it headed out over the ocean: reflecting the afternoon sun, hanging there, bright as a bauble. Out over the... over the...

Pacific. The Pacific Ocean. Another victory, of sorts — right now, remembering *any* name was a triumph, and the Pacific, that was a sweet one. But she kept forgetting them again too, the names. Even her own name refused to stay with her. Including now, for example, although in a few seconds it would be back...

She'd lost the coaster again; she'd been trying to keep it close, grateful she'd had the presence of mind to write her name on it, at some earlier point in time. Except she kept thinking it was her writing, but it wasn't. That was another thing: whose writing was it? And at what earlier point in time exactly had they written it?

Points in time, they were part of the problem. They kept shuffling and rearranging themselves. Wouldn't stay still. And kept hiding from her. Especially the points in time before today. Everything before today was... a black lagoon, vast and deep.

And its waters were lapping at her feet.

29.

The woman – Agatha, she now knew that much – looked at her phone: 4.02pm, Thursday 24 October. So she knew that as well.

She'd been glancing at her phone all day, once she'd found it. There were all kinds of clues in it, including names, places. *Sydney*. But most of all, it was the *time* that she clung onto. Like a kind of lifesaver (but wasn't that something you sucked on?). Somehow knowing the time helped keep things in place.

She was starting to remember some things now too. Bits and pieces. Today was clear enough. Like waking up naked on the floor that morning, although why was still a mystery.

The telephone rang, her landline, and it startled her. Her heart raced and she wasn't sure why the phone should cause her so much stress. She answered it anyway. Thinking it might be important, but at the same time realizing she probably wouldn't recognize what important looked like.

'Hello?'

There was the sound of a sudden great wind, a gale. Or that's what it reminded her of. It was a person, she realized, exhaling into the mouthpiece of their phone.

'Agatha, hi, it's me.' It was a man's voice. It sounded a little strained. 'Sorry to disturb you. I'm outside your building.'

She walked to the windows and looked down, being careful not to be seen. Sure enough, there was a man down on the street on his phone. He wasn't looking directly up at her but at one of the other buildings.

'I tried you on your mobile earlier, but there was no answer.'

She could see the man speaking so it was definitely her caller. He was wearing a dark suit, which made her feel uncomfortable. She didn't know why.

'I couldn't find my phone,' she said, just to say something.

'And I was going to press the buzzer, but you don't have one.'

She tried to get a better look at his face, to see if he looked familiar, but he kept turning away.

'So I thought I should ring you, rather than just knock on your door.'

'Sure, no, that's fine.'

'Which could have been a bit creepy.'

There was an uncomfortable pause. She wasn't sure what she was meant to say, or what she *should* say.

'I've been worried about you. Um... can I come up?'

She didn't know what to do, she had to make a quick decision. He knew her name, he was worried about her, he sounded like a friend, so the chances were it was OK.

'Sure, yeah. Come up.'

She walked quickly across the living room to the hallway beyond it. When she went to unlock the front door, she found it was already unlocked. Did that mean anything? She didn't have the time to think about it because the man was now walking up the stairs. And suddenly she was wondering whether this was a good idea and having second thoughts…

But it was too late because here he was.

Dark grey suit. Solid build, he looked fit. Dark hair. When he got to her floor she could see his face despite the interior gloom. He was good-looking. She'd have gone further than that and surprised even herself and said he was extremely cute. Handsome face, nice hair, with daring, green eyes. She felt an immediate physical attraction so strong it embarrassed her and she could feel herself blushing.

'Hi,' he said.

'Hi,' she said.

They stood there for a moment, looking at each other.

'Shall we…' He was obviously suggesting she let him in.

She hesitated and all at once a warm smile spread across his face.

'I get it,' he said. 'You're waiting to see the warrant. Well I don't have one. But I *do* have…'

He reached into his jacket and pulled out something and flipped it open. It was an ID wallet, with a large police badge on one side and he added:

'Detective Sergeant Peter Brearly, ma'am. Sorry to bother you but if it's all right, I'd like to ask you a few questions, would you mind if I came in?'

Which is when it all came flooding back, or at least a whole pool of them. Brearly. The Newtown police station. Perrick. Lutger. Terri.

Detective Senior Constable Agatha Ducatti.

Agatha Ducatti Durán-Delapeña.

30.

They sat down in the living room. He, on the red leather couch. She, on an adjacent chair (the one that had been on its side that morning). He did the detective thing of giving the place a good once-over. But she didn't mind about that. Not at all, because all she could think about was the attraction she'd felt for him before she'd known who he was. How embarrassing! She hoped he hadn't noticed. So he could look around as much as he wanted – the less he looked at her the better.

She became suddenly self-conscious about what she was wearing: turquoise harem pants and a white sleeveless button-up shirt. Had she left too many buttons undone? And when he *did* look at her, at her clothes and not her face, she felt like he was judging her dress sense and laughing at her.

'I'm sorry to drop in like this, Agatha. Invading your privacy. But when I rang you earlier today... as I say, I tried your mobile first... but when I rang your landline... was that you? That answered?'

Agatha genuinely didn't have an answer. She could only guess.

'Was I...?'

'I wasn't even sure it was you. You sounded terrible. Almost incoherent. Was that you? Anyway. I was worried.

I spoke to Perrick about it and he suggested I, er... pay you a visit. As they say.'

So now she was doubly embarrassed. Embarrassed about her thoughts when he turned up, and embarrassed about how she must have sounded when he rang earlier. Embarrassment as far as the eye could see.

'Yeah sorry about that. I'm not sure what...'

'Are you feeling OK? What happened?'

All she could feel was an overwhelming sense of shame.

'I'm fine. Thanks. Sorry you had to come out here. I'm not sure about... before.'

'I mean... you didn't even call in sick. Were you... was there...?'

'I'm sorry... Brearly.' At least she remembered that much. It was Brearly, not Peter. For some reason. 'I should have called.'

'Although from the way you sounded earlier, I'm not surprised you didn't.'

Brearly looked at her for a moment. She could feel his gaze on her, his green eyes exposing her soul, peeling back the layers...

'No.'

'Did you have a bad reaction to something? I didn't feel all that crash hot myself this morning and I drank more than you. Unless you...? Did you kick on, last night?'

Agatha shook her head. It would have helped if she could have *remembered* last night.

'No.'

'No?'

'I don't think so.'

'You don't *think* so? You don't know?'

All Agatha could do was slowly shake her head.

'That's not good. You remember having a drink in the Zanzibar and rushing out?'

'The...?'

'The Zanzibar.'

The Zanzibar. The beer coaster.

'Vaguely,' Agatha said, lying.

'You and I had a couple of beers, and then a round of spirits. You had a vodka and tonic I think. And that's it. You would have left around... it would have been 8pm maybe?' He was still looking at her closely. 'You don't remember? Leaving?'

She didn't remember *being* there.

'Not really.'

He looked away and sat back, exhaling air. Shook his head. 'I had a few more after you left. Margheritas.' He thought some more. 'I think I should take you to a doctor.'

'A doctor? What kind of doctor?'

'Just in case it's not something... I don't know. I mean look at Sam.'

Sam?

'Look what happened there. Don't think it didn't occur to me that could have happened to you, too.'

'Brearly, I'm fine. I don't need to see a doctor. I've obviously had a bad reaction to something. It'll pass.'

Her embarrassment was acute enough, she didn't need a shrink to pile it on. Nor to have her job put on the line.

What she needed was to find out for herself exactly what was going on, what *had* happened last night. And in the meantime, recover. It felt like she was improving by the hour.

'What if...? You might have been attacked on the way home. Hit on the head and don't remember it.'

'But my head's fine,' she protested. 'I think I'd know it if I'd been, what do you call it? King-hit or whatever. Attacked.' As soon as she uttered the words though, she could feel the soreness in her neck muscles.

'I spoke to a doctor yesterday about this kind of thing. You could be suffering from some kind of retrograde amnesia. Like Sam.'

Sam again.

'Apparently,' he added, 'even the *shock* of an attack or confrontation can do it. Mental trauma and all that. You forget stuff that happens around an incident, or just before it.'

'But nothing happened.'

'That you remember.'

There was an uncomfortable silence and then he continued:

'My first thought was that you narrowly escaped ending up on our list.'

List? What list?

She must have looked puzzled, because Brearly elaborated:

'Because I thought, Christ, amnesia, like Sam, who disappeared from the same area. Newtown. But then I

146

figured *naaaaah*, just a coincidence, because he'd have to be one dumb prick to have a go at the police who were chasing him.'

'He would be.'

Neither of them spoke for a few moments.

'Well anyway, at least you haven't hit your head,' said Brearly. 'And if there had been some kind of confrontation, you've sustained no physical injuries. And you know what? I wouldn't be surprised if someone spiked your drink. The Zanzibar. I always suspected there was something dodgy about that place.'

'Could well be.'

'At least you seem a lot better than you did when I spoke to you earlier.'

'I am.'

'Good. I've been told to tell you to take a couple of days off. Tomorrow's Friday. Don't come in until Monday at the earliest.'

'Oh. OK.'

'You ought to hit the beach if this weather continues. You're close enough.'

She just nodded, and smiled weakly.

'I can tell you one thing though, Agatha. If you'd been attacked in here, in your home, we'd have to think about putting a car outside. For your protection.'

'That would be ridiculous. And I haven't been attacked.'

As she said the words, the room seemed to drop a couple of degrees, as if to prove her wrong.

After Brearly left, Agatha felt suddenly exhausted. Shattered. Going out certainly wasn't an option. She double-checked the front door was locked, then lay down on the leather couch and tried to clear her head and think about nothing for a while.

She must have fallen asleep.

Almost three hours later, she opened her eyes. It was just after sunset, and she stared out the southern windows.

The deepening violet sky seemed full of bad intentions.

31.

The next day, Friday, turned out to be uneventful. No one called her, and for that Agatha was profoundly grateful. She was happy to recuperate, and gradually recover her memory. Wednesday night, though, remained a mystery, dressed in a heavy, dark cloak.

The following day, Saturday, was hot. A real stinker, with a forecast maximum of 35°C. But that was the least of Agatha's problems, given what this particular day had in store for her.

By midmorning it was already hitting 30, and with the ocean breeze still to kick in, and her flat heating up like an inner city bar on a hot Friday night in summer (now *there* were some memories), Agatha decided to go for a quick walk down to the beach. Not that the beach was much cooler, especially in the sun, unless you were going swimming which she wasn't in the mood for, but she had to get out of the flat, even if only for a short time.

She chose a circuitous route that took her through the local backstreets and then down through the cool of the forest in Tamarama Gully and over the road to the beach and the overpowering smell of suntan lotion. The deep blue waters of the horseshoe-shaped bay looked inviting, fringed as they were with only the barest of lines of dazzling white surf – the waves were small for a change – and she regretted not bringing swimmers and a towel. But the beach at Tamarama – also called Glamarama for obvious reasons – was crowded, especially for a weekday, and looking at strangers' faces from all corners of the globe – tourists mainly and almost all smiling – only made her anxious and she quickly retreated back up the steep streets to her apartment building. She didn't even buy her usual mango smoothie from the kiosk at the beach, but at least she could *remember* what her usual was.

She was dripping with sweat by the time she returned, and tore her clothes off and jumped straight in the shower. By the time she'd finished and was towel-drying her hair – at around midday – her mobile phone started ringing. It was Brearly.

'Sorry for not calling yesterday. Things got... busy.'

'Thanks, but... I'm fine.'

'You're OK? Feeling better?'

'Back to normal.'

'And Wednesday night? Have you—?'

'Yeah, yeah, all sorted. Just a bad reaction to something, or maybe my drink was spiked, although who'd want to... Probably intended for someone else. But thanks Brearly. I'll be in on Monday, I promise.'

'Well. Good. Pleased to hear it.'

'What are you doing working on a Saturday anyway? Or, is this...?'

'Yeah no I mean... Work, someone has to do it, huh? But I thought you might like to know... Just heard yesterday. Sam's gone. From the refuge. Disappeared again.'

'Has he.' She still couldn't remember who Sam was. She made a mental note to have another look for any diaries later.

'She. Samantha.'

'Oh *Samantha*. Right.' Still no idea.

'With any luck she'll turn up somewhere. Her mind still hadn't...'

He trailed off and there was an awkward pause. Which is when it clicked: Samantha Poole, the Pantyhose Woman. With the memory loss...

'One thing we did manage to get, though. A confirmation on the coaster. It was her handwriting, her phone number. So the death of Benjamin Deane looks like it's connected. I don't know where that leaves us. In terms of our Nowhere list, I mean.'

'No.'

Benjamin Deane. The body in the backyard. And more importantly, the Nowhere list, that came back to her now, too. What she and Brearly had been working on. Those girls, women, the ones who disappeared. The Nowhere women.

And all this led to a strange but powerful sensation: that she was observing a memory through the wrong end of a telescope. A memory, or a dream. And that what it was about she couldn't remember, and perhaps it was just a dream, but she sensed with a feeling of absolute certainty that it had already provided her with the answer to what they were looking for.

'Anyway,' Brearly said, 'we at least have a suspect of sorts now. That weasel, Shane Jeldry. Apologies to weasels. Now you're hardly going to forget *him*. Yeah?'

'I remember.'

'Skinny guy with the mullet?'

'Yeah yeah.' Finally, she wasn't lying. Shane Jeldry, and their trip to Maroubra. The 'Bra, as it was known locally.

'Lutger's decided our mullety friend has been playing a game of double bluff. Could be something in it too, his alibis don't fully check out... for any of the disappearances, not just for his ex's, Chalaise... but I gotta say, if it's true, I did not pick that one. The guy has a brain the size of a pea for a start, I don't care what his results at Uni were. I mean, are we seriously meant to believe that pathetic *runt* is the mastermind behind the Nowhere list?'

No we are not, she thought. Because something was suddenly bothering her. About the perpetrator. And 'skinny' and 'mullety' didn't fit. Definitely rang the wrong bells.

'If it's even a thing, of course,' Brearly went on. 'That list of ours. I'm still not convinced we're not barking up the wrong tree on that one. Oh but you'll like this. Perrick... in his infinite wisdom... has been looking into lining up an FBI profiler in the US. Can you believe it? He's already found a guy in California... forgotten his name... works out of Sacramento or somewhere... and *his* take on the perpetrator, his preliminary view, is that the person's most likely a male... well thanks for that *Inspector Poirot*... but he's a guy, he's highly intelligent, knows his drugs, his periodic table, he's probably an expert in chemistry, and... this is the good bit... he most likely suffers from feelings of inadequacy regarding women. Oh and he's either physically ugly or just plain nondescript. Well. Jeldry certainly qualifies on the ugly front I reckon, but Christ Almighty. A profiler.'

Despite the heat of the day, Agatha felt a chill all of a sudden. Maybe she was coming down with something.

'Also, I can't picture our Shane in a suit, can you? Mind you in this job, you do have to expect the unexpected. Anyhow, I've talked for long enough, I'd better let you go,' Brearly said. 'You need anything? I can drop by, if...'

'Well...'

'Sorry. I should leave you alone...' Something inside her said *No you shouldn't*, but it was fleeting, as was their conversation it seemed...

'Get some rest,' he added. 'Reboot that C drive. I'm sure you'll be fine by Monday.'

'I'm fine now! But thanks... Brearly.'

As they were ending their call, Agatha had begun to walk over to the southern windows, with all that hot coastal brilliance shining through from the outside. But now she slowed. Her limbs felt heavy. As if her body knew something her head did not.

A few hours later – at around 3pm – there was a knock on the door: three sharp, aggressive raps.

'Agatha! It's only me!'

It was a female voice this time.

Agatha opened the front door, revealing a woman possibly in her seventies wearing cornflower-blue pants and a white blouse, and with a face made up like a geisha's. She had bright, happy features combined with a dangerous smile. Agatha remembered her, too (a good sign): she was a neighbour. Whose name was...

'Isn't it hot?!' the neighbour said. 'Sorry to bother you. Are you all right love?'

'Yes. Thank—'

'Now I know it's none of my business...'

Agatha could see the woman's bra (*brassiere!*) through her blouse and found herself wondering whether that was appropriate for a seventy-year-old, and then thought of course it was, how could it matter how old you were?

'... and I know you can look after yourself and all but... well firstly I couldn't help but notice a bit of a commotion the other night... a bit of a sort of a racket a real ruckus and thought it might have been coming from your flat. Not that I mind of course we're all entitled to a bit of fun sometimes Lord knows I've had my fair share over the years... oh and... I still do I hope...'

The woman laughed. It was a high-pitched, soprano-style cackle, and when she really got going, Agatha could tell, it would've been something. Armour-piercing. Agatha did her best to smile back, but her face resisted, didn't want to get involved with all the necessary stretching and broadening – right now, it just wanted to be left alone.

The woman recomposed herself quickly. 'So anyway I said to myself "Bee you ought to just pop your head in and make sure there's nothing wrong."'

Agatha was grateful for the assistance with her neighbour's name. Bee. Beatrice. Beatrice Meehan.

'What sort of... commotion was it?' Agatha asked. She'd just twigged to what Bee had been saying, and the potential implications were making her apprehensive.

'Oh... some... look it was nothing really... it's usually the boys upstairs although we can't blame them every time can we?' Bee's grin was as broad as Bondi Beach.

'No we can't do that. Which night was this?'

'Which night? Oh it would have been let me think... it was... Wednesday night?... that's right because I had my dentist's appointment the next morning and I had to get up earlier than usual so I could get the... *anyway* you don't want to hear all of that now do you but I just wanted to make sure you were all right... because when I knocked on your door here the other night everything went quiet... I may have actually shouted something I don't know if you heard me... but after no one answered I walked back down to my place and I was putting my key in the front door when this... *man*... came charging past me he just went *whoooooooooooosh!* right past nearly knocking me over it was really most peculiar.'

'What did he look like?'

'Well he was... how would you describe him... so high I suppose...'

Her hand oscillated over a wide range of possible heights.

'... somewhat stocky or... *large*...'

Stocky. Large. Agatha started to get a bad feeling. A very bad feeling. Things were shifting around in the murky sludge in the depths of her consciousness.

'... and otherwise I'm not sure he had... mid-rangey sort of hair and... it was a bit hard to tell in this dingy old building the lighting at night is simply awful I can't tell you how long I've been at them to do something about it.'

'And the man? Was he...?'

'Oh yes well that man... I presume he's a friend?... I've seen him about and I'm not sure who else he might know here... not that I'm *implying* anything by that my dear!... goodness that came out poorly didn't it...'

Agatha was experiencing a distinctly unpleasant, nauseous sensation now, and the more Bee spoke about this man, the worse it got. She had no idea where the next question came from – she was speaking it, seemingly, before she thought it – only that it came from somewhere deep and true.

'And this man,' she said, 'What was he wearing?'

'Oh he was wearing a suit.'

'A suit.'

'Yes yes a suit.'

'Was it... dark?'

'Dingy as I say but I could see him well enough... enough of his clothes at least... his suit and his running shoes because I notice clothes it's the one thing I *do* see.'

'Running shoes? He was wearing running shoes?'

'I know. Friend of yours?... I'm only joking but really... A fashion blunder if ever there was one... you should have a quick word in his ear. *Anyway.* I'm sorry it's none of my business but you can't be too careful can you... this building needs better security I've been saying it for years and they keep saying we're getting it and we never do. I'll have to speak to them again I think.'

Agatha was, by now, having difficulty formulating words – speaking them or thinking them – and it was made all the more disturbing by her inability to pinpoint the precise cause of this unheralded onset of fear. Except that there was something significant – and terrible – about the man wearing a suit and running shoes.

When she eventually managed to say something, her words came out so quietly she was surprised Bee heard them.

'(You've said you've seen him around?)'

'Seen him my dear?' Bee asked. 'Is that what you said? Oh yes a few times I believe.'

'Since... Wednesday?'

'Yes yes I think so. I'm sure it was him and I don't want to pry I really don't it's none of my business who's a friend of anybody's. Goodness you're going to think I'm some pathetic old woman some scaredy-cat in the downstairs flat... that sounds like the name of a book or a poem doesn't it 'scaredy-cat in the downstairs flat'... and anyway I *do* feel silly raising these matters with you of all people... these security issues I mean with you being a *police*woman and everything but then again you're not always here are you.'

After Bee left, Agatha had to sit down to compose herself. She couldn't work out why this image disturbed her so much – this image sprung from a dark corner of her mind, the large man wearing a dark suit and trainers.

In an attempt to get to the bottom of things – and despite the heat which made her feel like not wanting to do anything – Agatha continued to poke around the contents of the living room: she'd been doing this on and off for the last two days, and she felt a compulsion to keep doing it until everything became boringly familiar. Because it was familiarity that she'd been craving, as much as anything else. Now though, she wanted to have a better look for any diaries or notes – she knew she had them, she'd just forgotten where she kept them.

And so she settled back into picking her way through the novels, and travel books, and other books on her bookshelves and through the miscellany of documents in the drawers of her wooden desk in the corner of the room.

At one point she paused and looked at her phone. Checked the time: 4.04pm, Saturday 26 October. Which wasn't so important in itself, but she remembered doing precisely the same thing at 4.02pm on Thursday. It was a good sign. Her brain was sharpening, making better connections, conscious as well as subconscious ones.

She walked over to one of the southern windows. In the midafternoon sun, the ocean was a deep blue. Heat rose off the bitumen on the road below, distorting, almost imperceptibly, the view of the street. The visible light. Reality. And standing there at the window reminded her of something else, something she could almost but not quite touch...

A plane flew overhead, heading east out over the water, and as she watched it, and thought of the passengers on board, she wondered who they were, those people jetting off on holiday perhaps or at least travelling somewhere else, and what sort of luck they had to have to be flying in that plane in the first place. And whether, if anyone knew the full facts of *her* predicament, they'd call her lucky or unlucky.

And then she reminded herself that she didn't believe in luck. That, in other words, you made your own.

To the south, dark clouds were just beginning to show themselves over the ridge of houses on the other side of the gully. Looked like a storm. She hoped so, it'd be a blessed respite from this heat.

When she turned to continue her searching, her eyes fell on the ottoman she kept over near the desk. It was topped with a moss-green padded leather seat and she'd completely forgotten it doubled as a chest and that she stored things in it. Notes, and her lists, her countless lists of things. She wrote notes to herself constantly, aide-memoires in a way, and the irony was that now, when her memory most needed aiding, they were next to useless. To-do lists, lists of books she'd read, wines she'd drunk, cookbooks she wanted to buy, garages for car services, train times, sunrise times, tide times (why? why? why?)... it was endless, but all she wanted was something – and she was certain it would be here somewhere – that might shed some light on what might have happened on Wednesday night.

It must have been about an hour later, while she was still in the process of sifting through all those papers and with her impatience growing with every fruitless minute, that a piece of paper fell to the floor and, carried by a burst of air from her oscillating pedestal fan, disappeared under the red couch. And when she then lay down on the floor – hot, bothered and annoyed – and reached under the couch to retrieve it, she found not just the piece of paper but something else as well.

It was her police notebook. It was her current one too, so finally something useful.

There was a rumble of thunder outside, and she looked up, only just realizing that the storm was almost upon her. The sky was black and the day was almost as dark as night.

Just as she was opening the notebook, her mobile phone rang. The caller was Peter Perrick. She continued, with one hand, to flick through the pages of her notebook as if there was something so urgent there that it couldn't wait, even for a call from her boss.

'Hello?'

'Agatha? It's Perrick here.'

White flashes outside her window, like being ambushed by a mob of paparazzi.

'Hi, how are you?'

'I was wanting to ask you the same thing.'

'I'm fine. I'm sorry about—' There was a sharp crackle and boom presaging the arrival of the approaching storm cell. 'There's a big storm about to hit here, how is it where you are?'

'It can't get you on your mobile,' he said, more condescending than she would have expected from Perrick. She flicked through a few more pages, keen to find the recent entries. In her nervous haste, the notebook slipped from her grasp and she had to pick it up and start again.

'That's true.'

'I just thought I should make sure you're on the mend from whatever it was.'

'I am,' she said, her diary open again, but at May. October was what she wanted. 'And I'll be good to go on Monday.'

'Very pleased to hear it. You just need to reboot that C drive.'

Which was what Brearly had said. She didn't know why exactly, but it creeped her out a little, hearing Perrick say that. It would hardly have been surprising if they'd been comparing notes, but the thought made her uncomfortable for some reason.

'And when you do,' he continued, 'and get back to the Nowhere List, just remember... Well. I'm leaving no stone unturned on this one, Agatha. And I want to stress...'

There was silence at the end of the line and another flash of lightning, immediately followed by a sharp and deafening crack of thunder that sounded like it must have hit the building next door. She almost jumped out of her skin.

Had he said something then?

She'd jumped ahead to September, but she was having trouble turning the pages, her fingers felt like bananas.

Was he still there?

'Hello?'

When he finally spoke – it had to have been after a good fifteen seconds – he continued heedless of the lengthy pause:

'I want to emphasize Agatha that I place great faith in your instincts. I get you. I really do. You have a talent that's rare and not fully appreciated by others.'

In her mind's eye, she could see his face. And his dark brown eyes. Her father's eyes, and that's what he really was, she realized. Her de facto father, replacing her absent one. Her Sydney father.

'It means a lot to me that—' she began.

'So when you get back to work on the Nowhere List, remember this. At the early stage of an investigation, the most important thing is not to rule stuff out. The smallest clue. Half the time they're in your dreams. It's a strange job we investigators have and you never know where your next lead is going to come from. Especially with those who are more... intuitive, like you. Sometimes, often, the answer's there, hidden away in your own head. So here's an idea. Make a note of them... your thoughts, your dreams... write them down. Because the nightmares could be real.'

'I'll remember that,' she said, feeling the weight of his words more keenly than she would have liked.

There was a long pause, as she waited for Perrick to say something.

'Hello?' she said. But there was no answer. 'Are you there?'

She waited, but he was gone, properly this time. Odd. Maybe it was the storm. But despite his praise, the call had unsettled her.

The nightmares could be real.

The phrase echoed around her head as she returned her attention to her police notebook.

She was in mid-October, and now she had the use of both hands again. She flicked straight to the latest pages with writing on them and found two entries dated Wednesday 23 October. The day! The last of the entries was headed 'Eliza St., 3pm' and described how she'd attended a crime scene with Brearly in a backyard near the Newtown police station where they'd viewed the body of a young man. Unnamed, but it was obviously Benjamin Deane.

There was no entry after the Eliza Street one, just blank pages – a bit like her mind over the last couple of days – but the entry before it caught her eye. Because the name 'Sam' had jumped out at her. Samantha Poole. This entry was headed 'Woolloomooloo, women's refuge, 1pm' and it contained notes about their discussion with Sam herself, including her amnesia. There was also a reference to a discussion with the woman in charge, Fiona, and it was here that Agatha came across something that chilled her to the bone. It was a name, consisting of a single word, and it was contained in a note of what Sam had said about the man pursuing her, that she thought he was called 'Smeedon or Smeeton'.

Smeeton.

And it all came back to her in a rush. Dreams, visions, memories, all indistinguishable, none of which she fully understood at first. But all of it featuring the man in the dark suit and trainers, and all of it terrifying.

This process of recovering and sorting her thoughts and memories wasn't helped by what was now going on outside: great gusts of wind had arisen, accompanied by strobe lightning and bone-juddering thunder and giant raindrops, and the raindrops had turned into hail, which in turn was now being replaced by sweeping rain, and she only just managed to close the southern windows in time before the rain began angling in from the south and hitting the windowpanes.

Against this tumultuous background of sound and vision, her recollections gradually sorted themselves, distinguishing dreams from real events.

And now she remembered: Wednesday night. And the assault. An assault by a man who called himself Smeeton. The plump, pale man in the suit and trainers. A man who at once seemed to be both sprung from her nightmares and real.

She realized, too, that Bee's knocking on her door that night must have been what interrupted the attack and probably saved her life.

She immediately tried to call Perrick back, but he didn't pick up. Then she thought it through: maybe it had been just as well he hadn't answered. If she spoke to him now, or to Brearly, about these dreams and sudden recollections, she'd just sound confused and they'd worry she'd lost her mind. She at least needed to get everything straight in her own mind first. But equally she couldn't do nothing at all, she had to set something in motion, so she opted to send Perrick a text message. She typed out:

> *Took ur advice & may have something. Gut instinct! Think POI may have been in my building here in Tamarama on Wed night. Large man in suit and trainers. Witness is neighbour below me, Beatrice Meehan, flat 2. Someone else should question her asap re what she saw.*

Agatha read over the text a number of times before sending it. Once that was done, she retired to the leather couch and lay back and watched the storm play out, allowing her swirling recollections to do the same.

Gradually the storm subsided – the rain withdrew and the wind dropped off leaving an eerie, post-storm silence, with only the sound of dripping water – and once she'd opened the windows again, she was overwhelmed by the pungent smell of petrichor lifting off the road and the vegetation. The ocean remained grey.

The gunmetal clouds had remained that way as well, and despite sunset still being almost two hours away, it was still dark enough to have kept the nearby streetlight on, and the houses across the street had surrendered to this storm-imposed darkness, their otherwise sharp outlines having faded to a crepuscular graininess. As if they were fading away, along with the rest of reality. Fading away like poorly tended memories.

The more she thought about it, the more she realized she had to get out of her flat. Today. She had to get to safety. Regroup. Collate evidence. Collate her *brain*. But there was one thing she felt sure of: she was in great danger if she stayed where she was.

She checked her phone: it was already 5.33pm. How long had she spent wading through those useless notes and lists earlier?

Suddenly she was almost in a panic – because something told her she had no time – and she grabbed a bag she used for the gym that was lying on the floor and threw in the notebook, along with her handbag, which had her wallet and keys in it, and headed for the bedroom to get changed and pack some basic clothes and toiletries. She didn't have a plan, just to leave and gather her thoughts. The flat no longer felt like safe ground. No longer felt like home.

After she'd quickly slipped into a pair of jeans, a T-shirt and trainers, and stuffed into the gym bag some underwear and toiletries, and a change of clothes, and a book that was beside her bed (*Maigret At Picratt's* by Georges Simenon), she stopped for a moment to think. Threw in an umbrella. She remembered her phone was in the living room, and she made a mental note to pick it up on her way out.

She looked up and could see, over the tangle of cushions and clothes that lay scattered across her bed, a view of the greenery in the backyard outside. It had brightened slightly, and the greens were lusher and richer after the rain. And still the only sound was the dripping of rainwater from the overflowing gutters.

For some reason her attention was abruptly, almost rudely, drawn – as surely as if someone had grasped her head from behind and turned it – to the door to her bedroom, which was open, the way she always left it. It opened inwards into the bedroom and back towards the corner of the room, touching the adjacent wall. There was room behind it to store things, although she could no longer remember what she kept there.

There's something in the corner behind the door. Go on, have a look.

Where was this voice, or this instinct, coming from? She wasn't certain what scared her more, the sight of the open door hiding the corner of the room or the voice telling her to close it and check what was behind it. She stared at the door for a while until she couldn't stand the inertia any longer. Made her way over to it, reached out, her heart in her mouth, and swung it free.

There was nothing there but a collection of cardboard poster tubes, containing posters or paintings which she hadn't got around to hanging.

Right at that very moment though, in the post-storm silence, she heard a noise coming from the hallway just outside her bedroom.

It was the sound of a kind of scratching at her front door, or more specifically at the lock. As if it was being tampered with.

Needing no time to think about it, Agatha quickly closed the bedroom door and locked it. Luckily – or by design (was that the real reason she'd checked behind it?) – the door had been almost closed anyway, and she was able to close it and lock it before the front door opened.

She heard the sound of the front door clicking shut. And then nothing, not a sound other than the water dripping outside and, she imagined, her heart thumping in her chest. She knew though that buried in the silence, along with the thumping of her heart, was the sound of malevolent footsteps noiselessly padding through her flat.

She strained to hear breathing – they'd just come up the stairs after all – but there was nothing. She was barely breathing herself.

And then, to her horror, she noticed that the doorknob on the bedroom door was slowly rotating. For a moment she wondered if she'd really locked it or had that been another faulty memory?... but it held fast and the door remained closed. For now. Because then the doorknob began turning rapidly, back and forth, so quickly it was rattling, as if all the impatience outside the door was pouring itself into the doorknob. It was made all the more frightening by the intruder's vocal silence.

After about five seconds of this the rattling stopped, and just as Agatha dared to believe they'd given up, there was a startling, silence-shattering *bang* as someone or something slammed into the door. And then, a few moments later, there was another one, even more ferocious. They – he, she, it, but who was she kidding, she knew exactly who it was – were clearly trying to break the door down. Voicelessly, methodically, ruthlessly.

She glanced at the open window and knew what she had to do. Grabbed her gym bag from the bed, slung it over her shoulder, but then remembered. Her mobile phone. It was on the couch in the living room. Clearly though, retrieving it now was out of the question. She quickly climbed out the window and onto the ledge as the regular, crashing bangs became louder. The lock on the door surely couldn't hold out much longer.

She contemplated the garden bed below. It wasn't such a big drop – maybe four or five metres – and the thought of the door bursting open behind her made the choice an easy one. After a fleeting moment contemplating the sense of how, with the latest commotion, Bee would now have something more to complain about, she eased herself down over the edge and let go.

She landed without injuring herself, crop-circling a patch of wet lamb's ears, and she picked herself up, not even stopping to brush off the damp soil, and ran. Ran for her life.

Because she knew after what now appeared to have been a lucky break on Wednesday night, she was unlikely to escape a second time if her assailant managed to get his hands on her again.

32.

The large pale man in the suit and trainers.

The image of him was just about the only thing in Agatha's head as she lay on the maroon-and-mustard paisley bedspread in Room 112 of the Marco Polo Motor Inn.

It was well and truly night, now. It had been about three hours since her escape from her flat in Tamarama, and almost the whole time all she could think about was the plumpish, pallid-faced man with the dull grey eyes, and in the dark suit and trainers. And that his name was Smeeton. And that he'd been there all along, in the dark recesses of her brain, lurking there. Biding his time. He was a fantasy – a nightmare – and he was real, at the same time. The more her memory recovered, the more she knew that everything that mattered right then was somehow connected with Smeeton.

The motel was situated in Summer Hill, a part of Sydney she wasn't overly familiar with, despite its proximity to Newtown, and the place itself wasn't exactly five-star. It was situated on a major arterial road, and it was what it said it was – a motor inn, or motel – and you could park your car, if you had one, directly outside your room.

The building looked like it had been built in the sixties or seventies, with its dirty-white bricks and faded coral panelling and black-tinted windows and a large neon sign outside proclaiming variously '*Marco Polo* MOTEL' and '*NO* VACANCIES' (with the 'No' unlit) and 'OPEN 24 HOURS'. That it was positioned on one of Sydney's busiest roads and nestled between an auto repair shop and a store which sold everything from outboard motors to night-vision goggles only added to its allure if the smell of petrol and opportunity was what turned you on.

Her room, Room 112, was one level up, but you were still able to drive up to it and park outside your door, just as you could on the ground floor – the building was like the bereft offspring of a small motel and a split-level carpark – although she didn't have her car with her. She couldn't remember how she got there, but presumed by taxi. Apart from the man in the reception office, who was distracted by his miniature TV and kept his words to a minimum as if he was paying for them, there was no one to be seen. There were cars dotted around – mostly SUVs and tradesmen's utes – but no people (were they in their rooms, or out?). It was poorly lit and there was a darkness about the place that you could almost reach out and touch.

Why Agatha had chosen this particular motel was, at this point, a mystery to her. Maybe she'd stayed there before, conceivably when she and her family had first moved to Sydney from Caracas twenty-one years ago. She had no idea. But right now it was the last place she wanted to be. Not counting her flat in Tamarama.

The room smelt of wet dog and stale cigarette smoke.

The events of three hours ago were still a blur. Had they really happened? Had someone really broken into her flat? Had she really jumped out the window? The thought now seemed insane. Although so did her surroundings.

She knew she should be ringing the police, meaning the police station nearest her flat, the one at Waverley, or even Brearly for that matter, but she couldn't, it all sounded too ridiculous, especially after what had already happened. Maybe she'd imagined it? Maybe she was losing it? Or was still mentally impaired in some way? For the same reason, as much as she'd have liked to have had someone check on her flat – Bee, for example – it just seemed too crazy. She'd just be digging a deeper hole for herself. No, for the moment at least she was on her own, in this cheap hotel for lost cowboys and lonely businessmen...

Speaking of lonely, that pretty much summed up the way she felt at this point. Not even scared, not anymore – perhaps she'd been numbed to the fear factor – but all she wanted was to hear a friendly voice. She thought of ringing her parents, but she'd be tempted to blurt things out and they'd only worry. Same kind of thing with her younger sister, she owed it to her to be a bearer of maturity and wisdom. She knew Laura looked up to her and she felt that she had to continue to try to live up to that ideal. She couldn't bear the thought of disappointing her.

What about a friend? It was a depressing thought, but since the break-up of her last relationship a year ago, with the pressure of work, she'd neglected the few close relationships that she had, and now wasn't the time to burden any of them.

For a few unhinged moments she considered ringing her ex, Tomas, who now lived in London with his new girlfriend. She actually calculated the time difference before sanity prevailed and she ditched the worst idea she'd had in a long, long time.

She'd had plenty of boyfriends in her time, obviously, but the reality was that the fact she was currently single only exacerbated both her sense of dissatisfaction with her life caused by her feelings of social isolation, and the fear she'd been experiencing.

The fear. Yes, it was still there after all.

Which was when she suddenly remembered she didn't have her phone anyway, which, in turn, made her feel even lonelier still.

33.

The next day was overcast with the odd shower and gusty winds. It was bleak, indecisive weather – more proof, if proof was needed, of the notorious capriciousness of Sydney's weather – and it matched the way Agatha felt.

She needed a plan, but didn't have one. She needed a *phone* but was too nervous to go back to her flat alone. She didn't know Brearly's or Perrick's mobile numbers off the top of her head, and the best decision she could come to was to not make a decision. Or rather, she decided to lie low, and do nothing and wait until tomorrow morning, Monday, when she'd ring work, the station, and hope to enlist some help.

Which was a good plan, because she wasn't just nervous about going back to her flat, she was nervous about going out at all. It'd be a Sunday afternoon like the ones she'd had as a kid when it rained – in Caracas or Sydney. She'd stay in and watch TV. And because she didn't have a mother to cook her meals, she'd order them in. One of the miracles of modern living.

Having the whole day to think, meant she had time to consider her dreams. The ones with *him* in them. Was there such a thing as a prophetic dream? She doubted it. But how else to explain this latest development, with Smeeton appearing in her waking life? Unless there was something that had triggered her dreams – unless she'd met him before, but no matter how hard she racked her brains, how far she wandered down the dusty aisles of her library of memories, she came up with nothing.

34.

That night, Agatha slept badly. She dreamt of Smeeton but the content of her dreams – her nightmares – didn't stay with her. She tossed and turned and it wasn't until almost dawn that she eventually managed to get some proper sleep.

When she eventually awoke, it was barely light, but that turned out to be down to the weather. The first thing she did was to check the time on the radio console in the side table next to her bed:

11:06 AM.

She cursed herself and leapt out of bed. She was supposed to have been at work and she hadn't even rung to report in. Deep rumbling filtered through from outside – it was a combination of random rolling thunder and the heavy morning traffic along Parramatta Road.

It was also now pouring with rain, but she desperately needed a phone box, and staying put for any longer wasn't an option. The only good thing: she'd remembered to pack an umbrella. Wishing she had her car, she plunged into the maelstrom outside.

Her prospects of finding a phone box along the main road looked poor, so she headed up the hill and under the railway line, clinging to her umbrella, into the shopping area of Summer Hill.

It was almost midday by the time she finally got to ring the station and was put through to Brearly. He sounded distant, which in the circumstances probably wasn't surprising.

'We've been trying to get through to you.'

'I'm sorry, a lot's happened. I don't have my phone.'

'Are you coming in?'

'Well that's what I need to talk to you about.'

'Lutger's just reported in from speaking to your neighbour.'

It took her a moment to understand: Perrick must have passed on what she'd said in her text, and Brearly had then sent Lutger to interview Bee.

According to Brearly, it hadn't gone well. Bit of a nutter, was Lutger's verdict. All over the shop.

'What about the trainers?' Agatha blurted out, exasperated. 'The suit and the trainers?'

Brearly shook his head. 'I don't think Lutger got anything out of her at all, let alone who was wearing what footwear.'

'What about CCTV?'

'No cameras.'

'Around there? With all that money? Surely someone has one?'

'Nope. Nothing apparently. But just going back a step, what exactly are we supposed to be looking for here? What was this neighbour of yours supposed to have seen?'

Agatha first told him about the home invasion on Saturday night. He sounded concerned and puzzled at the same time. He would have had a lot of questions, she knew that, but time was short. Although she did tell him she was now staying in the Marco Polo Motor Inn.

'The Marco Polo? You've got to be kidding, why there? You do realize it used to be a renowned drug dealers' convention centre? And that the reception area's protected by bulletproof glass for a reason?'

'It does have a certain allure,' she said, although she immediately regretted her misplaced levity.

One question Brearly did ask was if she could describe the intruder.

'No. I didn't wait around to check him out.' She knew how that sounded too. She was a cop and she ran from a burglar.

'Right.' The disappointment was thick in his voice.

'But listen Brearly. I'm sure... don't ask me how... but I'm certain it was the same man as the one who attacked me on Wednesday night.'

'Wait, wait... you were attacked on Wednesday night? But you told me that—'

'I know, I know. I had no recollection then, because of the... whatever it was, but I do now, it's come back to me, I remember. And I remember *him*.'

She went on to describe her attacker in detail and how he broke into her flat.

'And his name's Smeeton,' she added. 'The same name that Sam gave us.'

'How do you know? Did he introduce himself?'

And she immediately realized her error. It was from her dream. With nothing to corroborate it. She'd lose Brearly's trust completely if she started using her dreams as sources of information.

'No. And don't ask me how I know, but I do.'

'You don't want me to ask you how you know the name of your attacker.'

She could visualize him shaking his head.

'Anyway, I'll explain it all in more detail when I get there.'

'Agatha. Perrick told me that, when you rang, I was to tell you that you should take the week off. On full pay.'

'What? Is he pissed off? Because I didn't make it in?'

'Again. No, he's—'

'I can explain this morning. I can explain every—'

'He's not pissed off. He made a point of getting me to pass that on. He just thinks it'd be better if you took some time off. After everything that's happened.'

'But I've *already* taken time off! I don't think you understand that I absolutely—'

'No I get—'

'Brearly, I *need* to come into work—'

'He's made up his mind. And you know what Perrick's like.'

Brearly's voice had a softer tone to it now, but there was doubt underlying it and it cut like a knife.

'My *life* is in danger.'

'Then come in and give a statement.'

'Fuck that! You don't believe me, do you? You think I'm making this up?'

Brearly didn't answer.

'Let me talk to Perrick.'

'He's not in.'

'Bullshit, let me talk to him.'

'Agatha...'

'I'll just call his mobile.'

'You won't be doing yourself any favours. Trust me on this. I'll help you where I can. If you think you're in danger, you'll need to officially report it—'

'I'm not imagining this guy. You saw what happened to Sam. He's not a *ghost*.'

There was an awkward silence.

'So you say you'll help me?' Agatha asked. She had to calm herself down and realize any lack of composure on her part would only feed into the doubts Brearly already had.

'If I can.'

'I need to get my phone. It's in the flat and I'd get it myself but... I'm just not sure about going back there on my own.'

'And you want me to get it.'

'Or meet me there?'

There was a pause.

'It's a bit tricky right at the moment,' he said. 'But Lutger's still in the area, I could get him to get it and drop it in to you.'

'That would be great.'

'How will he get in?'

'It won't be locked, I heard him break in.'

'Him.'

'The guy.'

Another pause.

'OK,' Brearly said. 'Call me back in an hour.'

Agatha hung up and realized how hungry she was. Bought a paper, found a cafe and ordered an orange juice, an egg and bacon roll smothered in barbecue sauce and a strong flat white. Glorious.

What wasn't glorious was the feeling she got looking around. The passing faces in the rain-soaked street outside, and patrons inside the cafe. Certain she was about to spot Smeeton. Luckily there weren't too many men in suits in the area. And none wearing a suit and trainers.

Just after one o'clock, she called Brearly again.

'No luck,' he said. 'He couldn't get in. It was locked.'

'Locked?'

She couldn't understand it. You could only lock it with a key. He couldn't have had a key, surely. And now Brearly had yet another reason for doubting her.

'He must have got hold of a key somehow,' she said. 'Could you tell Lutger I don't mind if he breaks in? I just need my phone.'

'Too late. He's back in Newtown.'

His bluntness confirmed her fears – he was losing patience with this circus of hers...

'OK. Don't worry about it. I'll have to get it myself.'

'Or... I could do it. But it would have to be after work. I'll pick you up at seven. How's that?'

'Are you sure——?'

'In the meantime... sit tight.'

'Thanks Brearly. I really appreciate it.'

Sit tight? she thought, after hanging up. It hadn't helped before.

She now regretted not going to the doctor with Brearly when he'd offered. Just like Sam, she'd obviously been drugged with something, and just like Sam she'd foolishly refused a medical examination. And now Sam had vanished again, and she, Agatha, had been targeted again. So did the same fate await her? Would she end up on the Nowhere list for good next time?

35.

Agatha was standing under an awning near the Summer Hill telephone box she'd just stepped out of, watching the rain coming down in bucketloads. Harbourloads. She knew this weather. It bore all the hallmarks of a black nor'easter.

A taxi pulled up to let someone out. Agatha made a spur-of-the-moment decision, easily justified in hindsight: she knew she couldn't wait until the evening for her phone, she needed her car anyway, and she didn't want to put Brearly out any more than she already had. A woman dashed for cover and Agatha took her place and directed the driver to Bondi Junction.

After picking up her car from the garage there – a small, light-blue Renault whose conspicuous colour suddenly seemed to stand out a little too much – she drove to her flat in Tamarama. Being in her car, at least, made her feel slightly more in control.

The rain was still coming down when she pulled up in her street and turned the engine off. Looked up at the building she'd once regarded as home but which now, in the bleak conditions, was a dark planet. It did occur to her that forensics could be brought in, but she knew with one hundred percent certainty they'd find nothing.

She did a thorough visual check of her surroundings, then stirred herself into action and told herself to make it as quick as an F1 pit stop.

She took a plastic bag out of the car and dashed in, up the stairs, unlocked her front door – she should have been more cautious, should have stopped and listened for out-of-place sounds, but easier theorized than done – and tore through the flat, grabbing her phone (which was still precisely where she'd left it, unobtrusively leaning against a corner of her red leather couch), a few T-shirts and bras, and a fistful of panties, stuffing everything into the plastic bag, and after relocking the front door was out again and down the stairs and in her car in sixty seconds flat. Not quite F1, but good enough.

Lucky she never got that cat.

Inside her car again, she switched the ignition on, and then the wipers to keep a better eye on her surroundings. She texted Brearly to tell him that he was off the hook, that she'd got her phone, and received a simple 'Great' in response. It was just after 2pm.

She then drove off down her street and was relieved to be out of there. Back up to Bondi Junction, she found a park in the street and got out of the car, umbrella held low over her head, keeping a wary eye on the pedestrians around her. She found an appliance shop and bought an electric frying pan, and then bought some food.

Her last stop was a pharmacy, and she passed one on the way back to the car. It wasn't one she'd been to before, and hadn't even been aware it existed. It was a compounding chemist, and she decided it would do and was in the process of closing her umbrella and stepping inside when she froze.

Smeeton.

He was standing in the middle of the store, talking to one of the assistants, in a navy suit, blue business shirt, and black trainers. There was no mistaking him. The large pale face… he was even pulling on his cuffs as he spoke to the woman.

It all happened quickly, she kept her umbrella open enough to hide her face – which was difficult, with the two parcels of shopping she was carrying – and backed out of the store. No time to open her umbrella out fully, she backed out into the pouring rain, pedestrians cursing and stepping around her, and all the while trying to keep an eye on the entrance she'd just backed out of.

But he didn't emerge. He mustn't have seen her.

She then walked away quickly and turned around just one more time, before breaking into a half-run, with her useless, partly opened umbrella, and her bags of shopping, plunging into puddles and generally getting drenched from the bottom up and the top down, trainers, jeans, T-shirt, bare arms and hair, now a dripping mess of dark, sodden ringlets.

She jumped in her car, quickly pulled back her wet hair, and headed straight back to the Marco Polo, wipers at speed in the rain and traffic and headlights, and only narrowly avoided two collisions. Drove up to level one and parked directly outside her room, Room 112, and didn't calm down until she'd turned the engine off.

And she just sat there, in her car, in the rain, on the point of losing it completely. Because she'd seen him again. And yet again, it was as though he'd jumped straight out of her head.

36.

That night, in her motel room, listening to it, it felt like it would go on raining forever.

It wasn't just the heaviness of the rain that was getting to her, but the loudness. It may have been her heightened senses, but to her, now, it was deafening. She'd have preferred to have the traffic noises back, but they were mostly drowned out, other than the occasional roar and splash of a distant semitrailer.

And even in the room, with its all-pervading damp mustiness, the weather was inescapable.

She had to face facts: no one believed her. Even Brearly was having trouble and he was her closest ally. And what had happened to Perrick? He'd been supportive up until now, more so than Brearly in a way, and suddenly he was MIA. And missing in action was exactly where she was heading, along with the rest of the Nowhere list...

Or was she? Everyone else thought she was simply losing it and maybe they were right. In the chemist's today, had he really been there? Or had she dreamt him? Daydreamt him?

No. He had to be real. Because someone identical to him had attacked her on Wednesday night. And something had caused her to lose her memory afterwards, just as it had to Sam. And Sam mentioning the same name as the one mentioned by the man in her nightmares, was that just a coincidence?

Coincidences didn't exist, they were just a lack of imagination, any good detective knew that. Once again she tried to think of something that had happened to her, someone she might have met, that could have fed into her dreams, given birth to her nightmares. And once again, in vain.

She turned the TV on to distract her from her thoughts. And from the rain.

It had to be flooding somewhere.

It would be terrible being flooded, being inundated, at night, in the dark, wouldn't it?

When she woke up the next morning, Tuesday, she had no idea of the time and couldn't even be bothered checking. It was her third morning waking up in the Marco Polo, and the rain had now largely gone, but its absence had left her with a feeling of inertia and listlessness. Of *apatía*.

A gap in the curtains revealed another grey day. The traffic continued to trundle along the main road outside. When sleeping seemed no longer an option she reached for the remote and turned on the TV. She didn't really watch it, but turning it on was becoming a habit. Maybe she just liked hearing human voices. Maybe the TV was becoming her only friend.

Just after 9am she got a call from Brearly. Her spirits lifted the moment she saw his name on her phone.

'Big news,' he said. 'Even though you're on leave, I figured you'd want to hear this. They found Carol.'

'That's great! Where did—?'

'Dead.'

'What?'

'They found her dead.'

'Dead?'

'As a dodo. They found her body in a shipping container in Botany. In one of the yards down at the Port. It was a bit of a fluke. The Customs officer who found her had accidentally opened up the wrong container. He was meant to have been checking a container slated for a different ship.'

'How did she die?'

'It looks like asphyxiation, or possibly dehydration, they're not yet sure. She might have been drugged at some point, we'll see. But either way, it looks like she was incapacitated to start with. Temporary strangulation leading to unconsciousness. There's some injury to her neck muscles. Remind you of anyone?'

'Yeah...'

'Our Backyard Man in Eliza Street. Benjamin Deane.'

A hundred thoughts were flying around in Agatha's head. She automatically raised a hand and felt her neck.

'I have to say Agatha, I was a bit sceptical about our Nowhere list, but now with this... There might be something in it. Given the similarities with Benjamin and Sam.'

And me, Agatha thought.

'So anyway,' Brearly continued, 'I tried to take over Carol... Botany are currently handling her... but nuh. Can't convince anyone this is connected.'

'What about Perrick? I thought he was the one pushing our list?'

'So did I. He seems to have gone off the boil for some reason. You can never tell with Perrick. He blows hot and cold, it's his modus operandi. Although I reckon it's more like his modus vivendi.'

'There you go with the Latin again.'

'Means way of life.'

'I know. *Modo de vida.*'

'Huh? Oh right. Argentinian.'

At least the old Brearly was back.

'So why a shipping container?' she asked.

'Mystery. The shipping company claimed ignorance. As you'd expect. But our bros at the Botany Bay LAC assume an independent actor accessed the container as a way of disposing of the body. I'm not too sure about that though. Especially if the cases are linked. Look at what happened to Benjamin, *his* body was dumped in a side street behind a police station. Now whether that particular location was opportunistic or not, why would the same perpetrator, or any perpetrator for that matter, go to the trouble of breaking into a shipping container to dispose of a body? The chances of being caught in the act would be huge. There'd be heaps of places way more suited to dumping a body.'

'So you said the guy from Customs opened the wrong container and it was slated for another ship. So which ship was that?'

'I don't recall the name, but it was headed to... Nouméa I think. New Caledonia.'

Nouméa. That was significant somehow, but why?

'So what appears to have happened,' Brearly continued, 'the container's been accidentally put in the wrong location, and confused with another ship's cargo. And the ship it was meant for, the Nouméa ship, has already departed.'

But Agatha was barely listening. Nouméa was the key to something. Something critical.

'Call me if you need anything,' Brearly said before hanging up. 'Or if you're worried. For any reason. Be careful, OK?'

But she had to do more than be careful. She had to hold on to Nouméa. And work out what it was a key to.

It seemed connected to her dream. Of Smeeton in the South Pacific, somewhere they spoke French. And Nouméa was the capital of New Caledonia, which was French-speaking... But she'd never been to Nouméa.

As she was thinking this, she was staring at the TV. She hadn't turned it off, only down, and the news was on. It was a cheerless item about the steady growth of China's nuclear arsenal, and mention was made of a particular intercontinental ballistic missile, the Dong Feng-4, along with other types of ICBMs.

The abbreviation, she thought, should really be IBM, and not ICBM. Because intercontinental was one word...

A spark. And then an explosion, ignited by two ingredients.

The InterContinental, and Nouméa.

She remembered where her dream must have come from.

38.

It was just over two years ago. On the morning of 14 July 2011, to be precise, because it was Bastille Day, the French national day, celebrating the key event of the French Revolution. Agatha and Detective Sergeant Dan Jeffries were in the lobby of the InterContinental Hotel in Sydney's CBD, near the harbour. The lower section of the hotel was housed in an elegant sandstone building from the colonial era – the old Treasury Building of circa 1851 – and the eastern side faced onto airy Macquarie Street with its gentle leafy incline down to the Opera House and Circular Quay.

They were investigating the disappearance of what would turn out to be an early entrant onto the Nowhere list – possibly the first, although they obviously weren't aware of it at the time. Agatha was a junior detective then – still a Detective Constable – and she'd been newly assigned to the case, along with Dan, her senior officer. It was effectively day one of the investigation. The woman who'd disappeared had last been seen in one of the bars in the hotel three nights earlier. She'd been drinking with friends and afterwards they'd all gone their separate ways. She'd said she was on her way to the bathroom, and that was the last anyone had seen of her.

Agatha remembered it happened on a Bastille Day because it was impossible to miss: there were French-flavoured decorations everywhere – tricolour flags, red-white-and-blue streamers, Eiffel towers – and the hotel was running a number of celebratory events. She and Dan were talking to the hotel manager at the time, when she was momentarily distracted by a hotel guest at the reception desk. He was either checking in or out, she couldn't be sure – although as it was morning he was most likely checking out – but what initially drew her attention was him saying in a loud voice to the receptionist something in French. As far as she could remember, it was something like 'Bonjour!', an obvious tilt to Bastille Day, but she could tell he wasn't French and there was something crass or bombastic about it. And she distinctly remembered hearing him say something about having recently been in, or being on his way to, Nouméa.

She could no longer remember exactly what he looked like – which was strange because she could remember so many other details – except that he was larger than average and was wearing a dark suit, blue or navy. It was particularly strange because she now vividly remembered how at one point, after she'd returned to the conversation with the manager and Dan, she'd looked over to see him leaving, and as he was doing so, this now faceless man threw a pointed look in her direction, accompanied by a wry, knowing smile.

39.

She could see it now, the link between the InterContinental Hotel incident, and her dream.

The Bastille Day decor would have inspired the French Revolution elements of her dream. The mention of Nouméa presumably begat the French South Pacific setting at the end. The Sydney sandstone from which the hotel building was constructed must have given rise to the way the buildings in her dream morphed from their Parisian grey to a sandstone colour. And the hotel guest in the dark suit, Agatha felt convinced, was the Smeeton in her dream. There'd obviously been something about the guest's demeanour that had lodged itself in her subconscious. It was odd that in her recollection, the hotel guest was faceless – it was almost as if her dreams had taken his features and left a blank in her conscious recollection. This would explain why she hadn't connected the InterContinental Hotel incident with her dreams before.

If she was correct about the incident generating her dream, then it was safe to assume that the elements of her dream she couldn't now specifically recall from the InterContinental – such as his face, his trainers, the way he tugged on his shirt cuffs, and his name – were all in her dream because they'd been planted in her subconscious mind. Just because she couldn't recall it now, didn't mean she hadn't witnessed it two years ago. And with the name Smeeton, for example, he'd probably said it to the receptionist.

So what had inspired the remark he made in her dream about Tchaikovsky? *Tchaikovsky's your man*, he'd said.

Obviously it was possible she had this all wrong, and the hotel incident hadn't given rise to the dream at all – although every bone in her body said otherwise – and at the very least it was something worth following up. It would be easy enough to test: she'd go in there right now and test her theory in person. What had she got to lose?

She considered inviting Brearly to come with her, but she couldn't take the chance she had this wrong. She couldn't afford to make a fool of herself just when she had Brearly on her side again.

She leapt out of bed, got herself ready, jumped in her Renault and drove into town, and thirty minutes later she was taking a slight liberty (given she was supposed to be on leave) and showing her police badge to the valet in the hotel drive-in entrance.

As she stood at reception in the hotel lobby, it occurred to her that she was standing almost exactly where Smeeton had been standing – or the guest she was hoping would turn out to be Smeeton – two years earlier. She also thought of her light blue car parked in the hotel entrance outside and it reminded her how visible she was. How nervous it made her feel just being out in public. Not an ideal handicap for a police officer, on leave or not.

The other thing on her mind was she was hoping they didn't ask to see a search warrant. If there was a problem, she'd tell them it was a homicide investigation – which was technically true, if not officially – or else bat her eyelids and hope for the best.

The hotel manager came over to her. Different from the manager she and Dan had spoken to two years ago, this one had black hair with a perfect part on one side, was slightly tanned and sharply handsome – he could have been French himself – and neater than a pin.

'Can I help you?'

'Detective Senior Constable Agatha Ducatti.' She presented her badge for a second time in ten minutes, making her feel fraudulent. (She shouldn't have: she was only on leave, she was still a detective. But there was a name for it, and it was called imposter syndrome.) 'I need to know if you had a particular guest who checked in or out of here on 14 July 2011. With the surname Smeeton. With two Es.'

He seemed to hesitate, and she smiled her sexiest smile, hoping she had him down as a slightly effeminate heterosexual (of whom in her experience Sydney had many), rather than a cruelly handsome homosexual (of whom Sydney had even more).

'Two Es? Too easy,' he said with a killer grin, his Smeeton-like throwaway leaving her dumbfounded and without her smile, as he pivoted on one heel and headed for a computer in long, graceful strides.

'So... Smeeton? he said eventually, after much tapping away. 'With a double e?'

'Yes?'

'No one by that name, I'm afraid. Sorry.'

Agatha was devastated. 'Are you sure? Have you—?'

'I've checked every variation of the name I can think of. But nothing even close.'

'OK. Thanks for trying.'

She was almost out the front entrance doors when he caught up with her. He must have run across the lobby, clearly not wishing to call out her professional title in earshot of the guests.

'Detective, I'm so sorry. I'd been checking 2010 by mistake. It's our ridiculous computer system. For some unknown reason everything's separated into calendar years. You would have thought they could have managed to combine them all in one file by now, wouldn't you? So anyway, yes, we *did* have a guest by that name who checked out that day.'

It was like being told all your numbers had come up on the weekly national lottery, and then that there'd been an error, and then that there hadn't.

They returned to the manager's computer, and this time Agatha had a spring in her step.

'The only thing is...' the manager said, tapping and reading, '...here it is... Smeeton. Checked in 13 July 2011 and out the next day.'

'First name?'

'There doesn't... seem to be...'

'Address?'

'Unfortunately... that particular field doesn't seem to have been populated...'

'Has *any*... field been populated?'

'Not that I can...'

'So a surname is all you have?'

'It does look that way.'

'Hang on,' Agatha said. 'Credit card. You must have his credit—'

'He paid with cash.'

'You have to be fucking *kidding* me,' she said, forgetting herself. 'Sorry.'

The manager threw a quick and pretty smile in her direction as if to say *don't worry, I get far worse than that, honey.*

'Wait a minute,' he said suddenly. 'I don't know what's the matter with me today. We'll have a copy of whatever ID he provided scanned into our system. It was only two years ago, not twenty. I'm so sorry, just give me a moment.'

More tapping, and before Agatha's pessimism had a chance to take over (because he was nothing if not quick, this one), he was swinging his screen around for her to see. Not only that, he uttered the best two words imaginable:

'Driver's licence.'

It was a scanned copy of a New South Wales licence with an expiry date in 2014, so it was still valid. The great thing about driver's licences, they came with photos. And it was him all right. Light hair. Pale complexion. Large round head. Fleshy face with small features and dull, grey eyes. She cringed, and felt nauseous, and made herself tear her gaze away from the image.

The even better thing about driver's licences was that they contained the driver's full name, date of birth and street address.

In this case, the driver was revealed to be Neil Harold Smeeton, born 2.4.69, making him currently forty-four years old.

And had him living at Unit 6, 25 Courland St, Randwick NSW 2031.

Gotcha.

40.

It had been a depressing, overcast start to the day but the sun was finally breaking through. In more ways than one. Even though she was still under cover – literally, she was standing in deep shadow next to her car in the hotel's drive-in entrance – Agatha could see the sunshine on the road outside and on the tourists strolling down to the ferries and the bars down on Circular Quay.

The valet, standing off to one side, watched on nervously, clearly anxious for her to remove herself and her inexpensive, bright blue car from his otherwise car-free driveway.

She checked the time. It was now lunchtime, just after 1pm. She wasn't exactly sure why, but it felt like time was of the essence. It was logical though, she supposed, given the danger to her and to others. Perhaps one of the others, one of the Nowhere women, was currently under a threat of imminent pain or death? And maybe, for all she knew, *she* was?

She called Brearly and was thankful she was able to get through first go. He was on his lunch break in a cafe somewhere. On his own, which was a bonus.

The fidgety valet had, meanwhile, been edging closer, and the sight of her standing next to her unmoving car and pulling out her phone to make a call had obviously been too much for him. He was tentatively gesturing towards the car, about to say something, when she flashed her police badge at him for the second time that day – a reminder in case he'd forgotten, that he was a valet and she was a detective and sorry to say, but he was well down the pecking order from her.

She explained everything to Brearly: the dream, the incident two years ago, the details she now had on Smeeton. Smeeton, the same name that Sam had mentioned. It had to be the same person. Everything aligned. She was still not expecting him to buy it straight away, but he did. Or at least he was receptive, and agreed to meet her at the Randwick address. In the meantime, he'd run a check on the licence.

She could have kissed him if he'd been standing in front of her.

Courland Street wasn't the leafiest street in Randwick, but there were trees. And number 25 wasn't the prettiest block of flats in Courland Street, but it had flats. Maybe a dozen or so, throughout the building's three stories. Ochre-coloured brick, typical of the area, with white trim on the balcony railings. Gum trees. Peaceful enough, no traffic. And only a kilometre from the beach.

What more could a psycho want?

Agatha's bright blue Renault had arrived there first. She'd remained in her car, although didn't feel quite as nervous as she probably should have. She was relieved though when Brearly turned up and they had a quick discussion next to his car, a dark blue BMW. He kept it clean, kept it looking newer than it possibly could have been. Detectives didn't exactly rake it in. Except the dodgy ones.

'His licence is still valid,' Brearly said. 'And it's clean. He hasn't even lost any points.'

They both looked at the building across the road and took it in for a few moments.

'He could be watching us now,' Agatha said, sounding more anxious than she'd intended, and more than she was.

'You still in that motor inn?'

'Yeah.'

'That's some weird shit.'

'It is.'

Brearly was clutching a printout of Smeeton's licence. From where she was standing, Smeeton's eyes seemed to be on *her*. And maybe the real ones were too, the pair up in that building.

'You're still convinced,' Brearly said, 'that this guy attacked you on Wednesday night?'

'One hundred percent. OK. Ninety-nine, because there's always a chance isn't there that—'

'Why did it take so long for you to remember?'

'I was drugged with something and lost my memory for a while. *Remember?*'

'Yeah...'

He paused, acting oddly. It also hadn't escaped her attention that the whole time they were standing there, his gaze hadn't once dropped below her chin. This was abnormal for Brearly at the best of times. But he hadn't seen her in five days, since last Thursday when he'd dropped in to see her. Was he ill?

'You don't think the substance mightn't've... messed with your recollection?'

'No.'

Agatha could now see where this was going. He was still sceptical. She supposed it was understandable.

'But you still don't want to give a statement about it.'

'No. Not yet. I've thought about it, but it'd hamper things. And I'd be taken off the investigation. And we're nearly there, with this. And by the way, I'm not going back to my flat until we get him.'

Brearly said nothing, just nodded.

They crossed the road. As with Agatha's Tamarama building, this one had an unlocked front entrance. Flat 6 was on the first floor.

'Careful of this one,' Agatha said quietly as they climbed the first flight of stairs in the internal stairwell.

As they stood outside number 6, and Brearly went to knock, Agatha got his attention and mimed him pulling out his gun. Hers, of course, was still under lock and key back at the station. Brearly hesitated then nodded, and produced his Glock 26, although she sensed his reluctance and that he was only doing it for her peace of mind.

He pressed the buzzer as well as knocked, and kept his gun lowered and pointing towards the base of the door. Agatha stood to one side, out of the peephole's line of sight.

A man's voice responded quickly, as though he'd been standing behind the door all along.

'Who is it?' He sounded cranky and South African.

'Police. We need to ask you a couple of questions. Please open the—'

'Where's your warrant?'

'That's my warrant,' Brearly said, holding up his police ID and badge with his free hand. 'This is a matter of some urgency sir, and if you don't open the door, we'll have to open it for you.'

They heard the sound of at least two deadlocks being unlocked and finally the door opened.

He was Smeeton's general size and shape, but it wasn't Smeeton. He was probably in his fifties and had dark hair and dark brown eyes, and his expansive stomach was even larger than Smeeton's. He was standing there in his underwear too – a pair of white Y-fronts – so it wasn't a pretty sight. His back was as hairy as a mountain gorilla's.

'This better be good...' he began, before seeing the drawn gun in Brearly's hand. 'Oh shit. You're gonna shoot me as well, eh?'

Brearly looked at the printout.

'Is your name Neil Smeeton?'

'Of course it's bloody not!'

'Is this him?' Brearly asked Agatha. She shook her head. He looked back at the angry South African. 'Any idea where he might be? We have him listed at this address.'

'Of course you do. Another New South Wales Police fuck-up.'

'You live here on your own?' Brearly asked, although just by looking at the state of him, and the flat behind him, Agatha thought the answer was obvious.

'Yes. Will that be all?'

'How long have you—?'

'Now you listen to me. As you can see I'm not dressed. I'll tell you this and then you can fuck off. I've been here for around two years. I rent. I've never heard of any Neil Smeeton. And here...' whereupon he handed Brearly a business card that had been sitting on a table next to him, '... are the agents, so you can ask them whatever it is you want. OK? In the meantime you can piss off out of here, or I'll call the cops. Oh hang on, you *are* the cops. So if you don't like the deal, you can just shoot me. OK pretty boy?' And he slammed the door.

'Pretty boy,' Brearly said. 'That's the nicest thing a customer's ever said to me.'

'So that went well,' said Brearly once they were back outside.

They were standing next to her car this time, under a gum tree. Brearly didn't look happy, but if he blamed Agatha, he didn't say so.

Brearly rang the agents – the agent who'd looked after this flat two years ago was no longer there – and then the landlord, who was more receptive than her current tenant. She confirmed the flat had been rented to a Neil Smeeton, the previous tenant, but that it had only been a short lease, maybe six months or a year, and she'd never met or spoken to him. She did recall however that the inspection report had shown very little in the way of furniture or possessions.

Brearly then received a message from Lutger – he'd had him look for any other record of this guy.

'Did he find anything?' Agatha asked.

Brearly didn't take long to finish reading the text.

'Nothing,' he said.

'Nothing at *all*?'

'No record of him anywhere, other than on the licence, and presumably the lease agreement. No record of him having been *born* even. Or growing up anywhere. Going to school. Enrolling to vote. Filing a tax return. No passport. He just... appeared from nowhere, it looks like, when he first got his licence in 1989, which has been reissued every five years since then. But no record of him before 1989, anywhere.'

'Like the man who never was.'

'Well frankly, right now, he's like the man who doesn't exist.'

'He's a ghost after all,' Agatha said, mainly to herself, feeling as hollow as Smeeton seemed to be.

'Except that ghosts don't need driver's licences.'

Agatha's detective brain knew he was right, but her fear was not convinced. 'Maybe they do.'

'I'll get Lutger to double check and see if he can't find anything else. In the meantime I'll try to find out the latest on Carol.'

'Lutger's OK with this?' Agatha asked. 'I mean he knows about my involvement? Even though I'm supposed to be on leave...'

'Lutger's good. Not sure about anyone else. But he won't say anything. I've sworn him to secrecy and... well I reckon he's a little bit autistic, a bit on the spectrum—'

'No shit.'

'... so a promise is a promise. Naturally I'm leaving Perrick out of it for the moment. Speaking of which, I'd better head back.'

Brearly began walking over to his car but stopped.

'With this... Neil Smeeton character...' he began. 'I mean it's not as if the licence could be a forgery. It's in our system. Validly issued, although I don't know how, since he doesn't seem to exist. It may be that... Well if nothing else comes up, then I'm afraid we're at a dead end, Agatha.'

He paused as they looked at each other.

'Excusing the pun,' Agatha said.

Later that afternoon, Agatha received a text message from Brearly telling her he'd received the results of the forensics tests on Carol's body and it was important enough to warrant meeting up about it. There was a funky little bar in Darlinghurst he had in mind, and suggested if it was OK with her, that she meet him at 7pm at the Shady Pines Saloon.

41.

Agatha was staring at a moose, and it was staring back at her.

She was sitting at a small table next to an oak barrel in the Shady Pines Saloon. It was a bar hidden away in the backstreets of Darlinghurst, and had a nineteenth-century wild west theme with dim lighting and an array of American whiskies on offer. A real honky-tonk – although of course it wasn't a real one at all – crammed full of antique wood and pale lampshades and old paintings. Stuffed animal heads burst forth from the walls, the moose's being one of them. It was cosy and there were plenty of people. Or punters, as Brearly called them.

Opposite her, apart from the moose, was Brearly. They were most of the way through their first drink and hers was already going to her head. It was some fancy American cocktail with bourbon whiskey and calvados and a sprinkling of cinnamon.

'So this is your local, is it?' Agatha said. She didn't know exactly where he lived, just that it was somewhere in Darlinghurst.

'One of many. Bit of fun, this one.'

'Fun's good.'

'Yes it is, isn't it.'

Was Brearly being a bit strange or was it her imagination? In the half-light, even when she was looking away, she could feel his eyes on her again, which was normal, but this felt different, as if there was more sexual tension than usual. Was that coming from him... or from her? She suddenly recalled the moment in her building, outside her front door, and the attraction she'd felt for him before realizing who he was. Maybe it was the sense of safety that he embodied, or maybe it was just the alcohol. Or maybe it was something else... She squeezed her eyes tightly shut.

'Are you OK?'

She was relaxed now, after the drink, but getting to the Shady Pines had put her on edge. She hadn't appreciated being compelled to make her way along gloomy, graffiti-lined alleyways – even the front entrance, which was hard to find, was neon-free and had virtually no signage. In calmer times, though, she would have got a kick out of it. Even though she'd lived in Sydney for twenty-one years, she still viewed it through the eyes of a foreigner. People born in Sydney told her they did too, it was that sort of place.

'By the way, Lutger's dropping in,' Brearly said. 'He rang just before to say he'd found something important.'

'Why didn't he just tell you?'

'That was my idea. Same reason I suggested you and I meet up. Or one of the reasons.'

He smiled – and was that a twinkle in his eye, or just the lighting? – and sipped his rye whiskey.

'What reason's that?'

'I just think we need to be a bit careful of our phones. Call it one of your feelings. Or what does Perrick call them? Pulses.'

'Pulses. Right. So... Don't keep me in suspense any longer. Tell me about Carol.'

Brearly nodded.

'I told you it looked like she'd been incapacitated first, rendered unconscious, and then possibly drugged second. So that's now been confirmed. The exact drug used hasn't yet been identified, but it looks like it could be something similar to fentanyl. Much like what the Russians are supposed to have used in the Moscow theatre siege in 2002.'

'How was it administered?'

'In a gas form first, they think... so after she was already unconscious from the strangulation, and then possibly injected.'

'As well?'

'Yeah. They found a tiny puncture mark. Possibly from a super-thin needle.'

'Where was the puncture mark?'

'Not too sure.'

Agatha resisted the urge to examine her arms, where they usually took blood from, the veins in the crooks of her elbows. No point in the dim light anyway.

'But it does lead to certain conclusions,' Brearly went on. 'Her body was found in a shipping container. What this is... and this might sound crazy, but no other explanation fits... what this points to is she was being transported overseas. Alive.'

'Overseas?'

'Like a shipment of cattle. What do they call it? *Live export trade.* Adds a whole new dimension to human trafficking, don't you reckon?'

They were both silent for a few moments. Agatha had to force herself to say it:

'But... why?'

'It's not hard to guess. You're the one that argued Carol was a suitable candidate for the Nowhere list. Meaning, "young, pretty females", as you put it. I'd say they were probably destined for overseas brothels.'

'Brothels.'

'Keep them drugged. Keep topping them up. It'd fry their brains eventually. So no memory to speak of. And that'd be the idea. With no memory, the victims don't even know where they're from. They don't know who they are. There's nowhere for them to go. These women could be controlled for the rest of their lives in some foreign country. Somewhere they're never going to escape from anyway, with or without their minds intact.'

'In Nouméa?'

'Or wherever the ship was really heading. It was probably going on. Going... further afield.'

'Jesus. The white slave trade. For real.'

They both sipped their drinks. A sudden clamour of voices and laughter erupted in one corner of the room.

'So Pippa?' Agatha said. 'And Chalaise? And all the ones on the list? And Sam, who's vanished again?'

Brearly was slowly nodding.

'So with Carol... you're saying...'

'With Carol they fucked up. Container went to the wrong spot, and Customs got to it before they did. But not in time to save her. Without the container stuff-up, she'd probably still be alive. Alive, but... gone for good.'

And he left that thought hanging.

'We have to do *something*,' Agatha said.

'What?'

'I don't know. Close down the port. Search the containers.'

'Port Botany? Do you know how many containers they have there? And the victims... they'd be gone by now anyway.'

'What if there are more? New ones?'

'We'd never find them. Not that way.'

The voices at the noisy table rose and fell like the passing of a large wave. After the solitariness of her room in the motor inn, being in a small room full of loud, cheerful people was both a blessing and a curse. At least it muted, to some extent, the dark implications of what Brearly was telling her.

'Listen,' Brearly said. 'I've found out something very interesting about our man Smeeton.'

Our man. He wasn't hers, and as things presently stood, he wasn't a man. Not as far as she was concerned. He was just *Smeeton*.

'Or rather,' he went on, '*possibly* concerning him. Depending on—'

He was interrupted by the sudden appearance of Lutger who seemed to materialize rather than arrive. He sat down in the spare seat at their small table without any preliminary greeting.

Peter Lutger was twenty-nine and trim, with short wavy blond hair and blue eyes the colour of a tropical lagoon. When they eventually managed to endow a 'robot' with convincing human features and mannerisms, a fair guess would be that Lutger was what one of the prototypes would look like.

He got straight down to it. Not even so much as a remark on their unusual surroundings. Maybe this was his local too. Maybe he and Brearly were honky-tonk men.

'I think you're going to like what I found.'

Brearly looked at Agatha. 'What have you found, Lutger?'

'I found the ID that was used for the issue of Neil Smeeton's original driver's licence. His birth certificate.'

'You found his birth certificate?'

Lutger nodded.

'You champion,' said Brearly quietly.

Lutger produced a photocopy and took them through it.

'Neil Harold Smeeton, born in Townsville, Queensland, on the second of April, 1969. No siblings. Father, Gareth David Smeeton, 31 years old, schoolteacher, born in Birmingham, UK.'

Lutger looked up to make sure the others were paying attention. They were.

'Mother, Elizabeth Anne Smeeton, formerly Mayfield, 28 years old, home duties, also born in Birmingham. They were married in Birmingham on 12 February 1968.'

Lutger looked up again. 'Unfortunately I couldn't find any trace of the parents. At least not in Australia. No deaths registered either.'

'Damn it.' said Agatha, under her breath. The parents would have been a clear path to tracking him down. Pinning him down. She realized just how desperate she was for proof of Smeeton's authenticity. Proof that he was real and not just some monstrous product of her imagination. Or a ghost.

'Step ahead of you, Lutger,' Brearly said. And to Agatha: 'This is what I was going to tell you before.'

'I did a search earlier,' he said, 'for any newspaper articles about a Neil Smeeton born in 1969. It was a bit of a long shot but I eventually found something. A 1972 news item in a Townsville newspaper. About the *death* of a Neil Smeeton, aged three. From drowning.'

He paused, to let that sink in. Agatha didn't need any encouragement. It was sinking in, all right.

'Three years old in 1972, so the age matches. Now there's nothing in the records about his death,' Brearly continued, 'or the relevant part of the records was lost, or destroyed for some reason. But I got our colleagues in Townsville to check it out, and sure enough, there's a grave up there.'

'So...' Agatha began, trying to get her head around this latest piece of information.

'What I'd been going to say earlier,' Brearly said to Agatha, 'was if we could get our hands on the ID that was used for the driver's licence, then we could confirm a hundred percent that this Townsville Smeeton was the same person. And thanks to Lutger here, we now know...'

'... that it is,' said Agatha.

'No doubt the parents are untraceable because they left the country after the tragedy. Losing their only child. Probably headed back to the UK.'

'So where does that leave us?' Lutger asked.

'It leaves us chasing a dead child,' said Agatha despondently. 'So he *is* a ghost.'

'No,' said Brearly. 'He's not a ghost. He's a tombstone.'

'What do you mean?'

'He's been tombstoned. In other words our young, dead Neil Smeeton has had his identity stolen.'

'Well if that's the case,' said Lutger, 'who's *our* Smeeton?'

'Whoever he is, he's obviously someone in need of a fake identity.'

'So a fraudster,' said Agatha.

'Or a mobster,' said Lutger.

'Or,' said Brearly, 'a trafficker of women.'

42.

It was around 9pm. Agatha and Brearly had finally called it a night and they were standing in the dark backstreet outside the front entrance of the Shady Pines. Lutger had left a while ago and Agatha and Brearly had stuck around and had 'one for the road'. Brearly's idea.

'Now what?' said Agatha.

'You mean... with Smeeton, or... you want to kick on. Which I'm more than—'

'God no. I'm shattered.'

There was a hiatus.

'Well with Smeeton, I guess we just sleep on it. Convene in the morning.'

'I'm on leave, remember.'

'We'll find a way.'

Another hiatus.

'All right then,' said Agatha. 'I'd better head off.'

'OK. Um...' Brearly was being uncharacteristically hesitant. 'Will you be OK? Getting home?'

'I'll be fine. Oxford Street's just up there. Plenty of taxis.'

'It's just that... I was just thinking...'

Was he about to put the hard word on her? He hadn't had enough to drink, surely.

'What *were* you just thinking, Brearly?'

They were standing in the shadows and she wasn't able to gauge the look in his eyes, but she could tell. He *was* going to.

'You're welcome to crash at my place, you know. I'm not far. And I have a spare room, so...' and he raised his hands in a gesture of surrender. 'You're safe.'

'I didn't think I *wasn't* safe. Although... we have been drinking...' Now she was the one digging herself into a hole.

'Don't worry,' he said, 'there wasn't enough time to drink *that* much.'

She imagined she could see his green eyes gleam, even though the only light was behind him and his face was barely more than a silhouette.

'Thanks for the offer, Brearly. But I need to get back.'

'OK. Well be careful. Because whoever we're dealing with, he's still out there.'

It was less than a hundred metres – not even a minute's walk – down the lane, around the corner and up to Oxford Street, but even in that short space of time, Agatha imagined she could hear footsteps behind her. They weren't Brearly's, as he'd gone in a different direction. And there'd been no one around when she and Brearly parted company.

So in the circumstances then, with the cocktails and the latest developments and the footsteps behind her, it came as no surprise to her that up on the main road, under the bright neon lights of Oxford Street and beside the six lanes of busy evening traffic, she should turn around and imagine she could see Smeeton's face in the crowd on the footpath behind her. She quickly turned away again, determined to get a grip. The alcohol was making her feel better than she'd felt in a long time, it seemed, and she never wanted that feeling to end.

43.

She let it all wash over her, in the taxi on the way home. Using the word 'home' loosely. Smeeton, Brearly, life... Let it all wash over her and away, as the city lights flashed past.

None of it mattered. Nothing mattered but the bed with the maroon-and-mustard paisley cover waiting for her back at the Marco Polo Motor Inn.

She thought of Brearly's eyes, and then she noticed the taxi driver's eyes, in the rearview mirror. Looking at the road ahead, and now looking at her. And a thought came to her, seemingly out of nowhere. It was more of a general idea: the idea of sex with strangers.

But it was gone almost as soon as it had arrived because she banished it, wondering where in God's name or whoever else's name it had come from.

44.

The man was standing outside the two-tone, brick motor inn, a preposterous abode for such a classy, beautiful woman. He'd missed seeing her arrive, missed watching her getting out of her taxi. He would've enjoyed that.

He looked up at the sad neon sign, and the shadowed facade of the building, half lit by the streetlights and nighttime traffic. Saw a light turn on in one of the rooms and wondered if that was her. Her taxi hadn't been far in front of his, so it could easily have been her. He pictured her closing the door and walking across the room. Throwing her bag down on the bed. Deciding she'd have a quick shower, pulling her T-shirt off over her head, and then her bra, and then her shoes (in that order), and then her jeans...

He was tempted to knock on the door of that room right now and hope that it was hers, and beg her forgiveness for interrupting her at such an ill-timed moment. So inopportune. With her like that, in such a state of undress...

He ached to do it.

But he knew he mustn't. Because there'd be no more risk-taking (not an easy ask for someone in his profession!), no more lazy wagers.

He didn't know her room number yet, but he soon would. And knowledge was power.

He smiled inside.

And then he'd have this one – have her and 'finalize her' – like all of the others.

Or almost all of the others.

Because he'd make sure of everything from now on. There'd be no more hiccups or fuckups. It'd be back to business and 'All aboard!'.

Yes, and then she would be his, for a while at least, but he was fine with that because nothing lasts forever. Because as the old saying goes, you can't take it with you! But in a sense, the temporary *is* forever, because once it's done, it's done, and it can never be undone.

He felt warm inside and he ached, oh how he ached!

He reminisced for a moment, thought back to when he'd first seen her in the hotel in the city that wonderful morning two years ago, and to the sweet realization that this woman, who was seeking him, would eventually get to have him. Talk about be careful what you wish for!

Soon, very soon, that wish of hers will come true.

Sticking with his favourite mode of transport, the man then simply turned and walked away into the shadows under the awnings of Parramatta Road.

All aboard!

45.

She was thinking it the moment she woke up. Had probably even been half-dreaming it. The *compounding chemist*. In Bondi Junction. Where she'd seen Smeeton. Assuming Brearly was right – about the trafficking of women and some drug being used – mightn't there be a connection? It was certainly worth checking out, they had little else right now. But not on her own.

She checked the time on the radio console – just after 7am, so not too early – but when she picked up her phone to call Brearly and pressed the phone icon, the phone's alarm went off. Except it wasn't the usual alarm, just a continuous flat beeping sound. Nothing showed on the screen either and she was unable to turn it off. After about ten seconds, it stopped of its own accord. Very odd.

She tried again and this time was able to call. Brearly picked up and agreed to meet her in Bondi Junction at 9.30am.

Agatha and Brearly were standing across the street from the pharmacy. The street itself was located in the heart of Bondi Junction, a block away from the pedestrian mall. Agatha had been relieved to find Brearly there when she arrived – it wasn't a place she wanted to be standing on her own, especially given what had happened the last time she'd been there.

And one good thing about still being on leave, she didn't have to wear the jacket she usually wore when she was carrying her gun. The day was warm and sunny, and uncomfortably humid. Even in her T-shirt, she could feel the drops of sweat forming on her brow and the middle of her back and under her arms. It felt more like February than October.

Across the road there were a variety of stores typical of the area. To the left of the pharmacy, a small Vietnamese takeaway, and on the right, a beauty salon that specialized in cosmetic tattooing. A ragged line of cars and vans where slowly making their way down the one-way street, occasionally impeding the view. The footpaths were well-populated with the shoppers and workers enticed out by the fine weather.

The pharmacy itself had a large sign on the face of the awning outside announcing:

Andrew Penney
COMPOUNDING CHEMIST

'So that's it?' Brearly asked.

He hadn't been overly talkative that morning. Perhaps he was sulking because she hadn't taken up his offer the previous night? Or maybe he'd kicked on and was simply hungover.

She nodded, and saw that he'd already pulled out his phone – the latest iPhone, the 5s – and was checking something.

'Well now. That *is* interesting.'

He showed her what he'd found: it was the first photo from an image search for 'andrew penney pharmacist'.

'That him? Looks like it to me.'

If it wasn't, it was uncannily close. It was Smeeton with slightly more hair, a slightly thinner face, but the same pale skin and small features and blank eyes. It was close enough to make her feel sick again.

'Yep. Pretty sure.'

So Smeeton was 'Andrew Penney'? A chemist? And this was where he worked?

'Let's say gedday then shall we?'

Brearly marched across the street, stepping out in a gap in the traffic, and Agatha followed and once again instinctively felt for the gun which wasn't there.

In the store itself – thankfully, if Agatha was honest (although her relief soon turned to disappointment) – Smeeton was nowhere to be seen. They'd already agreed on what their story was if Smeeton wasn't there, to avoid alerting him. Agatha remained separated from Brearly and pretended to browse, and listened as Brearly spoke to the young female shop assistant behind the counter.

'Is Andrew around? Andrew Penney?'

'No. I don't think so.' She looked over to an older colleague standing nearby who shook her head. 'Not today.'

'Ah. Missed him. I'm a friend of his and I was hoping to catch him.'

'Can I tell him who called in—?'

'Do you know where he is? Is he away? Or...?'

'He's...' and she looked at the older assistant again who piped up:

'He's on leave.'

'On leave? From when?'

'As of today.'

'As of today? Ah what a shame. Really?'

'I believe so. He called in earlier.'

'He's not sick is he? I could drop in on him...'

'No he's away.'

'Away. Hmm. Do you know when he's back?'

'I couldn't say I'm sorry.'

'So he was here yesterday and gone today? That is a real shame. OK, well, thanks for your help.'

'Let me leave him a message,' the older assistant said, 'He specifically requested we let him know if anyone called for him.'

'Did he? Oh well he wouldn't have meant me, we haven't seen each other for years. That's fine.' Brearly turned and headed for the door. 'I'll surprise him another time.'

Agatha remained, taking care not to be seen as being with Brearly.

'Can I help you?' the older assistant asked her.

'Do you sell swimming caps?'

'We don't I'm sorry, but you could try...'

Agatha caught up with Brearly at their prearranged spot, a cafe down the road. Small and buzzy and opened to the footpath, with lots of dark wood and imbued with the rich aroma of coffee.

'It's strange,' Brearly said as soon as Agatha sat down, 'that he just went on leave today. And suddenly too, by the sound of it. It's as if he knew we were coming. But no one else knew. I didn't tell anyone at the station where I was going.'

'Not even Lutger?'

'Nope. Not a one.'

Brearly called Lutger to check out this Andrew Penney. And to make it snappy, he was out in the field.

Twenty minutes later, Lutger called back. Brearly didn't bother to hide his impatience:

'What took you so long?...

... For Perrick? You didn't tell him about this, I hope?...

... Good.'

While Lutger was telling Brearly what he'd found. Brearly threw occasional glances in Agatha's direction. She couldn't decipher them, they were neutral.

'In a nutshell,' Brearly said after he finished the call, which had been quick, 'he's found out one key thing. This Andrew Penney, the chemist, appears to have originally been Canadian. Migrated to Australia in 1988. Twenty-five years ago.'

'The year before Smeeton... Neil Smeeton first got himself a driver's licence.'

'Good point.'

It was a good point and it strengthened the link between the Neil Smeeton and Andrew Penney personas. But one thing bothered her. That he was supposed to be Canadian. It didn't fit somehow. But why not? She wasn't consciously aware of what accent he'd spoken with in the InterContinental, or even in her dream for that matter. But once again, as with the name Smeeton, perhaps her subconscious brain was trying to tell her something?

And then she thought of the one thing that didn't yet make sense in her dream. The reference to Tchaikovsky. She'd been assuming there was classical music playing in the background in the hotel, although she wasn't too confident in her own ability to tell the difference between a symphony or whatever by Tchaikovsky and one by... one of the other ones. So maybe it wasn't to do with the music. What if it was a reference to nationality instead? She was well aware that Tchaikovsky was Russian – he'd have to be one of the most famous of them all – so was her subconscious trying to tell her that that's what Smeeton was? Russian? Maybe she'd subliminally picked up the trace of a Russian accent?

She could tell Brearly was now open to the relevance of the elements of her dream, and told him this latest idea.

'Russian, huh?' he said and thought about it for a few moments. 'Well if this guy... Penney or Smeeton or whoever he is... if he *is* Russian, and he's involved in criminal activities, he could well have come to the attention of our intelligence service. He's unlikely to be a spy, though. People smuggling's about the last thing you'd expect of a foreign agent, unless they're smuggling their own, but organized crime? You never know. He could easily be on ASIO's radar, so it might be worth giving them a call. What have we got to lose?'

Brearly smiled and their eyes locked just as Agatha was thinking, for the briefest of moments, how admirable this man was in so many ways.

46.

'... What have we got to lose?'

Talking about losing things, he could lose himself in those amber eyes. He really had to avoid staring at her. If he wasn't careful, she'd think he was trying to come on to her. Which wouldn't do. Still. Easy to say it, harder to do it. Agatha was so easy on the eye and in no way, shape or form could that be his fault. He was the victim here.

Agatha's Tchaikovsky idea was suitably wacky, but the InterContinental business was equally wacky with the dream and everything, and look at what that had uncovered. Agatha was in a category all on her own, no doubt about it. So taken in context, his idea to call ASIO wasn't as insane as it might have otherwise looked. A detective's job was to go down every rabbit hole and this was just another one.

The coffee wasn't too bad here either, and there was no faulting the company, so why the hell not while away a little more time here?

Brearly found a number for ASIO online – it looked like a Canberra number, or at least a national one – and dialled it. He first spoke to a female (he assumed, although you never could tell these days, could you), and then, after a significant time on hold, a male. He pictured a greying, middle-aged accountant type in an ill-fitting suit and with soup stains on his tie. Which no doubt was completely unfair. There were probably no soup stains, he probably only ever ate with a napkin tucked into his collar.

'This is Detective Sergeant Peter Brearly of the Newtown Local Area Command. In Sydney. I'm not sure if you're who—'

'And good day to you sir.'

The man spoke with a gravelly voice and in a patronizing tone, sounding like a cross between HAL, the computer in the film *2001: A Space Odyssey*, and a professional rugby league coach.

'Yes. Hello. We're running an abduction slash murder investigation with a possible overseas element and need to know if you have any information on someone.'

'On someone.'

'That's right. There could be a Russian connection and there's certainly criminal activity.'

Brearly paused and could hear nothing, no tapping, no paper shuffling, not even breathing.

'Hello?'

'What is the name of the person in question?'

'There are two names actually, we think they could be the same person,' Brearly said, and then read out all the details they had on Neil Smeeton and Andrew Penney.

'Is there potential law enforcement involvement?'

'What?'

'In relation to this criminal activity, is there possible involvement of any of the local or national law enforcement agencies?'

'Not that we know of. Or not our branch anyway, but hey, we're not ruling anything out. Could be ASIO involvement for all I know.'

There was a longer silence this time.

'Hello?... Are you still—?'

'Because of the nature of your inquiry, you will need to apply for this information in person. Are you able to do that?'

'Apply? We just need to know whether you have anything that—'

'I can give you the address. I see you're calling from... Bondi Junction in Sydney, from an iPhone 5s. Is that right?'

You have to be shitting me.

'Correct.'

'You will receive an encrypted notification on your phone in around two minutes' time. It will contain an address within a five-kilometre radius of your position. Please attend that address in sixty minutes, or let's say... 11.10am. Are you able to do that?'

'Sure. I'll be with Detective Senior Constable Agatha Ducatti.'

'Noted.'

'So this address we're going to, is it ASIO's Sydney headquarters?'

'Can I help you with anything else in the meantime, Detective Sergeant?'

'No. You've been wonderful.'

'Have a nice day.'

Two minutes later, Brearly received a notification on his phone containing an address in Surry Hills and an instruction telling them to 'wait outside and someone will be with you shortly'.

Brearly and Agatha travelled separately in their two vehicles and were soon standing outside the specified address, well before the appointed time. The street itself, one of the many backstreets of Surry Hills, was narrow and quiet, although not far from a major arterial road leading into the heart of the city two kilometres away.

The building was a large nondescript modern building with an abundance of dark glass, and a close inspection of the tenant list at the front entrance revealed a variety of businesses, including a high ratio of dental practices.

'So I wonder which one's ASIO's cover,' Agatha said as they looked over the list.

'I guess we'll find out,' Brearly said, 'but it makes sense having all those dentists. Their skills'd come in handy. For any ASIO agents in need of a check-up, and for any foreign spies in need of a little persuasion.'

They had half an hour to kill, so they grabbed themselves their second coffee of the morning from a local cafe. Brearly, for one, was beginning to enjoy the way this was all unfolding. He felt he could happily have endless coffees with Agatha, and he wasn't even a big coffee drinker.

Right on the dot of 11.10am, they were approached by someone, but to Brearly's surprise, they didn't emerge from the building, but came walking towards them up the street. To his even greater surprise, it was a conspicuously glamorous-looking woman.

'Detective Sergeant Peter Brearly?' she asked. 'And Detective Senior Constable Agatha Ducatti?'

Brearly and Agatha nod.

'Great. I'm Carla. If you wouldn't mind following me?'

No doubt about it. Carla was a knockout. She could have been a Hollywood star or a supermodel. Statuesque, with wavy, dark red hair, hazel eyes and flawless skin, she looked about thirty, and was wearing a figure-hugging dark green dress and shoes – some sort of cross between Roman sandals and high heels – that looked like escapees from a red-carpet event somewhere. Brearly couldn't help but notice that her dark green dress was so low-cut it looked like her small but perfect breasts were about to spring free at the slightest excuse. It was an impression that was, he guessed, the whole idea.

He found it hard to believe she worked at ASIO, even as support staff. Was she a full-time employee or helping out on some kind of work experience gig?

She turned and began walking back in the direction from which she'd originally come. Brearly and Agatha looked at each other, then followed Carla's shapely form down the street.

'So that's not your building, then.' Brearly realized he was stating the obvious but was keen to make conversation.

'No it's not,' she replied without turning around.

Coquettish. That was the word he was looking for. There was a reason the New South Wales Police didn't employ staff like Carla. Crime would start paying, put it that way.

Carla led them on a meandering journey, although at a cracking pace, across the street and then down a side street and along a series of narrow lanes, alleys and passageways.

'I was always wondering where um... your people's headquarters were in Sydney,' Brearly said to Carla at one point, two steps behind her. 'So that's where we're going I take it?'

He got no reply.

Their journey came to an end in a passage that led into a backstreet lined almost entirely with garage doors. Brearly had no idea where they were.

And I thought I knew every street in central Sydney.

They came to a halt in front of one of the doors, which was painted a drab grey like most of the others.

'Careful,' Carla said as she pressed a remote that she seemed to conjure from nowhere and the door in front of them began opening outwards. At this point Brearly noticed the well-camouflaged CCTV cameras dotted around this particular section of the backstreet.

Inside the garage there was, as you'd normally expect, a car, nothing special, and Brearly and Agatha followed Carla in past it and on into the ground floor of a house. Inside, it looked to be a fashion designer's studio with half-finished dresses and pieces of cloth and scissors everywhere. But no people. Then it was downstairs and along a small grey corridor and into a room with no windows. There was a table with four chairs around it and that was it.

'Just wait here a moment if you don't mind. Take a seat.'

'Thanks Carla,' Brearly called out as she left through the self-closing door, a little sorry she was leaving them.

Brearly and Agatha looked at each other and then around the room, although there was nothing to see. No furniture, nothing on the walls. No obvious cameras or recording devices, but he knew they were there – behind the air-conditioning vents no doubt. Speaking of which, despite the day's oppressive humidity, the temperature and air quality in the room were close to perfect.

So *this* is where our taxes go, Brearly thought. He nearly said so too, but refrained. It had a surprisingly deflating effect, knowing everything you said or did was being recorded. Agatha must have been feeling the same way because she remained silent, although she did smile at him at one point, which most certainly helped to counter the oppressive atmosphere.

And then Carla paid them a return visit. She was carrying two thin black folders, presumably setting up for the meeting or whatever this was. Brearly had to try very hard to not stare at her, it had to be said, very beautiful breasts.

'So who will this, er... interview be with today?' he asked.

'This interview will be with me,' Carla said. 'My name is Carla Stark, and I'm an intelligence officer with ASIO.'

Well. You could have blown Brearly down with a
feather.

47.

'My name is Carla Stark, and I'm an intelligence officer with ASIO.'

Agatha was as surprised as Brearly seemed to be that Carla was their assigned officer. She'd assumed Carla was someone's PA or even the station's receptionist. She wondered how many staff were in the building. Maybe it was just a safehouse? A safehouse for one? For Carla?

And it was only moments later that she became equally surprised by something else: it dawned on her that Carla was a trans woman. The telltale signs were there, and it appeared she still had a little way to go on with her transition, but even so, she'd clearly gone far enough for Agatha not to have noticed, and Agatha guessed that Brearly hadn't twigged either. She'd have liked to be able to enlighten him about this little titbit, so to speak, if only to see the look on his face.

'By the way,' Carla said, 'we're down here because you indicated a possible Russian connection. This room is an SCIF.'

'A...?' Brearly asked.

'Sensitive Compartmental Information Facility. A secure room to prevent eavesdropping, essentially. So you'll have no phone signal.'

'No problem.'

'Normally we make you leave your phones outside, but this meeting will be brief.'

'OK.'

Carla opened the first of her two black folders.

'As to the Neil Smeeton identity, we have no information.'

'So, no existing file on him?' Agatha asked. 'Nothing at all?'

'Correct. As to the other identity... the Andrew Penney identity...'

Carla opened the second of her black folders.

'... we *do* have some information on him. Not much though, so don't get too excited.'

'We'll try not to,' Brearly said. With a bit of a flirty smile, Agatha noticed.

'The only reason we have a file on... information on him, is because he's an immigrant and has become a highly regarded member of society. So what we have is... He migrated from Canada as you know in October 1988. Canadian passport. Born in Canada, in... Calgary, Alberta, on 27 August 1962, making him... twenty-six years old when he arrived here. He then... studied at Sydney University and went on to become a qualified pharmacist in 1995. By which time he'd already become a naturalized Australian citizen. He's now seen as a prominent member of the community. Unmarried, no children, no suspected...' Carla paused for a moment, and sighed. 'I can't believe we still do this... *no suspected homosexual tendencies.*' She shook her head and continued. 'Owns his own pharmacy,...'

'Compounding chemist,' Brearly interjected.

'... a house in Vaucluse,...'

'Wait. In Vaucluse? Do you have the address?'

'This may well be out of date, but... 141 New South Head Road.'

Brearly scribbled it down, as did Agatha.

'He's currently a member of the Australian Club, where as you know, the powerful and the once-were-powerful... *males*... of Sydney society mingle.'

More note-taking.

'But other than that... we have no... contraindications, if I can put it that way. A term we've adopted, but anyway, nothing to indicate he's anything other than an upstanding, law-abiding citizen, loyal to his adopted country. If we find out more, we'll be in touch. I'll call you and leave my first name only, Carla, and a phone number.'

'What if we find something that you need to know?' Brearly asked. 'Is there a number we can call, to reach you in the meantime?'

'If you find something that we need to know,' said Carla smiling, 'we'll know it already. But thank you for bringing your suspicions to our attention. If it wasn't for good citizens like you, we'd all be out of a job.'

Carla closed her folders, indicating the meeting was over. She led them back upstairs, through the still-deserted fashion designer's studio, and to the front door of the house this time – it was a terrace house – which opened out onto another unfamiliar street.

'You know your own way back?'

'Of course,' Brearly said. 'And thank you Carla,' he added, 'you've been a great help.' But she'd already disappeared back inside.

Agatha remembered his claim that he knew every street name within a ten-kilometre radius of the GPO, so it didn't escape her attention when she then saw him go straight to the map on his phone. *Nearly* every street name, perhaps.

'So what have we got,' Brearly said, once he'd got his bearings and they'd begun walking back to their cars. 'First. Do we have the wrong guy?'

'No,' Agatha said. 'Penney is Smeeton. And Smeeton is definitely the guy.'

'Right. So Smeeton... or Penney slash Smeeton... has been here twenty-five years, was originally a Canadian, is now a qualified pharmacist or chemist, a respected and upstanding member of blah blah blah... and attacks, drugs and abducts attractive young women. Correct?'

'Correct.'

'And the evidence suggests he's operating a people-trafficking operation, sending his female victims overseas, possibly to the amnesiac oblivion of a brothel somewhere at the ends of the earth, and in any event far from the reach of the long but not infinitely long arm of the law, never to be seen again. Is that about the size of it?'

Agatha nodded. 'Since Bastille Day two years ago.'

'For two years.'

They continued on in silence.

'Obviously we'll get this Vaucluse address checked out, but it's probably an old address. And even if it's current, he'll no doubt have cleared out by now anyway, just as he cleared out of his store. Gone to ground.'

'And become Smeeton,' Agatha said glumly. 'Full time.'

They both considered this for a moment.

'So you think he's some sort of Jekyll and Hyde?' Brearly asked.

'Not really. I think he's always a Mr Hyde.'

Brearly nodded.

'That's the bad one,' Agatha added.

'I know.'

'I think he does the upstanding citizen stuff as Penney, his original name, and the criminal stuff as Smeeton.'

They said nothing to each other after that, just kept walking, until they were almost back to where their cars were parked.

'The thing that gets me,' Brearly said suddenly, 'is that even if he or his associates are paying off someone in the Port Authority, they're still doing it under our noses.'

'You mean you think there could be... some sort of police cooperation?'

'I don't know. I'll tell you what though... I wouldn't put anything past the Botany Bay LAC. Those guys are the wild west down there.'

'Shit,' Agatha said.

'I hope I'm wrong. But we'd better keep this thing under wraps for now. Certainly make sure it doesn't leak out of Newtown. I suppose I'd better tell Perrick what we've found.'

'You don't think he's going to be pissed off we did this without telling him? I'm still on leave remember.'

'I could keep you out of it.'

'I don't see how. Given how this unfolded.'

'You're probably right. Let's shore up the facts first. I'll check out Vaucluse this afternoon, and then we just continue to focus on this Andrew Penney character. That's our best bet. What's today? Wednesday. Let's aim to get this guy in for questioning by the end of the week. If he hasn't left the country, that is. He can't be that hard to find by the sound of it. Then we can let Perrick know and get you back in. In the meantime let's keep this between us. So leave out Perrick, Terri too in the circumstances, Lutger's obviously with us... not sure who else... so just between the three of us. Until we know more.'

'OK. And this afternoon? Can I do anything?'

'Put your feet up. You're supposed to be on leave, remember?'

Agatha nodded and was about to head off when a thought occurred to her.

'So what did you think of Carla?'

Brearly raised his eyebrows and nodded, and said:

'Yeah, where did they find *her*? Bit of a bombshell, huh?'

'She was that,' Agatha said, deciding this was an instance where Brearly would be happier in a state of blissful ignorance.

48.

Agatha was doing what she was told to, for once. Perrick had ordered her to go on leave, and she was on leave. Brearly had told her to put her feet up and that's exactly what she was doing.

It was around 8.30pm and Agatha was on top of the maroon-and-mustard paisley bedspread in her room at the Marco Polo, half watching TV and thinking about what she felt like for dinner.

After leaving Brearly earlier that day, she'd done some quick food shopping in Summer Hill (the area was beginning to grow on her) and returned to the motor inn and made herself a late lunch – an omelette cooked in her electric frying pan, a simple salad, and a couple of slices of soft, beautifully fresh, white bread. Finally she had a chance to read a little of her Simenon novel before falling asleep for a late afternoon siesta.

And now, thinking about dinner, thinking about food instead of Smeeton or Penney, was a welcome relief. She'd only just opted for takeaway again when her phone rang. It was Brearly.

Agatha spoke first, playfully second-guessing him.

'No Brearly, it's not too late.'

There was a pause, then half a chuckle.

'Good,' he said, 'because I was proposing to drop in.'

'Drop in?' She hadn't meant to sound quite so alarmed.

'Sorry. A bit... forward, I know. But desperate times call for desperate measures, and all that.'

'You're not too desperate, I hope. I might take that as an insult.'

She cringed at the innuendo in what she'd just said, wishing she could unsay it. But thankfully Brearly seemed to ignore it. He *was* in a serious mood.

'I've found out some stuff, Agatha. It's pretty huge, and I don't want to—'

'To do with Vaucluse? Did you find—?'

'No, no, that drew a blank. Something else, and I don't want to discuss it over the phone. And it can't wait. I assume you're still staying in that motor inn? And you're there right now?'

'I am.'

'Can I drop in? I can be there in ten... twenty minutes tops.'

Agatha hesitated, but only briefly.

'Ah... sure.'

'Great. In the meantime, talk to no one. And I mean no one *at all*. What's your room number there?'

'112.'

'Sit tight. Don't let the drug dealers bite. And don't let anyone in except me. I'll knock three times, two quick, one slow. *Knock-knock... knock.* OK?'

She wasn't sure how seriously to take that last instruction, but he certainly didn't sound like he was joking. She could detect the note of anxiety in his voice. What couldn't wait for the morning?

There went her relaxing evening.

She lay back on her bed and allowed her thoughts to drift for a while. A plane flew by somewhere overhead, reminding her that the motel wasn't so far from the Newtown police station. Or Port Botany for that matter.

And then her phone began to play up. Again, just as it had that morning, because the alarm suddenly went off despite there being no alarm set and no way to turn it off. And again, after a short time it stopped, but this time it started again. Like the worst type of car alarm. She scrolled through the phone's screens and came across an app she didn't recognize and it began to dawn on her...

She tried to access the Cloud but her password failed. Someone had tampered with her phone, and at the back of her mind there was a voice saying how easy all this was, how obvious. It was possibly some sort of spyware or phone-tracking app. Tracking...

She immediately knew she had to leave, and quickly.

She grabbed her handbag – there was no time to pack up everything – and just as she was about to head out, there was a knock on the closed door in front of her. Her heart nearly stopped.

Knock-knock...

Knock.

Brearly.

Relieved, she walked the rest of the way to the door, and opened it.

49.

As he pulled off Parramatta Road into the driveway of the Marco Polo Motor Inn, Brearly couldn't help but wonder if he'd still be doing what he was doing if he didn't have a mild case of the hots for Agatha.

If she was a bloke, for example. Would he still be doing this, driving across town after hours, just to give a male colleague a warning that really could have waited for the morning?

Of course he would have.

He drove up the driveway and into the bowels – a good description in this case – of the building. Dead creepy was what it was, even for a seasoned cop like himself. By the time he'd driven up the ramp and then along past the motley line of parked cars on the upper level, he knew he was doing the right thing. Particularly when he pulled into a parking space next to a black tow truck with bright, white lettering on the side, proclaiming:

> **Your cars...**
> **NOT WORTH JACK SH*T ??**
> **JUST CALL JACK SHIPPE !!**
> **Jack Shippe Towing – "We Tow Anything"**

This was no place for a lady. Copper or not.

As he got out of his car, he had a bad feeling, a *pulse* that he couldn't fully explain, even given what he'd discovered that afternoon. This one was a big, bad pulse indeed.

And then as he approached Room 112, he could see Agatha had put a Do Not Disturb sign on the door. Which made sense, but it felt wrong.

So with an overwhelming, not fully explainable feeling of dread, he knocked on the door.

Knock-knock...

But that was as far as he got – he didn't get to deliver the third knock. Because everything, all of a sudden, went completely black.

Blacker than black, if you can picture that.

50.

Agatha wasn't sure if she was awake, or if it was a dream.

Because it didn't feel so much as if she'd just woken up and opened her eyes. It was more like they were already open – although only partially – but all at once she was able to see out of them. And from the moment her vision switched on, he was staring down at her, with his large, round, pale face and his small, bland, grey eyes.

Smeeton.

Reflexively, she tried to scream, or to shout – to send out to the world an audible signal of distress, of panic, like a bird might, or a monkey, partly for its own sake and partly for that of its troupe – but nothing would come. She tried to move, but her limbs felt like they were encased in lead. For all she knew they were, because she couldn't move, not even her head. Not even her eyelids. All she could do was continue to stare back up at him through lidded eyes.

He smiled. Turned away, and as if looking at someone, he shook his head.

And then, all by themselves and not in response to any command from her brain, her vision and her other remaining senses, or what was left of them, shut down again.

When consciousness next returned to her, and her eyelids opened, fully this time, she had no idea how much time had passed. A minute, an hour, a day.

To her great relief, there was no one staring down at her. And she could move her head.

The air was stale. She was in a long and narrow, windowless room. The featureless walls were grey and there was harsh fluorescent lighting bolted onto the ceiling.

She was lying on the floor and it was hard. Wood of some kind, maybe plywood. Her head felt like a bag of rocks, her eyelids as though they had weights attached to them, and her tongue was dead and dry.

A couple of feet away, a bench seemed to hang in space, and seemed to serve as a workspace of sorts. There was more than one. They were industrial-looking. Heavy tools on them. A layer of grease covered everything like black snow.

She tried to lift her arm, tried to slap her face to stop her eyes closing again. Her arm weighed as much as a suitcase and she barely managed it. But she made contact and the sound echoed. Felt nothing. She tried again. Something. A little pain. And where there was pain, she told herself, there was usually hope.

The sound of a plane taking off nearby. She realized she'd heard another one earlier. Was she at the airport?

There was a broken window pane on the floor next to her, and next to that...

And next to that, there was a body.

It was a man's. With a herculean effort she managed to push herself up, maybe a few centimetres and just for a few moments, but it was enough to see the side of his face.

It was Brearly.

She managed to move her leg, and she nudged him with her foot, but got no reaction. And his chest wasn't moving. She tried to stretch her arm out and touch him with her hand, more of a gesture than anything else, but her hand would no longer do what she wanted it to. Her body was shutting down again.

Her eyelids grew unbearably heavy. Was she dying?

And just before she lost consciousness again, she noticed that the grey walls were in fact corrugated steel, and she realized that the room she was in was not a room at all, but a shipping container.

51.

The third time she woke, Agatha stayed awake.

She was immediately overwhelmed with a sense of panic. She was in a shipping container. That was all she could think for a while. A shipping container. And everything that went with that.

And then it occurred to her: given the planes she'd heard, she had to be near the airport, which probably meant the port at Botany. Which meant she had to escape before they put her on a ship.

And then she felt it. The floor was moving, and it wasn't dizziness.

She was already on a ship. At sea. It was too late.

And now there were voices. She kept her eyes open just a fraction, and slowly, in tiny increments, inclined her head, to surreptitiously take in her surroundings. Brearly's body was still there next to her. The overhead lighting was still on, but daylight was now finding its way in from somewhere, from a door or an opening at the end of the container behind her. The voices were coming from the opposite end, past where Brearly was lying.

A large man – not Smeeton – was doing something over by a workbench under a small light, and a skinny man was sitting on the floor next to him, with his back against the wall. The large man she'd never seen before, but the other one looked vaguely familiar. Not that she could get a clear view with her eyes only fractionally open, but she could tell there was something about the skinny man. He reminded her of Gollum from *The Lord Of The Rings*. He had a weaselly demeanour about him, and that in itself rang a bell.

The large one – fat, unshaven, with matted dark brown hair, big wet patches under his huge arms, a once-white, grease-stained T-shirt, army surplus khaki pants with bulging pockets, and steel-capped work boots – was putting something together or fixing something, something made of metal, something mechanical. He has his back to her. The skinny one, in a black singlet, blue boardshorts and thongs, was reading the sports section of a tabloid and picking his nose, not necessarily in that order. He had dark hair with blond streaks, and a mullet haircut...

The shaved meercat. It was Shane. Shane Jeldry.

'Hey Burger,' he said suddenly, uttering into space.

The fat man just grunted.

'I'm gonna rape her.'

No immediate answer.

'*Feel* like a fuck,' Shane continued.

'She's unconscious you douche.'

'Exactly. It's not rape when they're unconscious.'

'Fuckin' moron,' Burger said, under his breath and shaking his head.

'And as you know, I love doin' it legal!'

'Not countin' the twelve-year-olds.'

'Piss off.'

'So if you love doin' it legal, your girlfriend's in the next container, why don't you do her?'

'That slag? Wouldn't touch her with a ten-foot barge pole.'

'Of even a four inch one.'

'Get fucked Mister Cheerio. And go find some tomato sauce. Anyway, she's my ex, I don't do exes. The one here though, I've met her before and gotta say... she's my cup of beer.'

'Yeah well you better watch her. She's a slippery fish this one.'

'Ooh yeah. Just the way I like it. I'll be slippin' her a bit of slippery fish of my own.'

'Bit of slippery sardine, will you?'

'Get fucked.'

'And so you do this one, whaddya think the Chemist is gonna say about that then, eh?'

'He's gonna...' but Shane trailed off.

'You're gettin' a free holiday out of this remember.'

'Vladdy. Some holiday.'

'Our main *stopover* you idiot. Nouméa.'

'Yeah, well. Gettin' a bit sick of *that* fuckin' place. All that French shit. Nouméa ain't no Bali.'

'No pleasing some people.'

'Anyway. Half them end up *carkin'* it ya wanker, so it's not like the Chemist gives a fuck. She's not his fuckin' *bride*. And the dead ones, they go overboard, remember? Like where that cop's headed.'

'Which one.'

'So does the Chemist give a fuck? I don't think so.'

'Which *one*, I said. They're both fuckin' cops.'

'Well obviously *she's* not goin' overboard. She's a chick.'

'Exactly,' Burger said. 'He's the one going overboard. She, on the other hand, will be joining the others. Her services are required elsewhere.'

'Yeah, well, I'm not gonna fuck *him*, am I.'

'Wouldn't put it past you.'

'The Chemist ain't gonna find out unless you fuckin' tell him. And I know you. You're a cunt, but you're not *that* much of a cunt.'

Burger just shook his head and continued with whatever it was he was doing on the bench. A screwdriver was involved, and a hammer.

Shane seemed to take this as a yes.

'Right then,' he muttered, and sprang up off the floor, throwing his newspaper down. 'Smoko.'

'That implies you've actually been working,' Burger said, still with his back to the room.

Agatha tensed up as she watched, through her almost-shut eyes, Shane approaching her. He was rubbing the crotch of his boardshorts.

'Nice body... Hey. Don't look around, Burger.'

'Wouldn't dream of it. Be like watching a *cane* toad do it.'

'I didn't for you, last time.'

'She was conscious, you fuckwit.'

'Same deal.'

Shane knelt down next to Agatha and began removing her jeans. Top button, then zip – she could smell the stale beer and cigarettes on his breath – and then began pulling her jeans off. Agatha had let herself go limp and decided her best bet was to feign unconsciousness until a better idea presented itself. But how long could she keep that up for? And then what?

He roughly yanked her jeans down to her knees, and then completely off. His eyes sparkled ferociously. He began to lift her T-shirt up to pull it over her head, but impatience got the better of him and he returned his attention to her crotch. He rubbed his own, again, and then put his hand – and this was the worst part – *gently* on her. Gently, like he cared.

She felt like throwing up. He began to stroke. She wanted to scream but filled her mind with pure, bloody resolve. *Make a plan and stick to it.* She'd let him start things up, let him get things going, and then try something.

He ran his fingers lightly up the insides of her thighs and then over her panties again. He was salivating, she could have sworn it, and then, *oh save me*, she couldn't believe this, he bent down, hooked his arms under her legs, and began licking her inner thighs. Making the most disgusting noises she'd ever heard – he was actually *slurping*. She had to use all of that resolve of hers to shut out the sensations that were hitting her.

'I just hope you realize,' Burger said abruptly, his back still turned, 'that that's *lunch*. Don't expect anything else.'

Shane stuck his head up for a moment, twisted around like a demented animal – a demented meerkat, in fact, was exactly what he looked like – and looked over at Burger, laughing suddenly and exclaiming:

'You're just hanging out for sloppy seconds you fuckin' animal!'

When he returned his attention to Agatha, she saw her opportunity. Her plan may have been to let him get things going, but *fuck this*.

She found she'd already decided on a course of action – not consciously – and it was programmed in, an irreversible process.

She quickly yanked his face into her groin, so quickly he had no time to utter anything, all she heard was an exhalation of breath. She could feel his flattened nose and his open mouth and teeth against her skin, and she pulled so hard he couldn't have been able to breathe and she could feel the spasms in his abdomen. At the same time, with her legs, she pinned his arms, which were still awkwardly hooked under her thighs. He struggled but she knew she was stronger. She was lucky he was such a runt, such a weakling, and she knew she could hold him there. What she didn't know was how long it would take him to die or lose consciousness (she didn't care which), and whether she could make it happen before Burger turned around.

Shane was making fitful, muffled, snorting noises, and sounds of distress that might have been mistaken for moaning.

'*Hmmnnhn... nmmnnh...*'

'Having fun Shane?' Burger asked, chuckling to himself, as Shane's legs started thumping against the floor.

Seconds passed. They could have been minutes. They felt like hours. Agatha's muscles were burning. She felt some clicks in Shane's neck and hoped it was cracking, but he was still struggling, albeit noticeably weakening.

'Hey dickhead, I thought I asked you a question before.' Burger seemed to be enjoying this little game.

And then, a little later:

'What, Mummy teach you not to talk with your mouth full or something?'

More thumping on the floor.

'Whoop, there we go, foreplay's over. Not that a girl could tell the difference with you.'

A few more chuckles from Burger, and after what felt like an eternity, Shane went limp at last. Was he dead? There was still the odd twitch, so she couldn't be sure. And it was possible he was faking it. But she knew his pal Burger would be looking their way any moment. All she needed was a bit longer, just to be on the—

And then Burger turned around.

It didn't register with him straight away what was happening. A good three seconds. After that though, he reached for something and spun in Agatha's direction at the same time. It was the hammer.

Burger was a charging, hulking beast as he thundered across the floor, hammer raised, with Agatha thinking fast: could she get Shane in position as a shield? Was she strong enough...?

Suddenly there was the flash of reflecting glass, a scream and a crash. The scream was from Burger's mouth, and the flash of glass came from what was at the end of Brearly's outstretched arm – it must have been from the broken pane. The improvised weapon sliced through the ample flesh of Burger's left ankle. Burger crashed to the ground – through a wooden crate – giving Agatha her opportunity to slam Shane's head into the floor as hard as she could. When she looked up, it was just in time to catch Burger's angry riposte as he cracked the hammer down on Brearly's skull before turning his attention back to her.

All she could do now was save herself – it was obviously what Brearly had intended anyway. There wasn't a weapon in sight but there was an open door. Burger was pulling himself up off the floor. Blood was pouring from his wound and a series of guttural growls were pouring from his mouth. Agatha willed her legs to move and get her standing and down the length of the container and out into the sunlight on the ship's deck.

It was a medium-sized container ship – but huge, as far as Agatha was concerned – and there wasn't a soul in sight, just rows of blue and orange containers. She knew these ships operated with minimal crew these days. Not that finding any of them would do her any good – she knew there was no way they weren't involved.

The view that met her gaze out past the guardrails, though, was the sight she'd been dreading: as far as the eye could see, there was no land. Just a great expanse of ocean. As she'd feared, she'd left her bid for freedom too late.

She made it over to the guardrail and looked over the side, to the water below, sweeping past. It was a big drop, maybe fifteen metres. She could jump. She'd survive it, but then what? She was a good swimmer, but where could she swim to? If the sharks didn't get her, exhaustion eventually would. On the other hand, if she stayed on the ship, they'd kill her, or worse. And she already knew what the 'worse' was: a life sentence in a living hell.

She could hear the curses and mutterings coming from Burger, but thankfully he still hadn't made it out of the container. She desperately needed a weapon of some kind, but there was nothing. The deck was clutter-free, just rows and rows of twenty-foot containers.

And then, in the midst of this indecision, Smeeton appeared.

He seemed to come from nowhere, but it must have been from a nearby container or hatch. He was in his dark blue suit too, and black trainers. As always.

She'd stopped dead when she saw him, and he'd stopped too. He said nothing, just stared at her with those lifeless grey eyes. The beginnings of a grin appeared on his lips and he slowly shook his head.

She couldn't see a weapon, but she knew well enough the man himself was the weapon. When he got his hands on you it was game over. Shane was one thing. Smeeton was another.

Her mouth wouldn't function. She'd never said a word to him and she suddenly felt it was all she needed to do to break him, to break the spell, just speak to him, but nothing would come. What's this all about, she wanted to ask him. What are *you* all about.

He started walking slowly towards her, and she backed away along the guardrails of the ship, in the direction of the bow. Soon, he'd backed her to a point where she could go no further. Just forwards towards Smeeton, or to her left, over the rail and into the ocean below.

He began to pull something out of the pocket of his suit jacket. Agatha decided she wasn't going to hang around to find out what it was.

She turned, and with a speed and strength that surprised her, she sprang up onto the guardrail. Smeeton lunged at her and he was lightning fast, but not quite fast enough because she didn't hesitate, she just kept going, out into the space between the sea and the sky...

... and as she began to fall, she pushed her arms forwards, and downwards, and tucked her chin in the way they did in the Olympics, as if she, too, was looking for a perfect score, looking to slice, like a knife, through the surface of the dark, cold waters below.

52.

A plane thundered in over the building, interrupting her thoughts.

Outside, the sky had run amok and the glass panes were fitfully rattling in the wind. One of Sydney's notorious 'southerly busters' had blown in, the wind had just topped ninety-four kilometres per hour at the airport and the gusts were officially 'damaging'. Conditions at sea would be bad. White horses as far as the eye can see. If it had hit yesterday…

It was difficult to believe that it was only yesterday that she'd dived off a container ship into the Pacific.

Agatha was pleased she wasn't outside in the street, let alone in the ocean. She was sitting in the Big Room at the Newtown police station, waiting for the others to join her. Waiting for the 10.30am debrief.

The last twenty-four hours had been a bit of a blur. Or even the last thirty-eight hours, because that was when it had all started. With that knock on the door on Wednesday night at the Marco Polo. *Knock knock, who's there.*

The fact that she even remembered anything was down to the resistance she'd built up after her first dose of the drug nine days earlier. So the doctor had told her, at least. And maybe they hadn't kept her as drugged up as they should have. With all the excitement of having extra passengers, no doubt.

After she hit the water – as if she was a professional cliff diver, it was a miracle she hadn't been injured – she truly thought she'd never come up. She didn't fight it. At first she allowed herself to sink, like a stone in a pond, and imagined slipping all the way down to the ocean floor. In a way it would have been a relief, and at the time, she had the sensation that the bottom of the sea represented a place of safety, of refuge. Eventually though, deeper instincts took control, and she rose again, and the darkness turned to light and she surfaced.

It hadn't escaped her that there was an uncanny parallel between this dive and the one in her dream, but right now she was trying not to think about that. She was just relieved it was all over.

After she'd surfaced, she saw what she'd been expecting to see: the vastness of the ocean, and other than the ship, nothing but an empty horizon. She turned and watched the ship steam away, an impossibly long, dark silhouette with the morning sun behind it. Or what she'd assumed was the morning sun, because once the ship had moved on, she saw land.

In the distance, she could see cliffs. She realized that it must have been afternoon and not morning. She was now facing west, not east. And now she was looking at the sandstone cliffs of Sydney.

She later learned she'd been about three kilometres out. The ship hadn't yet travelled far after rounding Cape Banks at the entrance to Botany Bay, and notwithstanding the currents, and her level of exhaustion, she could probably have swum it, she was a strong swimmer. But she didn't have to put it to the test. A yacht appeared, with sails. They'd tacked east, across the stern of the ship, and someone had seen her dive. Seeing those sails, they were a wonderful sight.

After the yacht had picked her up, the police were contacted, which was when the water police vessel had come out to check on her. She had since been informed that the police vessel had then chased down the ship and boarded it, and that everyone on board had been arrested. Brearly was still alive and he was airlifted out. Agatha had then been picked up by a second police vessel and transported back to St Vincent's Hospital, the same one Brearly had been sent to, and she was kept there overnight for observation. She was tired, though, of being observed.

Two female captives had been found as well. Agatha had yet to find out who they were, although she already knew that one of them was Chalaise, Shane's ex.

While Agatha was in hospital, she learnt what big news it had all become: abduction of two detectives by a crime gang, the rescue of two kidnapped women, and the shutting down of a human trafficking operation.

Agatha was discharged at 8am the following morning – *this* morning – and on her way out, she'd asked to see Brearly. His head was heavily bandaged and he was still unconscious, or asleep, and she was told it was best not to wake him, so she gently placed her hand on his and silently thanked him.

She then left a message at work to say she'd be in, then headed back to the Marco Polo to collect her things, including her car, and she was hugely relieved to see the place in her rearview mirror for what was hopefully the last time. She drove back to Tamarama, dumped her things, had a quick shower and changed her clothes.

Leaving the flat, when she picked up her phone, she hesitated for a moment. For good reason, given what had happened at the motor inn and her discovery that her phone had been tampered with. She now realized Smeeton would have had the opportunity to do something to it when he broke into her flat last Saturday afternoon, and it occurred to her that maybe that was what Brearly had been coming to the Marco Polo to tell her, that her phone had been compromised. But it was all over now, and she'd have the phone fully checked out when she had a chance.

From Tamarama she drove to Newtown, and when she walked into the police station, she got a standing ovation from the officers and staff...

Knock-knock.

She froze, for an instant, at the sudden memory. Opening the door and the rush of the assault, the powerful arm around the neck. The flailing of limbs, the fall of the curtains, the blackout.

She twisted around. It was Perrick, followed by Terri and Lutger.

'How are you feeling?' Perrick asked.

'Much better, thanks.'

'I visited you. In hospital.'

'Did you? I didn't—'

'You were asleep.'

'It must have been terrifying,' said Terri. 'Not to mention the dive off that ship.'

'It's not something I'll be doing again in a hurry, that's for sure. By the way, what's the latest on Brearly?' She looked at Lutger for a quick visual assurance, but he just nodded and looked to Perrick.

'He's alive,' said Perrick. 'Which is something.'

'Fractured skull,' Lutger added. 'So not great.'

'Jesus,' Agatha said. 'He was trying to... He saved my life.'

There was a pause.

'Assuming he recovers,' said Lutger, 'there's a risk of permanent brain damage...' He let that sink in before adding '... although as I pointed out to the doctors, it may be difficult to tell the difference with Brearly.'

Agatha had to smile, not at Brearly's expense, but at Lutger's attempt to be stoic about it.

Perrick, as usual, kept a stiff upper lip. 'It was a monumentally brave thing he did.'

'It was,' said Agatha, thinking it was also monumentally stupid. Suicidal, really. And as she well knew, it was because of her. The only reason he was at the Marco Polo was because of her.

'Well with a bit of luck...' Perrick added, but didn't finish his sentence. 'He's as tough as they come.'

There was an awkward pause.

'So come on,' Agatha said. 'Tell me what happened.'

Perrick nodded, cast a quick glance over at Lutger, and began.

'After your... fortuitous rendezvous with the *Isla Bonita*, the—'

'The what?'

'The yacht that picked you up. After that, Marine Area Command came out to check on you and then proceeded to board the container ship. The *Sapphire Dawn*.'

'And that's when—'

Perrick held up his hand to her as a pause signal.

'First we found Brearly,' he said. 'He was in a critical condition, so he was airlifted.'

He said *we*. And then she remembered. Perrick had been on the water police vessel that had checked on her and gone on to board the ship.

'Two other captives were found too. Two of your Nowhere women, Agatha.'

'Who?'

'Chalaise Corlay was one. And Samantha Poole, the woman you interviewed.'

'Sam.'

'They were both in a poor state. Drugged, and barely conscious. They should be OK though.'

The wind outside seemed as if it was getting in through the cracks, and into the room, and whistling into the corners of Agatha's brain.

'But the main thing,' said Perrick, 'is that this criminal enterprise, the entire operation, has now been shut down. Thanks, in no small part, to you and Brearly. The mystery of the Nowhere women has now been solved. Unfortunately it does appear the other women on that list will never be found. They're possibly already dead, but in any event overseas, somewhere beyond our reach. Beyond anyone's reach.'

'So Brearly was right,' Agatha said. 'And we think they were... destined for brothels?'

'We really can't speculate. And we may never find out for certain. The federal police have been contacted and they've indicated as much. I don't think they want to know about it, frankly.'

'And so the others are lost. There were sixteen on that list.'

'I'm afraid so. But we've saved two, and most importantly, by nipping things in the bud, we've saved the lives of countless others.'

And the wind, the cold wind, was blowing through her veins.

'And the gang? Did you get—'

'Right. Well. One of them was already known to us. His body was found in the container where Brearly was found.'

'Shane Jeldry,' Agatha said.

'Correct. Cause of death yet to be determined.'

Agatha just nodded and said nothing.

'Another suspect, larger gentleman—'

'Smeeton?'

'... was found with a severe wound to his leg, apparently caused by Brearly. He would have bled to death but managed to successfully apply a tourniquet to himself. Gentleman by the name of—'

'*Gentleman?*'

'Pardon the idiom. Man by the name of Borg Rasmussen.'

'*Berrh-GEH*,' Lutger said, with a Scandinavian accent.

'Pardon?'

'*Berrh-GEH*,' Lutger repeated.

'Burger,' Agatha said, remembering what Shane had called him.

'What are you both talking about?'

'Rasmussen's first name,' said Lutger. 'It's not Borg, it's *Berrh-GEH*, spelt B.Ö.R.G.E. The O has an umlaut.'

'Right. Anyway, so Rasmussen's now in hospital under police guard and is, unsurprisingly, not being cooperative. Then there was the captain, a Russian by the name of Voronov or something, and a—'

'Vodyanov,' Lutger said.

'Right. There was also a skeleton crew, but none of them is cooperating, none of them claims any knowledge of you or Brearly or the two women being on the ship. Needless to say, they've all been taken into custody. The evidence of a conspiracy is strong. And we believe Rasmussen was the mastermind.'

'But what about Smeeton?' Agatha asked. 'Or Penney, or whatever he goes by. A large man in a suit and trainers?'

Agatha turned to Lutger who shifted his gaze to the floor. For a moment there was just the sound of the wind impatiently strumming the windows.

'Agatha,' Perrick said softly. 'There was no sign of him.'

'What? No sign?'

'They had your description, but there was no one—'

'Did they check the ship thoroughly? All the holds? The containers? Or the crew, maybe he was—'

'There was no one matching your description. No...' and he turned to Lutger. 'The name on the licence?'

'Neil Smeeton,' Lutger said.

'No Neil Smeeton, no one wearing a suit and trainers.'

'He can't just have disappeared! They've got to go over that ship with a fine-tooth comb. Every nook and cranny. Where's the ship?'

'Back at port, at Botany. It's been impounded. With a police guard.'

'Well tell them to get the hell in there and search it again!'

Perrick sighed. Agatha knew what was coming.

'Agatha, is there *any* chance you might have been—'

'No.'

'That you might have been confused in some—'

'No! No way.'

'You'd been drugged, remember.'

She could see what she was up against. All she could do was shake her head.

'I wasn't imagining him,' she said.

Again she looked to Lutger, and again he wouldn't meet her eyes. Everyone was silent for a few seconds, and the only sound was the wind – it continued to shake the building as if trying to wrench it from its foundations.

'Where was the ship heading?' she asked Perrick.

'Nouméa.'

'Logical. Just like Carol's ship. And after that?'

'We don't—'

'Vladivostok,' Lutger said.

'Do we know that?' asked Perrick.

Lutger nodded.

Vladdy. Shane had mentioned it.

'But what about Andrew Penney?' Agatha directed her question to Lutger. 'Smeeton's alias, or vice versa. Have you tracked him down yet?'

'Who?' Perrick asked.

'Our best information,' Lutger replied to Agatha, 'is that he's away for a month on an overseas holiday.'

'What a coincidence.'

'Yes, exactly.' Lutger turned to Perrick: 'A chemist called Andrew Penney. It's possible that he and Smeeton are the same person. Brearly had me looking into him.'

'Well when this Penney guy shows up, we'll question him,' said Perrick.

Agatha was still stunned. Couldn't believe it. That Smeeton hadn't been found. She hadn't been dreaming or hallucinating. Or had she? Was he simply a product of her very active imagination? Was he a ghost after all?

A siren went by somewhere, a reminder that the dramas don't stop for everyone else just because you're involved in one of your own. And as the windows continued to shake and judder, threatening to explode inwards at any moment, they continued to hold their ground as well. They, and Agatha. They were hanging in there.

53.

The thought that they might never find the complete answer to the Smeeton question – and that the man himself, real or imagined, could still be out there, roaming the streets or the oceans – was almost unbearable. She had to try to remind herself that if he was imagined, she had nothing to worry about. And assuming he was real, then whoever he was, he was beatable. Because she'd beaten him. Twice. And she'd beat him again.

She'd keep telling herself that.

She was back in her office – the office she shared with Brearly – and was sitting at her desk. The meeting had ended with Perrick suggesting she take the rest of the day off, pointing out she was technically still on leave, but she'd demurred, saying she was keen to get back to work and Perrick hadn't resisted.

As she sat there now, she knew that despite her concern for Brearly, her overwhelming feeling should have been one of relief, but two things were bothering her.

One thing that *wasn't* bothering her was the fact she'd killed someone the day before. In other circumstances it might have. It might have bothered her if it had been her first time, but it hadn't been. A few years back, she'd shot dead a gun-wielding motorcycle gang assassin after he'd killed a rival gang member. She'd never forgotten that, but she'd processed it and was now able to sleep without having nightmares about it. And it might have bothered her if Shane Jeldry hadn't been one of the most odious creatures that had walked the face of the earth, and hadn't been about to do to her what he'd said he was going to, and hadn't been about to kill Brearly. But he had.

But she had bigger things to worry about besides the possibility of some more PTSD to deal with. After she'd left the meeting and gone to her office, her sense of unease had only grown. Because of the two things that *were* bothering her.

Not only had Smeeton not been found – a fact that was puzzling and disconcerting enough on its own – but there was something else. What had Perrick been doing on the water police vessel? That was a Marine Area Command operation. It was highly unusual for Perrick to be there, even with the officers in jeopardy being his. Apart from anything else, no one knew she and Brearly were on that container ship. Who could have known this, and then known to contact Perrick? And how did Perrick get to the vessel in time? The Marine Area Command vessels usually operated out of Balmain. There were too many question marks.

She didn't know what to do. Her mind wandered: she thought about the expression 'all at sea', about how that was precisely how she felt, and about how the expression had now taken on added weight. She absent-mindedly flicked through some files, but couldn't concentrate.

She leaned back in her chair and swivelled and faced the window. Recalled how she'd done the same thing one evening – when had it been, over two weeks ago? – and had watched her reflection morphing into Smeeton. Thinking about that now only made the doubts creep in again even more. Was this man forever going to appear before her eyes? Night and day?

She looked over at Brearly's desk and noticed the pile of telephone memos. Without knowing exactly what she was looking for, she went over and leafed through them. One of them stood out. It said 'Call Carla' and there was a phone number. It was dated yesterday, Thursday 31 October, and time-stamped 11.35am.

Suddenly there was something Agatha could do. And there was one thing she did know, and it was that she had to do something.

She picked up her mobile phone, and was about to call the number, and then, for the second time that day, hesitated. Earlier, she'd dismissed her worries about her phone, but that was when she'd assumed the danger had passed. Now it seemed maybe it hadn't. She'd have to call Carla on another phone, and preferably from somewhere else.

She put her phone in her desk drawer and Carla's note in the pocket of her jeans. She then grabbed her jacket and wallet, and her car's key card and headed for the firearms room – now that she was back on duty, she was able to pick up her handgun, a Glock 26, same as Brearly's, nice and light. Luckily she'd thought to bring her green jacket to wear over her T-shirt, so she'd be able to carry the gun unobtrusively.

So as soon as she'd signed out her gun, checked it, and strapped it on under her jacket, she said goodbye to no one and marched straight out of the building and into the street. The day was still windy and bleak, but now that she was carrying her gun again, she felt significantly better.

54.

At three minutes to midday, under a grim sky, Agatha was in position. She'd found, with some difficulty, the gravestone Carla had described, and now she was facing into the strong south wind to stop her hair blowing over her face. She was standing in the Waverley Cemetery, at the designated meeting spot. A stone's throw from the cliffs that plunged down to the waves crashing on the rocks below. To her left, whitecaps, all the way to the eastern horizon. Low scudding clouds and an all-pervading mist that seemed to have blown in all the way up from the Southern Ocean.

It was hard to believe that only yesterday she'd been out there. The days couldn't have been more different. Yesterday was sunny and blue, and now it was wild and grey, and little droplets of moisture were pricking her face in the driving wind.

After walking out of Newtown police station, the first thing she did was to buy a burner – a prepaid mobile phone – and then telephone Carla. It had been Carla's idea to meet at the cemetery with the ocean view. When she arrived, which was right on the dot of 12 noon, she explained the choice of location:

'There's no better place for being sure you're not being listened to. The wind and weather mess with eavesdropping devices and you can spot a peeping tom a mile off.'

Carla was wearing another figure-hugging dress – this one was purple, which went equally well with her hazel eyes and her wild red hair, which miraculously stayed in place in the wind. That was not your average hairspray.

'And I'll bet you live locally, too,' Agatha said, 'like at Bondi,' but Carla just smiled and said nothing.

Carla had arrived with two takeaway coffees and handed one to Agatha. Agatha hadn't asked for a coffee but was grateful for it. It was exactly what she felt like.

'Flat white with one sugar,' Carla said.

'How did you know?' Agatha asked.

Carla gave her another of her smiles.

'One thing I *didn't* know about you,' she said, 'was that you were a platform diver.'

'Neither did I.'

'Impressive stunt. You might have missed your calling.'

'I think I just got very lucky. I wouldn't advise trying it.'

'Oh no chance of that. Heights terrify me. The *ocean* terrifies me even more. Land creatures belong on the land, sea creatures in the sea. As far as I'm concerned, when you mess with that formula, nothing good ever happens.'

'You may have a point,' Agatha said. 'So tell me. Have you found something?'

'We have. After your inquiry, we made a few of our own. And we found out from the CSIS... the Canadians... that your Andrew Penney is believed to be... or rather, is believed to have *been*... I'll explain... a Russian agent.'

'As in... FSB?'

'KGB. This was pre '91. He and his allocated wife were probably sleeper agents in Canada from as early as 1987.'

'So his real name isn't Andrew Penney.'

'The real Andrew Penney only lived to be a few months old.'

'And was tombstoned.'

'Exactly.'

'Just like Neil Smeeton.'

Carla frowned. 'As I said last time, we have no information on a Neil Smeeton, but according to the Canadians, this Russian male, currently known as Andrew Penney, along with another Russian, his female companion, arrived in Canada on fake passports and then took on their new identities. Then at some point the woman vanished and there was no further record of her.'

'Vanished,' said Agatha. 'Sounds familiar.'

'It's not known whether she was recalled to the Soviet Union... although that seems unlikely... or if there was a breakdown in their relationship and she left him, or, more likely, she met with some ill deed, possibly at the hands of this man himself.'

'Right,' said Agatha, 'And so this man... Penney, or whoever he was... was a sleeper agent in Canada. Who possibly killed his allocated sleeper agent wife. So why did he come to—?'

'I should say that the Canadians weren't aware of any of this at the time, which is why we had no record of him ourselves. But as we all know, he migrated to Australia in 1988 on his Canadian passport.'

'As Andrew Penney.'

'Yes. And to answer the question you were about to ask... Why did he come to Australia? Because it was around this time that he seemed to have gone rogue.'

'Gone rogue?'

Carla nodded. 'Parted company with his handlers. You see...' She sighed. 'We've made some inquiries of the UK's SIS... MI6 to you... I don't know why we're always the last to be told these things, but... it looks like ever since his arrival in Australia, he's been off his leash. MI6 believes... they're not sure and they have no definitive proof... but they think that Andrew Penney may be an ex-KGB agent by the name of Igor Kuznetzov.'

'Igor Kuznetzov.'

'He'd originally been earmarked for sleeper duties in the US. But something seems to have gone wrong. Maybe the disappearance of his wife. Maybe it was the historical context, with the collapse of the Soviet Union beginning around 1988. Maybe it was his disappointment of missing out on the best spy jobs and being designated a sleeper. Maybe he was just a piece of work. Maybe all of the above.'

'Well he's certainly a piece of work. So Andrew Penney's real name is Igor Kuznetzov.'

'Depends what you mean by real. Not much is, in this business. But his birth name, yes. It would appear so.'

'It would appear so. But he's no longer a sleeper agent.'

Carla shook her head. 'Hasn't been taking instructions for at least… twenty-four years.'

'Just doing his own thing.'

'Living his own life.'

A seagull that looked hard-done-by flew low overhead, battling the wind, and then gave up and shot out of their field of vision.

'What does MI6 know about this Igor Kuznetzov?' Agatha asked.

'About Kuznetzov, quite a lot. Born on New Year's Day, currently 49 years old. From Novosibirsk in southwestern Siberia. From a large family. Middle child. Due to his weight he was often made fun of in school. His physique and lack of charisma, incidentally, may have been why he was ruled out of the top spy jobs and led to a resentment towards the KGB. Anyway, what else. He got tattoos at a young age… probably suggestive of criminality to give him some street cred or whatever… but when he joined the KGB, when he was 20, he had to have them removed. Surgically, with skin grafts, but it was botched and would have been painful, and their removal and the resulting disfigurement is, according to MI6, why he always wears long sleeves.'

'Which would explain his habit of tugging his shirt cuffs,' said Agatha.

'In Canada, his story was that he'd been in a car accident and suffered burns. But anyway despite his problems, he was intelligent and good at chemistry, and that was probably what drew the attention of the KGB in the first place. And with the military training the KGB provided, he's learnt to use his weight to his advantage. He's no doubt highly trained in close combat. Dangerous, in other words.'

'You don't say.'

They were silent for a while, and Agatha let the wind buffet her face.

'So what do we do?' she asked.

'We?'

'Well... You mean you're not intending to do anything?'

'He's not a current concern for us. Is he stealing state secrets? No? Look... We'll augment our file, I suppose, and that's about it. To be honest.'

'Augment...? But he's abducting *women*. And transporting them overseas to work as *sex slaves*.'

'I'm not aware of that. There might be information I haven't seen, but even if he is, that's not really our field. Hate to say it, but that sort of general murder and mayhem stuff... that's what the cops are for, to put it bluntly. Right up *your* alley, in other words.'

55.

With Brearly down for the count, there was only one other colleague she could trust and straight after Carla had walked away through the headstones, she called him.

'I didn't recognize the number,' Lutger said. 'Almost didn't pick up.'

'I'll explain later. Can we meet?'

'Sure. You mean now? Somewhere other than work?'

'Yes.'

'Well... have you had lunch yet?'

Agatha suddenly realized how hungry she was. 'No.'

'Can you come to Chinatown? That's where I am now.'

Agatha was watching the lobsters in their tank. Scuttling away and amassing in a corner whenever a net came in to take one of their number away.

It was hard not to draw parallels.

She was sitting in the Golden Century restaurant in Chinatown. Yum cha was on offer and Agatha was so hungry she didn't wait for Lutger to arrive before ordering from a passing trolley a serving of sesame prawn toast, one of Chinese broccoli in oyster sauce, and one of roast duck. Lutger was only five minutes late, but they immediately secured for themselves a plate of seafood dumplings and one of salt and pepper calamari.

'Must be hungry work, whatever you're doing.'

Lutger munched on a piece of prawn toast, completely at home with his chopsticks. Which was more than Agatha could say for herself. She could never quite get the grip right, and appreciated she was possibly overthinking it.

'Well I have been a little busy the last couple of days, in case you hadn't noticed.'

Lutger nodded.

'Any news on Brearly?'

Lutger shook his head as he finished his prawn toast. 'Not since this morning.'

'I love this food,' he added, as he examined the other plates. 'Have you ever been to Macao?'

Agatha shook her head, attempting to negotiate a piece of the Chinese broccoli.

'It's the best,' he said. 'They have the Portuguese influence there as well. Best of both worlds.'

'Right. When were you there?'

Lutger shook his head, his mouth now full of salt and pepper calamari. Agatha didn't wait for his response.

'What's this about Smeeton not being on the ship?'

'He really wasn't, Agatha. They searched the ship top to bottom. Inside out.'

'But you believe me, right? That he was there?'

'*I* believe you. Not sure about the others. You may need to work on them a bit more.'

Agatha told him about her meetings with Carla, and what she'd just been told at the cemetery.

'And I'm assuming you think Smeeton...' Lutger said, 'born... what was it?... Igor Kuznetzov... alias Andrew Penney... you think he's really the mastermind behind this, and not Börge Rasmussen?'

'Burger? He's a moron, believe me. One baby step up from Jeldry.'

'And that Smeeton's at large.'

'For want of a better word, yes.'

'And he's the one that's developed this drug... pays off whoever... and personally abducts the victims, who are transported to... where, do we think?'

'Well as we know, the ship I was on was heading to Vladivostok, after Nouméa. So maybe Russia. Or maybe China or North Korea. Somewhere we can't get them back from, as Perrick said. Somewhere they can just disappear without a trace.'

'As captive sex workers. In brothels.'

'Best bet.'

'And what's he doing it for?'

'Money for one thing,' Agatha said. 'The universal, timeless incentive. But you know what I also think? He resents women. For whatever reason. Too fat to get a girlfriend when he was young, would be my guess. And that as a sleeper agent in the KGB, he was denied a past. And so he resents others having one too. So he kills two birds with one stone. The first dead bird is he gets back at women, which he does by wiping their memories and forcing them to acquiesce, and then the second dead bird is he gets to leave others without a past, just like him.'

Lutger nodded and picked up a piece of crispy-skinned duck, held it between his chopsticks and examined it, dipped it in a small dish of hoisin sauce and then slipped it into his mouth and chewed it gently and slowly, clearly savouring every moment.

'Sounds feasible,' he said once he'd finished. 'It certainly fits.'

Agatha obeyed the dictates of her hunger and requisitioned a serving of the barbecue pork buns as they went past. Lutger returned fire with another serving of roast duck before they'd even finished the first, but by the same token there was no objection from Agatha.

'So we know Smeeton's been getting help,' Agatha said. 'He must be, right? Unless he's superhuman.'

Lutger nodded with his mouth full of dumpling.

'And there has to be at least one person at the Port Authority, and no doubt we'll find out who that is in due course. But what I'm worried about... he'd need to be getting police assistance as well, wouldn't he?'

Lutger's expression said 'maybe'.

'Brearly thought the Botany guys could be a bit suss.'

'Could well be,' Lutger said. 'The Port's their turf. And they've always been a bit of a law unto themselves, that lot.'

'That's what Brearly said. I've never had much to do with them.'

'Keep it that way.'

Agatha picked up a pork bun in her fingers and took a bite. She'd always loved the soft texture of pork buns. Meanwhile, Lutger snaffled the last piece of prawn toast.

'I guess that'll come out in the wash too. But what's really bothering me... and you have to keep this to yourself...'

'Agreed.'

Agatha hesitated before continuing.

'What was Perrick doing on the water police vessel?'

'I was actually wondering that myself.'

'Do you think *he's* helping Smeeton? And maybe that was how Smeeton was able to disappear?'

Lutger nodded and considered this, and took a while before answering.

'We're going to have to be very careful how we play this.'

'We are. But we can't do nothing, either.'

'What do you suggest?' Lutger asked, slipping another dumpling into his mouth.

'Well first we keep this strictly between ourselves for the moment. Meaning just you and me.'

Lutger nodded and added emphasis by raising his eyebrows.

'And second, we need to track down Smeeton. My gut instinct is we need to find the next container ship headed to Nouméa. So get onto that straight after lunch and I will too. And get yourself one of these,' and Agatha produced her burner phone, 'and text me your new number. This is mine.'

She wrote down her number and handed it to Lutger.

'My phone was tampered with after the Tamarama break-in,' she said, 'so you never know, yours could be too.'

'OK.'

'We need to act really quickly on this, so phone me as soon as you find anything. Smeeton's out there and I know he's close.'

Other than receiving a text from Lutger confirming his new phone number, Agatha didn't receive any further information from him. As things turned out though, she didn't need his help after all.

It was almost 2.30pm when they parted company outside the restaurant. Agatha decided to do a bit of research of her own and to head for a nearby internet cafe she knew of, close to Paddy's Markets. Her car was parked around there too, but there was no way she was going back to Tamarama.

She took a slight detour to clear her head and made for the red green and gold ceremonial gate at the top of Dixon Street and strolled down the tree-lined pedestrian mall in the heart of Chinatown, with all its life and electric colour. Swirling aromas of ripening fruit and roast duck and sweet pastry. Happy faces and loud conversations.

And halfway down the first block, in this storm of gaudy neon, it happened again, just as it did three nights earlier in Oxford Street. She saw his face. Or imagined she did. Not behind her this time, but passing by, in the stream of humanity. He stood out, too, in the mainly Chinese crowd, but when she turned around, he'd gone. Or was never there in the first place.

Undeterred, she continued on, but she quickened her pace and snatched backward glances every ten steps.

Of course the doubt was still fresh in her mind – not so much her own doubt, but Perrick's, made plain in the morning debrief, as emphatic as a Chinatown neon sign.

You might have been confused.

She wondered if Lutger believed her, despite his assurance that he did. There'd been something strange about his manner at lunch. Still, there was *always* something strange about Lutger, and so what if he didn't believe her? So what if *no one* believed her, what difference did it make? She knew what she knew and had to trust it would all come out in the end. Somehow. If she was honest with herself though, she was still rattled by the absence of any sign of Smeeton on the ship.

The internet cafe, when she reached it, was well-patronized – she was relieved in a way – but she was able to find herself a quiet corner. Necessary, in case she needed to make some calls.

Her initial research drew a blank: she checked up to a week ahead and there were no container ships due to depart Port Botany for Nouméa. Presumably this was why she still hadn't received anything from Lutger.

She clearly needed a different angle on this, and she sat back and thought for a moment. Her own words to Brearly came back to her: *I think he does the upstanding citizen stuff as Penney, his original name, and the criminal stuff as Smeeton.* It occurred to her that instead of looking for a ship, she'd be better off focusing on Smeeton himself, on his name. And so where might he have needed to use his name in the course of his illegal activities? What was something that every good criminal needed, preferably on a regular basis?

Transport.

And transport meant a motor vehicle, especially when your occupation required getting to odd locations, getting there fast, and often getting there with a *body*, alive or dead.

Motor vehicles could be bought, stolen or borrowed. He wasn't likely to waste his time or money buying a car. He could certainly steal one – and for the Chalaise job he probably did – but stealing was high risk, and in any event the use of ID was hardly a requirement. *Borrowing* however was a different matter. All he needed for that was a fake licence...

Agatha began calling the handful of top-tier car rental companies, but before she spoke to anyone, she made a quick decision to not use her own name, just in case.

'Yes, hello. This is Detective Senior Constable Terri Spedding, of the Newtown Local Area Command...'

None of them, though, had a booking in Smeeton's name.

She was on the verge of giving up when she decided to try a few of the smaller ones, restricting herself to the eastern suburbs, given the location of the pharmacy in Bondi Junction. Amazingly, she got lucky with the second one she tried, a small outfit in Rose Bay.

'In fact we *do* have a rental in the name of Smeeton.' He sounded male and young. 'Being dropped off today...'

'Is it a *Neil* Smeeton? Neil Harrold Smeeton?'

There was a pause.

'Could I put you on hold for a second?'

After subjecting her to a minute of mind-numbingly repetitive hold music, he returned.

'I'm sorry, but, um... I'm not allowed to give you any further information over the phone.'

'Just the first name. It's kind of... it's an emergency.'

'I'm sorry, but I shouldn't have even told you what I did, to be honest. But if you come in with your police ID...'

'OK. I'll do that.' And after confirming the address, it occurred to Agatha to ask one last question before hanging up.

'By the way, where are your drop-off locations?'

'Sure, um... there's here, in Rose Bay, there's one in Bondi, and there's one in the CBD. And we also do Wollongong. In Port Kembla.'

Port Kembla. Of course! They'd been confining their enquiries to Port Botany, but Port Kembla, less than a hundred kilometres further south – or about an hour and a half's drive – was also close enough to justify a check.

And sure enough, after a couple of carefully placed phone calls, she found what she'd been looking for.

The *NV Zenegger* was due to depart at midnight for Nouméa-Shanghai-Vladivostok. It was not a common route, and for it to be heading to both Nouméa and

Vladivostok, just like the ship Agatha had been held on, was too much of a coincidence.

She'd have to drive to Port Kembla to investigate this ship as soon as possible. She would have liked to have checked in on Brearly to see how he was faring, but this couldn't wait.

She called Lutger on his new number just after 5.30pm, telling him her plan.

'I'll come with you,' he said.

'No.'

'You can't go on your own.'

'No, you're more use to me where you are. And this has to be low-key surveillance. But keep this phone with you. I'll call you by 11pm at the latest. If you haven't heard from me by then, call for back-up and don't let the *NV Zenegger* leave port. And in the meantime, don't tell anyone. Least of all Perrick. OK?'

'OK. And Agatha... be really careful. You don't know exactly what you're dealing with here.'

56.

It was around 7.30pm, just after sunset, and Agatha was driving south along the Princes Highway in her bright blue Renault in the fading light. She'd reached Loftus and had been driving for almost an hour – Friday evening was never a great time to be leaving the city – when she suddenly hit a bad stretch of heavy traffic.

It looked like there'd been an accident and an electronic sign indicated delays. Up ahead however, was signage to the Royal National Park. The detour normally added around 30 minutes, so probably wasn't going to save any time overall, but it was a beautiful drive and the absence of traffic would help calm her nerves and clear her head.

So she turned off.

And the drive *was* beautiful, even in the eerie crepuscular light. There was no moon, but the treetops against the darkening night sky felt like a crowd of old friends.

Until they didn't.

The snaking detour, through the world's second-oldest national park, passed through towering, ancient forests punctuated with fern-filled gullies, and was about a 40-minute drive to where it rejoined the highway. But 20 minutes in, Agatha noticed a pair of headlights behind her.

She'd been vaguely aware of the headlights of a vehicle that had been some distance behind her since the turnoff –

not unusual, as it was the only alternative route and she'd assume they were doing the same thing as she was – but suddenly they were close behind. And whenever she slowed on the straight sections to let them pass, they slowed down too. And then the pattern would repeat itself on the bends. It wasn't as if she was a slow driver, and there was only one conclusion she could draw: there was bad intention involved.

Her options were limited. Pulling over would be too risky, even though she was armed: they could be armed too, and there could be more than one of them, and they'd have the element of surprise. Her best option was to keep going and run down the clock and hope to be able to make it back to the highway. Twenty minutes of anxious driving, but she was up for that.

On one hairpin bend it looked like they were attempting to pass her on the inside. The headlights suddenly swung out to the right, and then just as abruptly they dropped back again. It was more of a threat, than a genuine attempt to pass her. Or else it was an attempt to run her off the road.

It was too dark to get a good view of the vehicle, let alone the driver.

And then the headlights abruptly dropped back again.

By the time she rejoined the highway, she couldn't see the headlights at all, and she managed to arrive at Port Kembla in one piece just after 9pm.

57.

Agatha knew the berth where the *NV Zenegger* was docked, and after slowly driving through the approaches to the port – where the intermittent streetlights cast spaced pools of light on the deserted roads – she parked the Renault about a hundred metres away from her destination and got out.

There were few parked vehicles around. The great bulk of the *NV Zenegger* rose up before her, faintly lit by sparse dock lighting.

She walked towards it.

On her left was a factory straight out of the nineteenth century – it could have been a steampunk concoction. There was a gigantic metal, pipe-like structure, nine or ten metres wide, running horizontally in front of the building and then, in a ninety-degree turn, curving straight upwards and stretching into the sky to a height of maybe 90 metres. There was another equally tall chimney next to it, and behind the complex there were vast mounds of coal, like black sand dunes on a faraway planet.

To her right, the waters of the port were preternaturally calm, and small lines of light from the docks on the other side lay across the mirroring surface.

She'd been expecting a cacophony of sound – semitrailers, forklifts, conveyor belts – but there was near total silence.

There were small, sharp stones on the uneven road that made walking uncomfortable, even in her trainers. And they magnified the sound of her footsteps, which seemed unnervingly loud in the enveloping silence, and encouraged her to tread lightly. And although the night air was crisp but not cold, the atmosphere – as in the vibe, or ambience of the place – was frigid. She pulled her green jacket in around her, more for the reassuring feel of her holstered gun beneath it, than for warmth.

As she drew closer to the ship, she could see it was much the same size as the ship she'd escaped from, the *Sapphire Dawn*. It was about 250 metres long and it seemed enormous close up. Memories of the *Sapphire Dawn* came to her, and were not welcome and she shut them out.

Multiple large cables ran from the bow of the ship to the dock. There was little movement anywhere and she guessed the ship had already been loaded. She wondered if there were any more Nowhere women on board, but doubted it. There was a feeling of finality about the evening which she couldn't have explained if you'd asked her.

She warily watched the entrances to the factory to her left, and she occasionally glanced behind. The pools of light were smaller here than back where she'd parked, but more numerous.

When she reached a point roughly halfway down the length of the ship, she paused and took stock. There was a gangway towards the stern of the ship, and no sign of anyone boarding or disembarking.

Just as she was turning to check behind her, she caught sight of something out of the corner of her eye. It was the figure of a man emerging from one of the factory entrances.

She'd stopped in a poorly lit section of the dock, so was confident he couldn't see her. He was heading in the direction of the gangway, and as soon as he passed under one of the lights on the dock, she recognized him straight away.

It was, without a doubt, Smeeton. In his dark suit and black trainers. And his untucked shirt.

She immediately reached for her gun, half-expecting it not to be there, like before, as if some terrible trick had been played on her, or she was in another dream. But it was there. And as it was a Glock 26, there was no safety to unlock. And she'd already made sure, before she'd left the car, that there was a round loaded into the chamber, ready to be fired.

She started walking, at an angle to him in order to cut him off, with the gun in her hand pointed 45 degrees to the ground.

He soon became aware of her and slowed. There was something about his movements suggesting a lack of surprise, which both concerned her and told her she had the right person.

She closed in on him with her gun raised now, pointing at him.

'Police. Move your hands away from your body and place them on your head.'

He did nothing, just stood there, now tugging on his shirt sleeves, and smiled at her – creases forming around his grey, washed-out eyes – and said nothing.

'I said put your hands on your head. *Now*. I will gladly fire this weapon, just give me an excuse. Make any sudden movement, I will shoot you, and shoot you dead.'

'I wouldn't do that, Agatha.'

It wasn't Smeeton talking, though. The voice came from behind her. It was Perrick's voice.

'That would not be a good idea,' he added.

She turned and confirmed who it was.

'What are you doing?' she asked.

He had his gun trained on her.

'I don't know what you think *you're* doing,' he said, 'but just put your gun down.'

'What do you mean you don't know what I'm doing, it's *Smeeton*.'

'Who?'

She looked back and Smeeton had gone. Seemingly vanished into the night air.

'He was just...'

'You're imagining it, Agatha. Just as you have been all along.'

'You know I haven't—'

'Just put your gun down.'

'You *know* he was there!'

'You're overwrought. Just put... your gun... down.'

'OK, I'm putting it away...'

'No. I want you to put it on the ground.'

'On the ground?'

'I should have kept you on leave. Should have known you weren't thinking straight after what happened. Big mistake. But right now, I need you to hand over your gun and I'm putting you on a week's leave as of now.'

'So why do I need to hand over the gun? Am I being disciplined? What's the charge?'

'You're delusional Agatha, but right now, you need to put your gun on the ground and slide it over to me.'

'Slide it? Like a criminal?'

'*Do* it.'

Agatha could see the fierce look in his eye, and with his gun pointed directly at her, could see she had little choice. She slowly placed her gun down on the ground.

'And now slide it.'

He was standing about ten metres away. With her foot, she slid the gun towards him but it stopped about halfway.

'You're making a very big mistake, Perrick.'

She realized it was the first time she'd called him Perrick to his face. She'd never called him anything.

'Superintendent, to you,' he said as he pulled a pair of white latex gloves from his coat pocket and put them on.

'What are you doing?'

Without answering her, he walked over to Agatha's gun. Holstered his own and picked hers up. He then removed the clip, checked it, and put it back in.

'I'm really sorry,' he said. 'But I have no choice.'

'Oh my God. It was you following me in the national park, wasn't it. You're helping Smeeton.'

Perrick then racked the slide to ensure a round was in the chamber.

'What are you going to do?' Agatha asked. Starting to feel a rising panic now. 'Are you going to *execute* me? Here?'

'Don't be ridiculous,' he said coldly and did a final visual check on the gun.

'Don't do this!'

Perrick looked around, as if to ensure there were no witnesses, then raised the gun and pointed it at Agatha.

And in those fractions of a second, Agatha's brain did some calculations and came up with two conclusions: there was absolutely nothing she could do to stop this, and she was about to die on a deserted dock in Port Kembla.

'Freeze! Police!'

It was Brearly. Sprung from the shadows. Perrick must have been as shocked as she was, but if so, why was there a trace of a smile on his lips just before he turned around?

'Put the gun down Perrick, or I'll blow your fucking brains out.'

Brearly's head was still bandaged, but he was in his usual work clothes, his suit. He'd edged forward and was now standing in a pool of light, with his gun aimed at Perrick in a double-handed stance, and his green eyes shone from beneath the white of his bandages.

'Brearly?' Perrick said calmly.

'*Now*, Perrick. Put it down *now*.'

'All right, all right,' Perrick sighed. 'Keep your knickers on.' And he placed the gun on the ground next to his right foot and raised his hands again.

'Push it away with your foot.'

Perrick complied.

'That was my gun,' Agatha said, as Brearly closed in. 'He's still got his own. In his holster.'

'Very slowly,' Brearly said to Perrick. 'Remove it, and put it on the ground away from the other gun.'

Perrick did as he was told, and slowly and calmly placed his own gun on the ground off to one side.

'Now back away from the guns.'

'I think you two both need to calm down.'

'Oh I'm extremely calm, Perrick. I've had a nice long rest. And you'll be getting an even longer one if you don't back away.'

'No problem,' Perrick said and backed away a few steps. 'So what are you up to, Brearly?'

Brearly continued to walk towards Perrick. 'Back off some more.'

'Sure,' Perrick said, and then Agatha saw him turn his head slightly off at an angle, and nod.

Brearly frowned.

A gunshot rang out, and what followed happened quickly.

Brearly was hit, in his left shoulder, and twisted around, partly from the force of the impact and partly to face his attacker.

And his attacker was Lutger.

Lutger was by now standing with his gun pointed at Brearly. He fired a second shot, which missed completely, and Brearly fired back and his round hit Lutger just below his throat, and his gun flew out of his hand and he fell.

At the same time, as soon as Lutger had fired the first of his two shots, Perrick had sprung forward to grab his gun. Agatha rushed to stop him. Perrick pushed her away, hard, and she fell backwards. Perrick scooped up his weapon, by which time Brearly had turned back and fired a shot at Perrick that missed.

Perrick then fired, hitting Brearly squarely in his chest. Brearly went down. When Perrick then turned to Agatha, she'd already picked up her own gun and was pointing it at him.

'I wouldn't do that, *Perrick*,' she said, mimicking his first words to her.

'OK,' he said, slowly lowering his arm, but it was a feint, and he ducked and fired, but in his haste, his shot went wildly astray, and she'd predicted his evasive action because they'd had the same training, hadn't they, and she shot him squarely in his head, straight into his right eye, which at that close range was never going to result in anything other than an ugly, fatal wound, and he jolted backwards, dead before he hit the ground.

Lying awkwardly crumpled like that, with his legs buckled under him and his outstretched hands still in their white gloves, he looked more like an abandoned marionette puppet than a superintendent.

After confirming that Perrick was now missing the entire back third of his skull, along with a good portion of his brain over the ground behind him – thereby leaving his wife a widow and his two mistresses to their own devices – Agatha went over to where Lutger was still lying on his back, keeping her gun pointed at him. When she got there, she could see the entry wound at the bottom of his throat, and that he was motionless, and that if he'd been alive after he'd been shot, he was certainly dead now. His open, inquiring eyes seemed to seek out an answer in the night sky as to how it had all gone so badly wrong for them.

Then she checked Brearly and she experienced a sense of relief she'd never known before. Because he was alive. In fact not only that, he was sitting himself up, using his good arm. Grimacing a lot, though.

'Proves these things work,' he said, undoing a shirt button and revealing a bulletproof vest. 'They both dead? Still alive?'

'Dead.'

'Shit, eh?'

'Yeah.'

It was a sorry sight. Two of Sydney's finest, one with half his head missing, the other gaping lifelessly at the heavens.

Meanwhile, back to the living, and there was blood beginning to soak through the left side of Brearly's jacket.

'You're bleeding,' Agatha said.

'Bullets will do that. And that's the trouble with these vests. They don't cover everything. At least it's my shoulder, and not my—'

'Heart.'

'No, my *groin*. Last thing my sex life would have needed. Pity Lutger's such a shithouse shot, he might have hit my vest like Perrick had the good manners to do.'

Agatha began dialling triple 0 for an ambulance.

'Then you would have gone down and Perrick would have shot *me*,' she said.

'Not sure why I'm the one that's always taking it for the team. One hammer and two bullets so far. How about you?'

58.

'Nice shot by the way,' Brearly said.

'Yours too. *And* after being hit. Impressive. How's that shoulder?'

'Went right through I think. No major arteries. But it hurts, getting shot.'

'Hang on...'

The Triple Zero operator had answered. Agatha told her the situation. Police? No thanks, we *are* the police, just paramedics at this point.

Three detectives shot, two dead and one injured, and no police required. Not a call they'd get every day.

After the call, Agatha continued:

'But what I don't understand is... what in God's holy name are you doing here, Brearly?'

'Thought you might have needed a hand.'

'No, really. I thought you were supposed to have a fractured skull?'

'Slight exaggeration. Not fractured. Worst headache ever though. And yeah, I guess I did discharge myself a little earlier than was ideal.'

'I'd be dead if you hadn't. That's the second time you've saved my life.'

'We all have our hidden talents.'

'I owe you.'

'You do. You can buy me a drink.'

Agatha smiled and looked around. The dock was still deathly quiet. It was getting on towards 9.30. She had it in her head that she had to do something and then remembered it: ring Lutger by 11pm. The memory left a queasy, hollow feeling.

But what she did have to do was find Smeeton. Once the paramedics arrived for Brearly.

'Tell me you saw Smeeton,' she said.

'Smeeton? No. When I arrived, you were having your little tête-à-tête with Perrick. Just the two of you, no one else. So was Smeeton here?'

'I wasn't seeing things.'

'No one's saying you were.'

'Perrick was.'

'Perrick's dead.'

'I can't have imagined him.'

'Did he... say anything? Did you talk to—?'

'No. Didn't say a fucking word.'

'Listen Agatha. If you say you saw him—'

'He *exists*.'

'I believe you. Where did he go?'

'Well that's just it. Perrick bailed me up. I turned around and he'd gone.'

'Could he have boarded the ship?'

'He'd had to have gone the other way, or I would have seen him. I'd go after him, but I'm not leaving you. Not until the paramedics arrive at least.'

'Don't hang around on my account—'

'That ship can't be allowed to leave though,' Agatha said. 'Not until every single container's been checked.'

'So what's the story?'

'It was a bit of a stab in the dark. I decided to check to see if anyone had rented a car using the name Smeeton. And I eventually found one. A rental for a Smeeton with a drop-off today.'

'For a *Neil* Smeeton?'

'Don't know but Port Kembla was one of their drop-off locations. And then I find there's a ship docked in Port Kembla called the *NV Zenegger* that's headed for Nouméa and Vladivostok, same as the ship we were on, the *Sapphire Dawn*. And that it's due to leave at midnight. And I race down here and sure enough...'

'And sure enough the gang's here too,' Brearly said. He was staring at the ship, and eventually said: 'You don't think there are any of our Nowhere women on board, do you?'

'I doubt it, but you never know. Another reason the ship needs to be thoroughly searched.'

Brearly nodded.

'I'll put a call in,' he said. 'Might be time to get the feds involved. Never thought I'd utter those words. But in the circumstances...'

They were both quiet for a moment.

'How did you know I was here?' Agatha asked suddenly.

'I didn't. Not exactly. When I left the hospital I knew I couldn't phone you and I didn't want to alert the others, so I had no easy way of finding you. But I guessed that Perrick was involved in all this, so I put a tracking device on his car. When he was out at lunch. And I knew something was up when I saw him heading south. At first I thought he was heading for the Botany port, but then he just kept going.'

'So when you were coming to see me at the Marco Polo, you said you'd found something big but couldn't discuss it on the phone. Was it to do with what happened to my phone, because—?'

'That was part of it.'

'At the time I assumed it was some sort of phone *tracking* app, but I'm guessing it must have been a phone *tapping* app.'

'Yeah, well. What set off alarm bells for me was the realization that Penney... or Smeeton... seemed to have advance warning we were coming to his store. It could only have been through a phone tap. I guess I shouldn't have asked you your room number. My mistake was to assume whoever was listening didn't already know you were in the Marco Polo. And that they weren't about to attack you. I thought they were just monitoring what we'd found out. But listen. That wasn't the main reason I was coming over. Something happened at the station that afternoon.'

'What?'

'Terri came up to me. Out of the blue. Asked me if I'd ever been to Macao.'

'Macao?'

'Mm. She'd been getting suspicious of Perrick. Not sure why exactly, women's intuition I guess... they still call it that?... but she came across his passport one day and it turned out he'd been secretly going on short trips to Macao. He had some little tart over there apparently... sorry, her word, not mine. Then she discovered Lutger had been going over too. So with both of them going, she figured it was probably more than just the girl. So she started wondering, was it gambling? Or some dodgy Triad connection? And that's why she confided in me. I then joined the dots. Or went with my gut, really. A bit like you. See what a good influence you are? But yeah no, especially after all our speculation about possible police involvement in a port conspiracy. Way I saw it, the writing was well and truly on the wall at this point. So I was coming over to tell you not to trust Perrick or Lutger until we knew more. And there you have it.'

'So what were they doing in Macao, do you think?'

'Probably where they were getting paid. It's a great place for laundering money over there. With all those casinos and Hong Kong and China on its doorstep. Perrick and Lutger, though. Who'd have thought. Perrick, maybe. Explains why he transferred Spanner and Dan out so quickly. But Lutger. I really thought...'

Brearly shook his head and Agatha thought of how it was only lunchtime that day that she and Lutger were eating yum cha together.

'Aiding and abetting human trafficking,' Brearly added. 'The fucking *slave* trade.'

'So... if it was for brothels in East Asia or wherever, why here? Why were they abducting them from here?'

'I assume because they wanted *white* women. And they wanted to grab them from somewhere far away so there was zero chance of anyone recognizing them. And they used shipping containers because it's the easiest way of avoiding detection.'

'They're never checked.'

'Only a tiny percentage, both here and at the destination. So given they're using ships, the logical thing is to source their targets from a port city, and the bigger the better. Sydney's an obvious choice. Ticks all the boxes.'

He paused.

'What I want to know is,' he said, 'who *is* Smeeton? Or Penney.'

Agatha told Brearly about her meeting with Carla at the Waverley Cemetery and the discovery of his other identity – and probably his real one – the Russian ex-agent, Igor Kuznetzov.

After she finished, Brearly just shook his head.

'He's a one-man band, that one,' he said. 'Pharmacist, chemist, opportunist, rapist.'

And then he added: 'Was that who mugged us at the Marco Polo? I never saw his face.'

'I didn't either, but I didn't need to. It was definitely him.'

'Hasn't this guy heard of delegating?'

'We have to find him.'

'We've been trying, haven't we? The guy's as slippery as an oiled-up eel.'

'Yeah.'

'It'd make sense though, if MI6 is right. If he really is this Igor guy.'

Agatha nodded. 'Igor Kuznetzov.'

'The best spies cover their tracks and leave no trace that they ever existed. Barely even a photograph. That's why they call them spooks.'

They both stared out over the dark waters of the port. Not a ripple. Just a black mirror.

'Or maybe you're right,' Brearly said. 'Maybe he really *doesn't* exist.'

'Don't say that. Whatever you do, don't say that.'

A siren in the distance.

'I can't believe Perrick...' Agatha began, then stopped. Reflected for a moment. 'I mean, apart from anything else, he was actively *encouraging* us. With our Nowhere list. He was the only one who was backing us.'

They both listened to the sound of the approaching ambulance.

'Yeah, that's the trick, isn't it. Deflects attention away from him. Should things heat up.'

Agatha thought about that.

'I suppose when they're not the one actually *doing* it,' she said, 'when they're just turning a blind eye and getting paid for it... it's so hard to prove. To even detect it.'

'You follow the money. That's why the payments will be the key to unravelling this. And they *will* unravel it, especially with Perrick out of the picture, no longer blocking things. And now we've got Terri's evidence too… Some task force, the feds as I say, they'll be the ones to do it. They'll unravel it and mop up the rest. Whoever's been helping. Port authority employees, customs officers, anyone getting paid off. Anyone taking a few too many trips to Macao.'

'Except for Smeeton,' Agatha said. 'They won't get Smeeton.'

They could see the lights of the ambulance now, coming around a corner at the far end of the road leading to the dock.

Something occurred to Agatha.

'The Vaucluse house,' she said. 'The chemist's house, Andrew Penney's. You checked it out, didn't you? You said on the phone you drew a blank.'

'Yeah, it was empty. No furniture even.'

'Empty?'

'Nothing. And certainly no Penney. No Smeeton.'

'That's weird. Was there a For Sale sign?'

'No, nothing like that. Just empty.'

This was significant, Agatha felt, but she couldn't have explained why.

The ambulance was almost there.

'Agatha, listen, I know you're chomping at the bit to get after this Smeeton character, but there's going to be a massive inquiry into this, you know. Two detectives were shot dead by two other detectives. It will tie you up. It will tie us *all* up.'

'Unless I go now,' Agatha said. 'Fade into the night, like Smeeton. Fight like with like.'

'You won't have long.'

'One night, that's all I want. I have to at least try. Then tomorrow I'll head into Newtown and face the music.'

The ambulance had now pulled up. The paramedics could see that Brearly was sitting up, and they weren't rushing. One of them was calmly gathering his box of tricks.

'I'll cover for you,' Brearly said. 'But you need to be really careful because—'

'Because I don't know what I'm dealing with. I know. That's what Lutger said.'

'Right. And look what happened to him.'

And as the first of the ambulance officers began walking over to them, Brearly said:

'So with Perrick and Lutger gone, I'll be the only one left. You'll be able to call me Peter, now.'

'I don't think so, Brearly.'

Agatha was smiling at him.

'You're one tough chick,' Brearly said, shaking his head. 'And it makes me wonder... Is that an Argentinian thing?'

59.

It was midnight, and Agatha was lying in bed in a hotel in the CBD and staring up at the ceiling.

Earlier that night, after seeing off Brearly in the ambulance at Port Kembla, she'd driven back into the city. She tried to figure out, on the drive, what she was going to do about finding Smeeton, but no clever idea came to her. She felt strangely certain he'd gone to the house in Vaucluse, but didn't know why she felt it, it was just there. In her bones, as they say.

She didn't want to go there at night, though, so she decided to check into a hotel and head there just before dawn. Unless she thought of a better plan in the meantime.

She pulled into an uptown overnight parking place. The bright blue Renault was too distinctive, she needed to jettison it. Her idea was then to find an anonymous hotel somewhere nearby, but the streets at that hour were creeping her out too much. Every shadow contained an assailant. Contained Smeeton. A cheap hotel was the last thing she needed.

So she made a beeline for the first nearby five-star hotel she could think of, the Sheraton opposite Hyde Park, and took a room with a view over the treetops.

When she finally turned out her bedside light, she lay back and listened to the traffic sounds hounding her from the street below, and watched as the trees outside cast strange and unsettling shadows on the ceiling.

She had a poor night's sleep – she kept dreaming that Smeeton was on the other side of her hotel room door, trying to pick the lock. Or he was down in Hyde Park, under a streetlight, staring up at her.

When her alarm went off at 4.45am, it was still dark outside. As soon as she woke though, as so often happened to her it seemed, she was already thinking it as if she'd been dreaming it: Brearly telling her Andrew Penney's empty house at Vaucluse had no For Sale sign outside. It was so obvious to her now. An empty house was perfect for a 'ghost' like Smeeton, or for anyone trying to fly under the radar. She should have thought of it earlier. And of course its proximity to the car rental place down in nearby Rose Bay made sense too.

When she left the hotel half an hour later, she avoided the concierge desk and a waiting taxi in the driveway, but instead hailed a taxi on the wide, sparsely populated street outside. She remembered the address as if it was imprinted on her brain, and told the driver to head for 141 New South Head Road, Vaucluse.

60.

It was around 5.30am – the beginning of what's known as civil twilight, just before dawn – when the taxi arrived in Vaucluse. Agatha told the driver to pull over a long block away from 141 New South Head Road. She didn't want the taxi's headlights to herald her arrival.

The night's darkness had dissipated, the cloudless sky was tinged with blue, but the streetlights were still on. The road was even quieter than the streets in the city and there were virtually no cars and not a single pedestrian in sight.

It was a three-minute walk to the house, and she slowed when she got close – a little warning light went off in her brain – and sure enough, when she was only about 40 metres away, the shape of a person – a large person, a man – emerged from the gate to number 141.

She stopped and didn't move a muscle. Luckily she was near a tree on the footpath, which she hoped would help camouflage her.

Although the man was not under a streetlight, he wasn't in the shadows either, and there was enough light now from the sky to tell: he was wearing a dark suit and trainers.

He stopped too. Hesitated. Had he seen her?

He then turned and began walking along the footpath in the opposite direction. To the east.

Agatha followed him stealthily, keeping her distance, but made sure she was close enough to react and to stop him if he attempted to get in a car. She wasn't completely certain he hadn't seen her and wasn't just playing for time, or wasn't up to some other ruse, but once again found the feeling of the bulge of her gun under her jacket reassuring.

He continued along the footpath, crossed the roundabout at the end of the road, where New South Head Road joined Old South Head Road, and walked across the reserve on the other side, towards the path that ran along the clifftops overlooking the ocean.

Agatha had increased her speed and was now closing the gap between them. By the time they'd both reached the cliff path, she was about 20 metres behind him. He still hadn't once turned around and she suspected he knew she was there.

She pulled out her gun.

They were both walking north: the conspicuously phallic Macquarie Lighthouse was up ahead on the left, and beyond that the narrowing peninsula of land that led eventually to South Head at the entrance to Sydney Harbour. To their right was the Pacific Ocean.

Just before the bitumen path drew level with the lighthouse, it curved left, then right, snaking through a short section of coastal scrub. Agatha saw the danger too late. She lost sight of him on the first turn, and increased her pace. When the path finally straightened again and came out of the scrub section, the lighthouse was there on her left, but he was gone. He was no longer ahead of her.

She cursed her own carelessness and hurried back down through the scrub section of the path again, realizing that he'd probably hidden somewhere and doubled back. She kept a close eye on the scrub when she passed through however, particularly to the left – the ocean side – where it was thickest.

A rush of man slammed into her from the right.

It was like being hit by a truck, more than a person. The force of the impact knocked the gun out of her hand, which landed with a clatter on the path, and drove them both through some temporary plastic fencing and halfway through the scrub. When she landed, he landed on top of her, punching the air out of her. Along this section of the path there was no other barrier beyond the temporary fencing, just the thick coastal scrub, which was patchy in places, and she was aware the cliff edge had to be little more than 10 or 15 metres further on.

He got off her and lifted her up like a doll – she was still winded – and with one arm between her legs he lurched through the remaining scrub, towards the rim. The greenery ahead of them now had a large gap of blue and orange in the middle: ocean and dawn sky.

Agatha realized she was seconds from being thrown over the cliff.

He was holding her facing outwards and against the right side of his fat, hairless belly that poked out through his untucked shirt and suit jacket, and Agatha had no way of hitting him or getting her arms around a leg. All she could do was look for something else to grab – a post, or a tree – but there was nothing within reach, and then she could feel the momentum building and the throw beginning, and suddenly she was being swung through the gap and out into empty space, and time decelerated and everything happened in slow motion as they do in times of crisis, and she flew so far out she could see over the edge of the cliff and all the way down the sheer rock face, the whole terrifying 80 metres of it, to the foam of the waves breaking on the rocks below.

She helplessly assumed it was all over for her, and that now was when he would let her go, but he didn't, not yet, and he swung her back again, apparently to build up to an even bigger throw to make sure she cleared the edge cleanly. As a result, this time he swung her lower, and her face came close to one of his black trainers, and the top of a dark-grey sock over a chunky ankle, and the pale hairless skin of his massive calf above that, and wondered if these were the last images she would ever see. If she could have, she would have grabbed his leg, clothed in its navy-blue trouser, but she couldn't and all she could do was feel the powerful muscle of his thigh against her hip, and picture a Tyrannosaurus Rex, and give in to the inevitability of it all...

But she refused to give up, and this time he'd swung her low enough for her also to see, and to clutch at, and to seize the lower, stronger section of the narrow trunk of a small tree which she was familiar with from her coastal walks and knew as a Black She-oak (*allocasuarine littoralis*), known, appropriately, for its resilience.

She clung to it like a lover.

And like a faithful lover, the tree returned the compliment and held fast. And this time his throw was caught before it got going and he stumbled and lost his grip on her. Her trajectory was still forward though, and her legs swung around and she felt her trainers and ankles strike out into clear space. The edge of the edge. Torn vegetation and dirt and pebbles fell away into the void.

She had precisely two seconds to get a foothold and roll away from the precipice and get clear before he grabbed her again, and she didn't waste them. She flung herself away and felt a hand clip her heel, but managed to escape his lunge and leap up and dart through the scrub dodging branches and back to the path. She could hear that he was close behind her, but she spotted her gun and snatched it up and turned, ready to shoot, expecting him to be upon her.

But he'd seen what she was doing and was now sprinting north, in the direction they'd originally been travelling. At that moment she would have fired if she'd had a clear shot, but his legs were already vanishing around a curve in the path.

She followed, but more cautiously this time, her gun at the ready.

When she next set eyes on him, it was after getting clear of the section of scrub. The lighthouse was visible again on her left and he was 50 metres ahead and running. She holstered her gun and ran after him.

Despite his size and her fitness, he almost matched her in speed, but she was determined not to lose sight of him this time. She knew it was probably her last chance. She managed to gain on him and reduce the gap and she sensed she had him, and thought of a lioness running down its prey. Until now, the prey had been her.

They reached a place where the terrain opened out, with grass extending across to Old South Head Road on one side, and on the other, between the path and the fence at the edge of the cliff, an area of mostly flat, exposed sandstone. She was expecting him to make a dash for the road at this point, and she altered course, running across the grass to cut him off, but he abruptly stopped and turned around.

She stopped too, about 20 metres away from him, and pulled out her gun and pointed it at him.

He was catching his breath and he laughed and then began to slowly clap.

She didn't let it distract her and she didn't take her eyes off him. Just willed him to rush her, to give her an excuse to shoot. She considered shooting him anyway, given he'd just tried to kill her, but she couldn't shoot anyone in cold blood, execution style. And anyway, she had to do it by the book.

Behind him, beyond the fence along the rim, the ocean stretched away to the edge of the sky and the sun was coming up over the eastern horizon and there was now an orange glow over everything, making the usually pallid skin of his face glisten like gold.

Keeping a close eye on him, she adjusted her position and circled around slightly, making sure he had no easy escape route. Just as he'd done to her, on the ship.

She said nothing to him. She didn't trust her powers of speech, not with him, and anyway she had to concentrate. She knew he was about to do something, she just didn't know what it was.

The angle of the sun was more behind him now, and his skin had lost its golden glow, and as his small grey eyes began to disappear, his eye sockets became two dark shadows. His mouth she could see clearly though, and she watched as a smile unfurled.

She started to move in closer, ready to fire, ready for the mistake that she knew he was about to make, perhaps hoping to precipitate it. At this range, she couldn't miss. At the same time, she pulled out her phone to call for back-up. She'd already decided to call Brearly first, he'd know who to call in, including PolAir – the police air wing – if necessary.

And then, incredibly, he spoke.

'Well done Agatha.'

He had an almost effeminate voice. If there was an accent, she couldn't identify it. Not Russian, not Canadian, not mid-Atlantic, it was a type of educated, global English, a multitude of accents blended in. He could have been from anywhere.

His words emboldened her. This time, finally, she was able to find her voice.

'I just want to know one thing,' she said. 'I want to know *why*. The rest you can tell them in custody.'

He turned his head, glanced at the ocean behind him, and then faced Agatha again. He took his time, before speaking.

'You were always my favourite,' he said. 'I want you to know that. But you *do* know, don't you. You've always known. Because you and I, we've always had a connection.'

'Was it because you couldn't get a girl? And they passed you over for the best KGB jobs? And because you were born Igor Kuznetzov? Common first name, common surname—'

'Igor Kuznetzov?'

'... and you always felt like such a nobody?'

The thought appeared to amuse him.

'That's right,' he said. 'I *am* a nobody. I'm nobody and I'm no*where*. And you see, there's your problem right there. You are inherently incapable of comprehending, in any meaningful way, who I actually am. Let alone what it's like to be someone like me. It's a little funny, when you think about it, that you should even try.'

'I don't care what you find funny. Because it's over.'

'Of course it is. ' He glanced over his shoulder again. 'But just ask yourself this. What's over? What is it, exactly, that you think is over?'

'This bullshit for a start. Because, *Igor Kuznetzov*, I'm placing you under arrest for the—'

'Just don't forget the name,' he said, not rushing his words. 'It's Smeeton. With a double e.'

Agatha could feel the blood drain from her face.

'Too *eeasy*,' he said. 'Do you get it Agatha? Do you *get* it?'

The slowness of her reaction was partly due to the effect his words had on her, seemingly straight out of her dream – although what could she have done, shot him in midair like a clay pigeon? – but she saw it unfold, as before, in slow motion, and as she still sees it now, over and over in her head: he suddenly turned towards the fence and ran at it, like a sprinter out of the starting blocks – an extraordinary sight with a man of his size, the bouncing flesh under the suit, the flapping clothes, the raw power – and in a continuous motion he leapt up onto the railing of the fence and kept going, out into the crisp morning air and rising sun, and over the edge in a perfect dive, with his arms out in a T and his head lifted to the horizon, as elegant as a fat man could be...

When she'd recovered from the momentary shock of it, Agatha rushed to the fence and then along it, to find a place where she could see down to the foot of the cliff. But by the time she'd found the right spot and climbed over the railing for a better view – being careful to hang on as she leant over – there was nothing to be seen. Nothing on the rocks at the base of the cliff, or in the white water of the crashing waves, or in the blue restiveness of the ocean beyond that.

She turned and looked along the path in both directions, north and south, but there wasn't a soul to be seen. No witnesses, in other words.

She looked back at the cliffs and the ocean and kept watching, desperate for something to appear. But nothing did.

He'd vanished.

In the following days, she was reassured in the knowledge that it would have been impossible for him to have survived. Or any human being for that matter. Everyone she spoke to said the same thing. Not with an 80 metre drop into the ocean, which in itself would be virtually unsurvivable, and certainly impossible to pull off without serious injury, but he couldn't have cleared the rocks at the base of the cliff anyway. She'd seen with her own eyes the exposed rock shelf at that spot, and how far it had jutted out (which she later verified on police satellite imagery, as well as on Google Earth). She'd seen how fast he'd been running. She was good at calculating that sort of thing. Trajectories. And an expert she'd approached – a professor of physics – had confirmed it. No person, regardless of size or gender, could have cleared the rocks, even with a long running start. And not only all of that, her long-distance vision was second to none and she'd stood there on the top of that cliff for an interminable period of time, watching without seeing anything – watching for so long, in fact, that when someone eventually did walk past they thought she was a potential jumper and asked if she was OK.

When she filed her report about the incident, she decided not to use any names – she couldn't prove who it was anyway. (Andrew Penney, unsurprisingly, still hadn't returned from his so-called overseas holiday and officially he remained sought-after for questioning.) She just described him as a pale, overweight man, around 50 years old, with light-coloured hair and grey eyes, and who was last seen wearing a navy-blue suit and black trainers, and was believed to have leapt from the cliffs adjacent to the Macquarie Lighthouse at Vaucluse.

What she left out was an image of his face she couldn't shake: it was from their stand-off on the clifftop, when the angle of the morning sun behind him had shifted and his eyes had disappeared and turned into shadows.

61.

Whenever she thought of the women who were saved, she'd think of the ones who weren't. And especially the ones who were still alive somewhere, but who'd lost their memories forever. Which would remind her of the importance of memory. And how without memory, we were nothing, as good as dead. And if actions and events and memories made a person, then perhaps you'd have to add dreams to that as well.

And then she'd think, dreams might play a part in making a person, but they can't, of their own, *create* a person.

Naturally, she told herself he was real. Of course he was real. Or had been. She simply had to trust what she'd seen.

And anyway, she wasn't the only witness. The fact of his existence – or of having existed – didn't stand or fall with her. It was, surely, a circumstantial case. Because there was other evidence too: the InterContinental, for example, and the driver's licence, and the encounters and sightings from other witnesses.

Even so, it hadn't surprised her, during those days and weeks afterwards, that despite the best efforts of the search teams, including the helicopters and police divers, no body was ever recovered. Nor any item of clothing. Nothing.

Because she knew, deep in the core of her being, that with any serious question there were no absolute truths, that there was always only a most-likely answer — that everything was a question of probability. It came down to the weight of the evidence, like Justice with her scales.

And when she thought about it, that's all it was, the Truth: whatever was most likely at any given point in time. It was a bit like quantum physics with its uncertainty principle and its alive-and-dead cats — the way particles could exist in different states and locations until they were observed. At the best of times, all you could do when it came to the Truth was take a stab at it. Take your best shot.

And thus it was with Smeeton. Almost certainly, he'd existed. And almost certainly, he was now dead. That was all that could be said about the matter, and she'd have to be content with that. And get on with her life.

On the plus side, her nightmares with Smeeton in them seemed to have gone.

So far.

e

www.markmacrossan.com